Edited by Harriett Thomas

First Printing   January 1991

Second Printing   March 1992

Third Printing   September 2010

Printed in Canada

Dedication

This volume is dedicated to the congregation of First United Methodist Church, Tulsa, Oklahoma, a friendly church where people care and serve and Jesus Christ is Lord.

PREFACE

This series of sermons was preached to the congregation of First United Methodist Church, Tulsa, Oklahoma, August 1978 through April 1979. In a preceding series on the Gifts of the Holy Spirit, Dr. Thomas had identified his own Functional Spiritual Gift as Exhortation and defined it as "urgently advising others how to apply God's truth to their daily lives." This is exactly what he does in these sermons as he presents God's answers for our daily problems in clear, logical, simple language, and "urgently advises" us how to appropriate those answers for our lives.

Harriett Thomas
March 1990

TABLE OF CONTENTS

I   *How the Bible Can Help You*

Subject: Introduction

Scripture: Ephesians 6:10-20

Text: *Put on the whole armor of God, that you may be able to stand against the wiles of the devil* (Ephesians 6:11).

All scripture is inspired by God... that the man of God may be complete, equipped for every good work (II Timothy 3:16-17).

If I have learned one thing above everything else in twenty years in the ministry, it's the fact that everyone must continually struggle with the temptations and problems of life. All of us must learn to cope with serious personal pains and hurts.

For that reason I want to talk with you about how the Bible can help you cope with the hurts and pains in all areas of your life. We'll consider how the Bible can help you deal with such particular problems as anxiety, fear, self-pity, tension, sexual problems, guilt, loss of marital love, resentment, impulsiveness . . . to mention only a few of the many problems and temptations which plague us as human beings.

Before we can receive help from the Bible in particular areas, we must first understand how it is that the Bible can help us. We can do this only by approaching the Bible with certain specific presuppositions. These presuppositions fall under two general headings:

I. God's Part, and
II. Our Part

Many of us are confused and fail to find help in the Bible simply because we try to do God's part instead of our own part.

I. God's Part

If we are to receive help from the Bible we must begin with this basic belief which underlies all else:

The enemy with which you and I are struggling today, no matter what it is, has already been defeated!

God has already done everything that needs to be done to give us the victory over this enemy. All we really need to do is to learn how to appropriate this victory for ourselves. Even though it may not look like it to you right now in your particular struggle, the place to begin is this: You are on the winning side!

That's the good news. You are on the winning side because of three things God has already done for you, and these three things make up the whole superstructure of Christianity. This is why you must begin with them as your presuppositions before you can receive any help from the Bible.

Justification

The first of these three the Bible calls "Justification." It is, and must be, the foundation for everything else in the Christian life. Finding the wisdom and the power to cope with whatever life deals out to us is what is meant by Christian maturity. Nothing is more crucial for going on to Christian maturity than a clear awareness of its foundation, which is this: Justification—the act by which God has already declared you and me to be acceptable.

If we are to become psychologically whole, emotionally stable, and spiritually mature—which all go a long way in making us physically fit—we must first understand clearly that our acceptability to God is not based on our own behavior. Rather it is based on the behavior of God himself in the person of Jesus Christ. It is based on the act of Jesus, who was and is perfect, and who never sinned. It's based upon the death of Jesus, who never deserved to die, but who voluntarily died on the Cross as the punishment which my sins and your sins deserve.

2

You see, in his love Jesus has provided for an exchange. When we give him our sins—when I give him my sins and you give him your sins—he pays for them in order to justly forgive us. Then he gives us the gift of his righteousness. God declares us to be righteous on the basis of what Jesus has done for us, and on that basis alone!

Now, because of this fact, each of us can shout with joy, "I have been declared just by God. I am justified. I am accepted just as I am, because my acceptability has nothing to do with how I am now or how I was yesterday or how I will be tomorrow. It depends upon the perfection of Jesus Christ alone!" Until we grasp and accept this basic truth through faith, God can do nothing for us and the Bible cannot help us. But when we do grasp and accept it through faith, it becomes the foundation for all Christian growth and the basic motivation for all of our thoughts, feelings, and actions.

Sanctification

Then we are ready for the second of these three presuppositions:

God mediates this victory to us through the ministry and work of his Holy Spirit.

Again, this is God's part, not ours. The Bible calls this process "Sanctification." This is how we mature as Christians—how we grow up in Christ. This is dealt with in detail in my series of sermons, *How God Ministers to His People*. All I will say here is that it is through the ministry and work of the Holy Spirit that God makes the justifying work of Christ a living reality for us today. It is the way God assures us of what Christ has already done for us. It's the way God imputes the victory of Christ to us. Until we grasp and accept this truth, Christianity can only be a sort of magic to us, instead of the life-changing reality God intends for it to be. That's the second truth: God mediates the victory of Jesus to us through the ministry and work of his Holy Spirit.

The Means of Grace

The third truth is this:

The Holy Spirit uses what John Wesley called "the means of grace" to accomplish this.

Of course, in one sense, everything in creation is a means of God's grace to us. But God has chosen to mediate the victory of Christ to us through certain primary means, such as worship, Christian fellowship, the sacraments, and prayer. However, the principal means of grace God has chosen to use to come to us and meet our needs is the Bible—Holy Scripture. Why? Because the Bible alone contains in propositional form God's truth and directions for living. The Bible alone sets out these propositions in a way no person can misunderstand, if he is honest. Only in the Bible do we find God's specific, special word to us about life—both his Word made flesh in the person of Jesus Christ and his written word set out in propositional form.

This is why, beyond any doubt, the Bible is the principal means of grace which God has chosen for our use. This is why John Wesley said that every truth must be verified by this test: *Is it scriptural?*

The reason Jesus calls the Holy Spirit the Counselor is because, as he says, the Holy Spirit will take his words— God's word—and apply that word to our lives. This is why the Bible can never be studied and understood apart from the Holy Spirit as our Divine Interpreter. On the other hand, neither can the Holy Spirit lead us, guide us, and enlighten us on any permanent and secure basis apart from God's written word in the Bible. The very mission of the Holy Spirit is to confirm God's word and to apply God's word in our lives today.

Being led by the Spirit, for instance, as the Bible speaks of it, should never be understood by a Christian as being led apart from, but rather by means of the Holy Scriptures. The word "led" can become very misleading and confusing when we use it to refer to feelings or hunches, or to visions or extra-biblical revelations. Rather, we should use it to mean that God's word to us—which he has already given us in the Bible—actually comes alive personally for us through the ministry and work of the Holy Spirit. It's the joining together of the ministry of the Holy Spirit with the ministry of the Word. We can never separate them without cutting ourselves off from the principal means God has chosen to help us.

II. Our Part

This brings us to our part in receiving this help. Our part is Faith—a threefold faith: faith in the ministry of Jesus, faith in the ministry of the Holy Spirit, and faith in the ministry of the Word.

- Faith in the ministry of Jesus, so we can be justified,
- Faith in the ministry of the Holy Spirit, so we can be sanctified,
- Faith in the ministry of the Word as the means by which God can perfect us, complete us, and equip us for his work.

We've already discussed what it means to have faith in Jesus so we can be justified, and faith in the Holy Spirit so we can be sanctified, so let's look now at what it means to have faith in the ministry of God's word as a means of grace. Again we must accept three presuppositions, and they are so fundamental and to the point that they need very little clarification. Let me simply state all three and then give two or three short illustrations.

First—before we can receive any real help from the ministry of God's Word—we must accept the Bible as God's inspired, infallible revelation of truth to us about life.

Therefore—and this is the second presupposition we must accept before the Bible can really help us in dealing with life's problems—we can keep life stable and successfully deal with life's daily temptations and problems only by following God's ways set forth in the Bible.

5

Consequently—and this is the third presupposition— we must always, without exception, recognize the Bible as our ultimate authority, not man's learning or suppositions.

Now let me quickly illustrate what I mean. All Christians recognize that God has revealed himself and his truth to us in two basic ways. First, God has revealed himself and his truth to us through his creation, which theologians call "General Revelation." Man has discovered many of the truths in God's creation by using the scientific method and logic. These truths are very important and must not be ignored by the Christian. Second, God has revealed himself and his truth to us through what is called "Special Revelation," which means his revelation in the special person of Jesus Christ and his special revealed word in the Bible. For the Christian this is the highest and ultimate revelation of truth and must always take precedence over General Revelation.

But don't misunderstand me. When we accept the presupposition—that the Bible is God's inspired word of truth, which sets out in propositional form God's ways for living and therefore must be our ultimate authority—it does not follow that we reject the truths about life which man has discovered through science and learning. On the contrary, it specifically means we do accept them.

For example, Dr. Eric Fromm, the New York psychiatrist, in his popular book, *The Art of Loving*, states that he has discovered our basic need to be the need for love. This is the thesis of this book. A Christian will accept that truth because it is supported biblically. Consequently, a Christian should then accept other new insights that Dr. Fromm uncovers about our basic need for love. However, the Christian cannot accept Dr. Fromm's method for becoming a loving person, because he does not recognize God as the source of all love. This truth, which is God's Special Revelation to us through the scriptures, is basic to Christian love.

6

Another illustration is the form of counseling called Transactional Analysis, popularized by the book, *I'm OK—You're OK*, by Dr. Thomas Harris, a practicing psychiatrist in California. Dr. Harris' thesis is based upon the sound biblical principal of individual self-worth—"We're all OK." And likewise the goal he points to for each person is the Christian goal of growing into true maturity. Dr. Harris' insights into these two basic truths can be extremely helpful for every Christian and especially to a Christian counselor or minister. That is, they can if—but only if—that Christian accepts Transactional Analysis as an adjunct tool to the Bible and not as his Bible—his authority. For you see, Dr. Harris totally omits from his methods the first two basic presuppositions of every Christian—God's part: *Justification*—the basic reason we are OK, and *Sanctification*—the way the Holy Spirit mediates this "okayness" to us.

Only confusion can result when man tries to do God's part. Certainly, we should accept all truth which man has discovered through General Revelation. But any time we make this truth our Bible to live by in place of God's Holy Word there can be nothing but confusion. This is exactly why there is so much confusion today about how to handle life's problems. We've tried to substitute man's learning and suppositions for revealed biblical truths instead of using them as adjunct tools to the Bible.

One final illustration. I know of no writer in this century for whom I am more thankful than Dr. William Glasser, the developer of *Reality Therapy* and author of the book by that name. In my opinion the greatest need in the field of psychology since Freud has been for a recognized authority to state unequivocally and show clearly that every person must take responsibility for what he does and says without blaming someone else. That's exactly what Dr. Glasser has done, and how thankful I am for him. This truth undergirds the basic biblical truth of individual accountability without leaving any loopholes for cop-outs.

Dr. Glasser's insights can be extremely helpful for every Christian; that is, they can be, if—but only if—they are used as an adjunct tool for the Bible and not as the Bible itself. You see, there is one very important difference between Dr. Glasser's position and the Bible's position and it has to do with the basic concept of sin. To Dr. Glasser sin is irresponsibility, while to the Christian irresponsibility is simply one symptom of sin. Therefore sin itself, the root cause of irresponsibility, must be dealt with before there can be a permanent deliverance from the symptom of irresponsibility.

As we look at *How the Bible Can Help You*, we shall use all of the applicable adjunct tools which are available to assist us in dealing with specific problems and temptations. But we shall use them only as adjunct tools. The word, adjunct, means something that is added to and is helpful, but is less important. Always our Bible and ultimate authority will be God's Holy Word.

Furthermore, as we search the scriptures for solutions to our problems, we need to remember our six presuppositions as the basic foundation. I want to share a secret with you that makes this easy. Although I did not begin this discussion by quoting the scripture on which it is based, I've stuck to that scripture almost verbatim. In the last chapter of Ephesians Paul tells us to put on the whole armor of God so we'll be able to stand against the wiles of the devil. Then he describes this armor piece by piece.

That's what I've really been doing as I listed these six presuppositions, and that's what I'm asking you to do too— to put on the whole armor of God so you can stand against the wiles of the enemy and learn to live victoriously. Join me right now as I go through the process of putting on this armor as Paul describes it. Do it again each day as we let the Bible help us live victoriously. For the sake of helping us remember it easily, I'll change Paul's order slightly so we can begin at the top of the head and go down the body.

1. First, let's put on the *helmet of salvation* with our first presupposition—our justification. Jesus has already won the victory for us and through our faith in him we are already justified before God. "I'm OK!"—this is what the helmet of salvation means.

2. Next we put on the *breastplate of righteousness* through the sanctifying work of the Holy Spirit. Through the ministry and work of the Holy Spirit the very righteousness of Christ himself is given to us and becomes a living reality for us as his own spirit lives in us.

3. Then we must gird ourselves with the *belt of truth* by accepting God's means of revealing the truth to us— especially the means of the ministry of his Word.

4. Now on our left arm we hold the *shield of faith* which alone can keep the enemy from breaking through and destroying us, as it covers us from head to foot: Faith in the ministry of Jesus Christ, Faith in the ministry of the Holy Spirit, Faith in the ministry of the Word.

5. Now with our right hand we pick up the weapon with which we must fight the battles of life. We pick up the *sword of the Spirit* which is the Word of God. The Spirit and the Word—they go together. To separate them is like breaking our sword. Then we're without a weapon. We're helpless. But to join them together as the Bible does gives us a two-edged sword, honed to perfection, with which to fight the battles of life. One edge is the inspired, infallible word of God as our truth to live by; the other is the power to follow God's Word as our own way of life.

6. Finally, we're ready to shod our feet with the *equipment of the gospel of peace.* That is, we're ready to step out into the world with assurance, because we have been equipped with the good news of an ultimate authority which cannot fail—the Holy Word of God. Christian Soldier, you're ready to fight the enemy and win—win every single battle!

We're ready now to look at God's winning tactics for each particular battle. If you're to participate in that victory there's one absolute prerequisite: You must always put on the whole armor of God before you go into battle. Start each day with it. And every time you are attacked check your armor before you counter-attack. Christian, the good news is that you don't have to be a casualty in life's battles with the temptations and problems of the world. You can win every battle when you put on The Whole Armor of God!

Subject: Self-Image

Scripture: John 4:3-30

Text: *If you knew the gift of God . . . he would have given you living water* (John 4:10).

             My grace is sufficient for you, for my power is made perfect in weakness (II Corinthians 12:9).

We begin our actual exploration of *How the Bible Can Help You* with the specific problem of your self-image. We begin here because the way you see yourself will determine, to a large extent, whether or not you have serious problems in many other areas of your life. If you think too lowly of yourself, you will inevitably struggle with many other problems, such as insecurity, fear, or anxiety, having as root cause a poor self-image.

On the other hand, if you think too highly of yourself it will cause just as many problems, such as poor relationships with God and with the people around you, a critical mind, or an argumentative attitude. The result is bitterness, resentments, guilt, and the like.

The Bible prohibits both thinking too lowly of yourself and thinking too highly of yourself, and tells us how to have the right self-image. But first let's see how we get our self-image in the first place. Let's see what truths man has discovered about himself from General Revelation in the field of psychology that can help us in our search for an answer to this specific problem. Psychology has shown us that every experience is recorded in detail, stored in our brain, and can be played back in the present. Not only is the event itself played back in our memory; so is the feeling which accompanied it. We project similar images and feelings about ourselves into the future through our

Imaginations. Although memory looks backward and imagination looks to the future, when they meet in the present of our lives they are so closely related that at times it's almost impossible to distinguish them. Together, memory and imagination tell us this one truth: We are what we see ourselves to be!

For example, if through memory we recall ourselves as a failure and through imagination we're afraid to try again for fear of failing, then our present situation is apparent. As Dr. Bill Lantz says in his course on Christian Personal Resources,

> "Sure 'nuff, we are a failure! Sure 'nuff, we are what
> we see ourselves as!"

But that's not all! Simply because of this poor self-image our present moments are also spent struggling with dozens of other problems, such as anxiety, insecurity, fear, guilt, defeat, depression, and many more enemies of the Spirit—all of which in turn undermine our self-image. A vicious circle!

Again the discipline of psychology has discovered through General Revelation that three things are essential for a person to have the right self-image. As Christians we accept these truths because they undergird three basic truths of our faith which have been given to us as Special Revelation in God's Word—both God's Word made flesh in Jesus Christ and God's written Word in the Bible. Before any person can have a good, healthy self-image, both psychology and the scriptures say we must first have a feeling of

> Worthiness,
> Competence, and
> Belonging.

When I say "a feeling of," please remember that feeling is always a part of the actual happening in our life, whether it's lived actually in the present or in our memory or in our imagination.

Now let's turn to the Bible and see how it can help us have these feelings of *worthiness*, *competence*, and

12

belonging. I want to take you to the encounter of Jesus with the Samaritan woman at the well found in the 4th chapter of John. This consists of a conversation between the woman and Jesus, flowing back and forth, as Jesus gradually unmasks her completely.

The story ends with the woman leaving her water jar at the well and excitedly running back into the town of Sychar, shouting to her fellow townspeople, "Come, see a Man who told me all about myself. Only God can do that. He must be the Christ!"

Why was she so excited? Because for the first time she knew who she really was. First, Jesus led her to see herself honestly in her memory so she wouldn't think too highly of herself. Then, he led her to see herself from God's point of view in her imagination so she wouldn't think too lowly of herself. Of course, this is exactly the way Jesus wants all of us to see ourselves. He wants us to see ourselves honestly in our memory as sinners, and to see ourselves from God's point of view in our imaginations as redeemed by the blood of Christ. Only this can make us truly OK—seeing ourselves as redeemed sinners. Paul called this "Justification." The psychologist or psychiatrist might call it seeing our own worthiness—our personal worth. Notice how Jesus begins the conversation with the woman at the well:

> *"Every one who drinks of this water will thirst again, but whoever drinks of the water that I shall give him will never thirst; the water that I shall give him will become in him a spring of water welling up to eternal life"* (Jn 4:13-14).

Jesus is telling her, "Woman, your problem is what the scriptures call worldliness. You live only for this world. But you can never be satisfied by the things of this world, for you are more than a creature of this world. You were created for eternity with God—for eternal life!"

Now don't misunderstand what Jesus is saying. He's not saying this woman is worldly because she is living with a man who is not her husband after she has already gone through five husbands. No! He is saying that she's doing this because she is already worldly. Her problem wasn't adultery. Rather, adultery was simply one of the symptoms of her problem. Her problem was that she didn't know herself. She didn't know who she really was. This is always what the Bible means by worldliness. It means lack of an eternal value system to live by. People are worldly because their priorities are all confused.

So the first thing Jesus says to this woman is the first truth we all must grasp in order to have the right self-image and it's this:

Know Yourself! Know Who You Really Are!

One of the tools which best helped me to know myself is a short seminar course I took nearly ten years ago, led by Dr. Bill Lantz, Director of our Heritage Services. This course, called *Christian Personal Resources,* is offered periodically in LIFE FM (Lay Institute for Equipping for Ministry). I guarantee you, after you take this course you will know who you are and you'll be able to utilize this knowledge correctly.

For example, I now have 36 Mental Practice Cards I have gone through daily for ten years. I credit much that has happened in our church during these past ten years to first getting the right mental picture. Let me read you Card #1, which is the first thing I read each day to program into my memory and into my imagination—the first essential ingredient of a healthy self-image.

> I am a redeemed sinner—a forgiven Christian! In Jesus Christ on the Cross, God released me from my sins—past, present, and future. Every sin I ever committed—past, present, and future—is totally and completely forgiven! Because the Living Christ dwells within me my sins are gone forever, and I accept all of God's blessings and gifts. I am filled with love, joy, peace, patience, kindness, goodness, faithfulness, gentleness, and self-control. I walk in the light and have nothing to do with the darkness. When I confess, I confess and reaffirm that I am in the light, and that Jesus Christ is the Lord of my life.

14

Isn't that what Jesus is saying to this woman at the well? "You're OK now, not because you're so good, or so smart, or so pretty, or so clever, or so rich, or so successful. You're OK now, because I've come to make you OK. You're OK because you're redeemed—you're justified! So start now seeing yourself as a redeemed sinner."

This is exactly what Jesus is saying to you and me. The reason Jesus wants us to see ourselves as redeemed sinners is because the word "redeemed" will keep us from thinking too lowly of ourselves, and the word "sinner" will keep us from thinking too highly of ourselves. Together they spell worthiness—individual personal worth!

The point is not for each person to sell himself a bill of goods about how great he is so he can begin to say, "I'm OK." The point is for all of us to grasp the reason why I'm OK. I'm OK because I'm a redeemed sinner! I'm OK because of Jesus! I'm OK because now, through faith in Jesus I'm justified! I'm OK because,

"Like the woman at the well I was seeking
For things that could not satisfy.
And then I heard my Savior speaking,
'Draw from my well that never shall run dry'"*

Now I'm OK because I let him fill my cup with himself. Now I know I'm OK because I know who I am. I am a redeemed sinner. The first step to the right self-image must always be: Know Yourself! Know Who You Are! The second step is this:

Be Yourself!

Psychology tells us that the second essential for a healthy self-image is a feeling of competence; that is, a feeling that "I Can." I can do something and do it well. I am adequate for whatever comes. What causes us to have a feeling of inadequacy and incompetence? Two things primarily:

Fill My Cup, Richard Blanchard, 1959

- Past failures, which we relive in our memories, and
- Comparing ourselves with others, which we see continually in our imaginations.

Before we can have a healthy self-image we must turn our past failures into stepping stones to successful experiences and we must stop comparing ourselves with others. This is exactly what Jesus tells this woman at the well and all who follow after her. First, he points up the fact that she has already failed five times in marriage and because she is afraid of another failure she's now living in sin with a man who is not her husband. In other words, her failures are dragging her down into degradation instead of being stepping stones to success. Inevitably, that's the life story of every worldly person whose priorities are twisted.

Of course, she knows it is true, but just like us today, she can't face up to herself. So, she tries to change the subject and begins to compare herself, a Samaritan, to the Jews. You see, she tries to justify herself, because she, as a Samaritan, hasn't had the blessings the Jews have had. She has a "reason" for her failures. Sound familiar? Anyway, she goes on, the Jews say one thing and her people say something else; how can a person know? In other words, she acts like she does because she's confused.

Then, Jesus drives home the point she needs and that all of us need before we can have a healthy self-image. Jesus looks at her and tells her to be herself—be the person God created her to be. This is the essence of his reply to her in John 4:21-24. He's telling her that what she needs comes neither from the ritual of Samaritans nor the Jews, nor from justifying herself because,

"God is spirit, and those who worship him must worship in spirit and in truth" (Jn 4:24).

God has not left us desolate. He comes to us as Holy Spirit to assure us of forgiveness, to cleanse us and to deliver us from bondage to our past failures. He comes to us as Holy Spirit to equip us with specific gifts and with power so we can do our own thing according to his will—not

16

someone else's thing. He comes to us as Holy Spirit so we can be ourselves! Paul drives home the same truth in his second letter to the Corinthians when he says:

"When they measure themselves by one another, and compare themselves with one another, they are without understanding" (II Cor 10:12b).

That is, because you are permitting others to control your life you cannot understand God's special revealed truth to you. Neither can you discern and use the particular spiritual gifts which God has given especially to you. Consequently, you must inevitably fail. To be competent—to be adequate—you must worship God in spirit and in truth. You must accept the assurance of forgiveness that the Holy Spirit wants to mediate to you. You must accept the spiritual gifts with which the Holy Spirit wants to equip you.

The point is, we are competent because the Holy Spirit equips us for competence—not because we are so smart or so great ourselves. But we can express this competence only when we are ourselves, which means when we are truly new creatures in Christ. When, through forgiveness, we put off the old person who trusts the things of this world for his competence, and we put on the new person in Christ through spiritual empowerment, then and only then do we have a feeling of competence. That's how we make stepping stones out of failures. That's how we stop comparing ourselves with others, and start being ourselves. That's how we start being the spiritual person God created us to be. That's how we become OK in our doing as well as in our thinking. That's how we feel competent. We can feel competent only when we honestly begin to sing,

"Fill my cup, Lord.
I lift it up Lord,
Come and quench this thirsting of my soul;
Bread of heaven, feed me till I want no more;
Fill my cup, fill it up and make me whole."

Since we are created in the image of God, and created for eternity with him, the feeling of worthiness must come through *Justification* and the feeling of competence must come through *Sanctification.*

This brings us to the final essential for the right self-image, the feeling of *Belonging.*

Worthiness comes through Justification.
Competence comes through Sanctification.
Belonging comes only through Participation. So...

Give Yourself!

See the difference? The first two God does for us through faith, but the last one we must do ourselves. We have seen that to feel worthy we must know ourselves, and to feel competent we must be ourselves, but to belong we must give ourselves. That's the third truth.

Notice that Jesus sends this woman back into her village with a mission and a message. She runs back shouting, "Come and see this Man . . . who is the Christ!" Now she is part of the community, no longer a bitter, hurt individual striking out at the mores and standards of her group. No longer is she just concerned about being OK herself; now she is concerned about others knowing they're OK too. This is simply another aspect of the teaching which Jesus repeats more than any other: You must lose yourself to find yourself; to become the greatest, you must become servant of all; it's through giving that we truly receive.

Is it any wonder that over half of my 36 Mental Practice Cards deal with my participation in this community of faith we call First United Methodist Church of Tulsa, and of my giving of myself to you, the members, to meet your needs? For example, I have cards which remind me that I preach to your need; I schedule my day to serve you; I get to know you by sharing your hurts and pains; I go on prayer retreats for you; I devote the first hour of my study time each day praying for you; I listen when you call. These are only a few of the ways I remind myself each day that I must give myself to you. Because I know only by giving myself in this way can I really know you and know that your hurts are like my hurts, your joys like my joys, your hopes like my hopes.

18

Only by giving myself to God can I ever know God; only by giving myself to you can I ever know you; and only by giving myself to both God and you can I know that you are OK, and know that you know that I'm OK, which enables me to actually feel OK too.

You see, the feeling must always follow the act of faith. This is what the Bible means when it says that a Christian does not live by feeling—he lives by faith. Consequently he finds the feeling as a by-product of this faith. Those who say feeling is not important neither know the scriptures nor psychology. Feeling is all-important because your self-image is made up of an homogenized mixture of facts and feelings.

So it's as important to program into your memory and imagination the right feelings as it is to program in the right facts. Perhaps it's more important, because our feelings are so much more subtle in the way they control our lives than are facts. Living by feelings is not the way to program in the right feelings. In fact, that is the one sure way to program in the wrong feelings! You do it, not by withdrawing to straighten out your feelings, but by giving yourself to God and to his church. The feelings will follow as surely as the harvest follows seedtime.

I don't pray for you or do these other things I mentioned because I always feel like it. Sometimes I feel like doing anything else but that! I do it because you need it and God's word tells me I can truly belong to God's people only by doing it. I can belong only by giving myself. I do it because it's the only way I can go through life with the right self-image, knowing that *I'm OK—You're OK!* For *worthiness* comes through justification and *competence* comes through sanctification which is God's part. But *belonging* can come only through participation which is my part!

It takes all three for any person to have the right self-image and know *I'm OK—You're OK!* You are worthy because Jesus Christ gives you his worthiness. You are competent because the Spirit equips you with his gifts. But you can belong only through your own participation.

Are you like the woman at the well? Do you find that many of your present problems are rooted in the wrong self-image? Are you seeking for worldly things that cannot satisfy? Is Jesus saying to you through his Holy Word, "Draw from my well that never shall run dry?" Are you willing to do your part and conscientiously say to him,

"Fill my cup, Lord. I lift it up, Lord!"

I lift it up by genuinely belonging to you and your Body on earth and being a full participant.

"Come and quench this thirsting of my soul."

Make me worthy by justifying me and make me competent by sanctifying me.

"Bread of Heaven, feed me till I want no more."

I want to give myself to you and to your church and truly belong to the redeemed of the Lord; so I can be the person I was created to be!

"Fill my cup, fill it up and make me whole!"

III   *God's Cure for Insecurity*

Subject: Insecurity

Scripture: Luke 12:13-34

Text: *Instead, seek his kingdom, and these things
               shall be yours as well* (Luke 12:31).

The Bible says clearly that God created us with certain
specific basic needs. In giving us these basic needs
God motivates us to become what we were created to
be. Different schools of psychology have emphasized
different basic needs as primary. Freud emphasized man's
need for pleasure. Adler emphasized man's need for power.
Jung emphasized man's need for selfhood or discovering
self. Frankl emphasized man's need for meaning. Glasser
has emphasized man's need for responsibility, and
Fromm—man's need for love. I believe that the Bible sums
them all up in four basic needs:

> The right self-image
> Security
> Freedom
> Purpose

As we look at *How the Bible Can Help You*, first of all we
must examine how the Bible can help us meet these four
basic needs. Any time we try to meet these basic needs in
the wrong way, that is, in some way other than God's way,
we cause all kinds of specific problems. We have already
considered the first basic need—the need for the right self-
image—in the sermon *I'm OK, You're OK*. Let's turn our
attention to the need for Security.

This basic need for security is seen in the first story in
the Bible—the story of Adam and Eve. What made the
Garden of Eden a paradise for the first man and woman?
There they possessed the three things which are essential
for security:

21

- *Peace.* Peace of mind, peace of heart, and peace of spirit;
- *Power.* Power to be themselves, power to obey God and to triumph over the circumstances of life;
- *Hope.* Hope for tomorrow and for eternity.

When we first see them in the Garden of Eden, Adam and Eve are secure on all levels of life—physical, social, political, psychological, and spiritual. That is, they are until something happens; and that event is what the Bible calls "the Fall." Then their paradise turns to hell. Why?

Their paradise is lost because, instead of being secure on these five levels of life, they are plagued by insecurity. Instead of having peace, they struggle with anxiety. Instead of having power they are plagued by weakness. Instead of having hope they are filled with fear. After the fall, insecurity becomes their way of life, and we see them desperately searching for *A Cure for Insecurity.* It's a curse with which all of us have had to struggle ever since.

Most people today are struggling with this problem of insecurity simply because they've tried to meet this basic need for security in the wrong way. To help all men deal with this common problem, Jesus tells a parable—The Parable of the Rich Fool —found in the 12th chapter of Luke. The man in this parable ate the forbidden fruit, and like Adam and Eve, gave in to the temptation to rebel against God and put his trust in himself. Then the devil whispered in his ear, "Listen to me and you won't die. Rebel and you will be secure. Take care of yourself. Forget about God's word. Get all you can as fast as you can, and you will be secure."

It's a very tempting challenge for all of us. The man in Jesus' parable gave in to it. He ate the forbidden fruit. He rebelled. He got all he could from the bountiful garden and stored it in his barns. But, like Adam and Eve, instead of finding paradise, he too woke up in hell. Jesus calls him a fool because he gave in to the sin of Adam, following Satan instead of God. Then, in a dozen simple words Jesus tells us how to keep from being such a fool ourselves. He tells us *God's Cure for Insecurity.* Notice he begins with the word "instead." "Instead of being like this fool," he says, "here's the way to find security."

"Instead, seek his [God's] *kingdom, and these things shall be yours as well"* (Lk 12:31).

What does that mean for you and me? It really boils down to one word, and that word is "stewardship." God's cure for insecurity is stewardship. Here is what stewardship means on each level of life.

The Physical Level

All of us have a basic need for physical security. We all need to feel secure about food, shelter, and clothing and our other physical needs. Dr. Abraham Maslow in his classical *Hierarchy of Needs* lists this as the most basic need in life. All animals have this need. But the physical security we human beings need goes much deeper than that. Certainly, we need to eat, like all animals. But when our working days are done, we also need to feel secure about our old age—to know that we can continue to live like a human being created in the image of God.

Today even the most financially secure are threatened. If you are older, you know what I mean, for the money you have wisely saved across the years for retirement suddenly isn't enough anymore. If you are young, you know what I mean, for saving is becoming harder and harder for young families. The house you dreamed of owning is getting further and further out of sight. Insecurity is a common malady for almost everyone. Could it be that we find ourselves in this predicament because most of us have played the fool like the man in our Lord's parable, instead of heeding God's word about stewardship?

You see, this man wasn't a fool because he worked hard and acquired possessions. The Bible says that we are created to have purpose, to be productive. In fact, this is the fourth basic need for all of us—purpose. The amount this man made is not the point here. In another parable— The Parable of the Talents—Jesus says that the wise man is the one who does work the hardest and does make the most

23

out of what he has. But the point here is motivation. Why does this man work so hard? Why does he make all he can? He does it for himself—for his own physical security. That is why Jesus calls him a fool. He missed the real point in life. He worked hard and laid up material wealth for the wrong reason! "Instead," Jesus says, "seek to be an honest, faithful steward for God first; and you will find physical security as well."

Perhaps the question each of us needs to ask himself is this: "What is my motivation for working and saving today? Am I following this fool, or am I following Jesus Christ?" How much you make, how much you save is really immaterial, if you've done the best you can with what you have. The real question is why you have made it and why you have it. The real question is your motivation.

The Social Level

All of us have a basic need for what I call social security, and I don't mean the need for a pension at age 65. I mean that all of us need to feel socially secure in our relationships with others. Everybody needs to be recognized and to find his niche in society. It's intolerable to be a nobody. Consequently we'll go to almost any length to get this recognition and be somebody. In this world in which you and I live, nothing will give us this recognition more quickly than success in our chosen field of work. It wins for us the approval and acclaim from our peers and satisfies this basic need for social security.

Surely Jesus didn't call this man a fool because he succeeded in his chosen field of work. God wants all of us to succeed if our work is worthwhile and legitimate. God gives us special gifts and talents so we can succeed.

The Bible tells us that God intervened again and again in human history to help his people succeed. He intervened for Moses, and Moses was a great success. So it was with Joseph too. Incidentally Joseph succeeded in the same way that this fool in our parable succeeded. But for his success Joseph was called the wisest and best man in all of Egypt! You remember; like this fool, Joseph filled his barns with grain, and like this fool, he even built new barns and filled them too. In fact, Joseph's stockpile far exceeded the stockpile of this fool. No, this man was not a fool because he succeeded. Far from it! God wants us to succeed.

This man was a fool because he succeeded for the wrong reason. Joseph did it so he could be a co-worker with God and feed God's people. This fool did it so he could feed his own ego. That is always self defeating, for fame is fickle. It puts us at the mercy of fickle people. Any man is a fool who lets fame be his motivation in life. Here is Jesus' message to us: "Instead, desire to serve God in your chosen field, for God alone is not fickle. God alone is eternal, everlasting, and secure. Then, not only will you have the right motivation for success; all these other things will be yours as well, including the recognition which gives you true social security."

Perhaps the question we should ask ourselves is this: "What motivates me to be a success? Am I motivated like the fool our Lord tells about, or like Joseph? What is my true motivation for social security?"

The Political Level

As long as we live on this earth we must live as dual citizens. There is no way to escape it. As Christians, not only are we citizens of God's kingdom, we must also be citizens of a particular nation as well. This need for national security is certainly a basic need for all of us. If a person doesn't feel secure on the political level of life, then everything he does is threatened. Without this national security life becomes almost unbearable. Do we need any examples other than life under Hitler and the Nazis in Germany and under the long, diabolical reign of Stalin in Russia or the mad Idi Amin in Uganda? To find this national security we must start with this: God's truth is eternal. It applies to nations as well as to individuals, because nations are made up of individuals.

In his monumental account of *The History of Human Civilization*, Arnold Toynbee says that throughout known history every civilization has fallen for the same basic reason—because they made violent power the basis of their security. Inevitably, no matter what the cost, another nation would rise up, become more violent, and overthrow them. On the national scale this is the way of the fool in our parable; that is, one who never learns from experience.

On the other hand, the weak nations—those without power—are trampled on and never have their day in the sun. Certainly the answer is not weakness—just lying down and waiting for someone to step on you. But neither is it violent power as the world has known it in the past. Jesus is teaching us: "Instead, take the offensive with the greatest and most dependable power on earth, God's power, and all these other things, including national security, shall be yours as well."

What does this mean? Well, certainly it means that when we as Christians go to the polls, our first concern should be to elect people who are committed to being co-workers with God in running our government. It means that God's way with nations is reconciliation, not violence, just as it is with individuals. But before this reconciliation is possible with nations as with individuals, Jesus Christ must live in men's hearts. It means every Christian must accept nothing less than a dynamic mission program that has as its goal, *Jesus Christ—Lord of Every Nation!* That, and that alone, can bring us true national security.

I wonder if a familiar scene has flashed through your mind as we've looked at these first three points? Perhaps you've remembered the scene of Jesus being tempted in the wilderness.

- On the physical level it's a replay of Jesus' temptation to turn stones into bread and make material things ultimate in his scale of values. All of us are tempted to do the same thing.

- On the social level it's a replay of his temptation to jump from the pinnacle of the temple, to win fame and make the opinions of others ultimate in his scale of values. All of us are tempted to do the same thing.

- On the political level it's a replay of his temptation to use violent force and make political control and power over others ultimate in his scale of values. All of us are tempted to do the same.

Our Lord turned his back on all of these temptations, for he knew this was Satan's way, not God's. This is what trapped Adam and Eve into a false security. Real security on these first three levels of life—the outer levels—comes as a by-product of real security on the remaining two levels of life—the psychological and the spiritual levels. Or to say it Jesus' way, "It's the inner man who controls the outer man, not vice versa. It's not what goes into a man that controls his actions, but what comes out of him. You must find inner security before you can hope to find outer security."

The Psychological Level

No matter how much wealth you accumulate, how much fame you win, or what country you call home, without peace of mind and peace of heart you will still be insecure and anxious. First find inner peace; then these other things will be yours as well. The fool in our parable was a fool because he thought he could satisfy the inner man by accumulating outer things. He was a fool simply because he never learned this lesson: Real security must begin on the inside with peace of mind and peace of heart.

Paul's answer for psychological wholeness is this:

"Let this mind be in you, which was also in Christ Jesus . . . and the peace of God, which passeth all understanding, shall keep your hearts and minds through Christ Jesus" (Phil 2:5 and 4:7 KJV).

Paul is showing us that Christ is our way to mental health—to inner security. Only when he lives in us can we have outer security too. This is the message of the whole New Testament: we seek God's kingdom by seeking Jesus Christ. When the Bible says, *"Instead, seek first God's kingdom,"* it is saying, "First of all seek Christ; then these other things will be yours as well." That's the key to real security in life.

27

The Spiritual Level

The Bible says that God created us in his image for eternity with him. No one has ever expressed what this means better than St. Augustine when he said,

"Thou madest us for Thyself, and our heart is restless, until it repose in Thee."

From a practical standpoint this simply means that we are created by our eternal God for eternity and there can be no real security until we find this eternal security. The things in this world—the finite which will pass away—can never satisfy this basic need in us for eternal security.

How can we find this eternal security? The Bible is clear about it. We find eternal security as God's Holy Spirit witnesses to our spirit that we are children of God and fellow heirs with Christ (Rom 8:16,17). Absolutely nothing else in all heaven and earth will do it! Our God created us in his image for eternity with him, and he will never let us meet this need for eternal security by simply possessing the temporal things of this earth. Only a fool could think that. God put this basic need in us for a purpose, and that purpose is to keep us from playing the fool and settling for false security. But in spite of that, if we do play the fool, he has given us the cure for that too.

"Instead, seek his kingdom, and these things shall be yours as well" (Lk 12:31).

Instead, seek Christ! Christ alone is the way to Peace, Power, and Hope, the three essentials for true security.

- *Peace.* - The mind, heart, and spirit of Christ. Peace of mind, peace of heart, peace of spirit. The peace that comes from knowing you are working with the divine plan of creation, not against it.
- *Power.* - Power from on high, from the Living Christ. God's power, the Holy Spirit. The dynamic of Love itself, personified.

- *Hope.* - Assurance of eternal security in Christ Jesus himself who died to give us eternal life and who awaits us in our eternal home.

Victor Frankl writes that sometimes he has helped his patients find meaning in life by asking them to jump time to their old age when they are lying on their death bed. Dr. Frankl asks them to imagine how they would feel then. Often, he says, this helps them discover true meaning in life and the right motivation for what they do.

I wonder if such an exercise in imagination wouldn't help many of us to realize that we have been playing the fool instead of being the faithful steward God wants us to be. I wonder if such an exercise wouldn't help us give up our foolish ways and begin to practice *God's Cure for Insecurity* which is this:

Instead, seek first his kingdom—through Christ Jesus. Then these other things will be yours as well!

Subject: Freedom

Scripture: John 3:1-21

Text: *Truly, truly, I say to you, unless one is born anew, he cannot see the kingdom of God!* (John 3:3).

              If you continue in my word, you are truly my disciples, and you will know the truth, and the truth will make you free (John 8:31-32).

In the opening pages of the Bible we are told that God's first gift to man, after life itself, was the gift of freedom—total freedom. On first reading, you might say, "Wait a minute! You'd better read that passage again, for the Bible does say that God restricts man's freedom!" All right, let's read it again together. Here it is—the 16th verse of the second chapter of Genesis:

And the Lord God commanded the man, saying, "You may freely eat of every tree of the garden;"

Semi-colon. That's total freedom so far, isn't it? God continues speaking,

"but of the tree of the knowledge of good and evil you shall not eat,"

That does sound like a restriction on man's freedom, doesn't it? But that's not the end of the sentence. Here we find a comma, then God continues,

"for in the day that you eat of it you shall die."

Period! That's not a restriction. That's a warning! That's a divine revelation in God's Holy Word of the only way we can keep the freedom—total freedom—which God has given us. In effect, God is telling us, "You are born to be free, so you can enjoy life in my paradise. But one warning: the very fact that you're free means that you can sacrifice even freedom itself. But if you do, you will sacrifice the good life

31

with it. For you must have freedom in order to enjoy life in my paradise."

Why is this so? It is so because we are created in the image of God; that is, we are created with a spiritual nature. Only by being true to our spiritual nature can we partake of the blessings which God has for us. When we use our God-given freedom to try to remake ourselves into a different nature, we are cut off from God's blessings.

Or to use the biblical words, when we try through our own knowledge of good and evil to take over our own lives, we're lost! We're lost because we corrupt the very nature which God has given us. We're lost because we are no longer a spiritual person, free to receive the blessings God has for us—that is, his spiritual fruit and gifts. We are lost because we take on the nature of a natural person, or natural man as the Bible calls it. This means that we must depend upon ourselves alone like all the other animals of the field—wholly finite. We are lost because then our destiny is set. We are doomed to loss of freedom! Bondage! Death!

There is no problem more intolerable than bondage, yet it is the common lot of all of us since the days of Adam. We're bound to the enemies of the spirit found in the finite, natural man—enemies such as fear, guilt, worry, anxiety, impulsiveness, anger, bitterness, resentments, strife, and the rest.

But, perhaps this bondage can be seen most plainly in what modern man and woman have done to another of God's most precious gifts to us—the gift of sex. Sex for man and woman is not meant to be like the animals of the field. Sex is meant to be the highest way a man and wife can communicate this God-image of love within us, so that every family can be founded upon that love. Sex is meant to be the coming together of man and wife in the true oneness of agape love—selfless love. It's meant to be the actual union not only of bodies, but of spiritual man and spiritual woman, joined together by God in his paradise of total freedom! Yet everywhere we look, men and women are in bondage to sex, treating it like the animals of the field,

32

instead of like spiritual men and women created in the image of God. No wonder Freud thought sex was man's basic drive, because its degradation is the cause of so much of man's emotional misery and mental anguish.

If Freud had gone to the scriptures instead of rejecting them, he would have found the cause, not in sex itself as he thought, but in man's fall from spiritual man to natural man. He would have also seen that God's answer is not found in dealing with sex, the symptom, but in redeeming the root cause—man's fallen nature. Most important of all, he would have seen that God gave us his answer to bondage in the advent of the Second Adam, who is Jesus Christ, the Perfect Man.

In Jesus, God comes to set us free by giving us a second birth. In Jesus, God comes to transform us from the natural man we have become through sin to the spiritual man he meant us to be. In one real sense, in Jesus, our Divine Creator finishes his creation in us by re-creating us as spiritual men and women, free to enjoy all the blessings of his paradise. Perhaps the most graphic picture of how God performs this divine transformation in us can be seen in the story of Nicodemus in the third chapter of John. Let's set the scene.

Nicodemus is a good man, a religious man, a respectable man, who, as a Pharisee, does his best to keep the law of God. But somehow, life is not what it's meant to be, so he comes to Jesus seeking the secret to divine transformation, and Jesus says to him,

> "Truly, truly, I say to you, unless one is born anew, he cannot see the kingdom of God" (Jn 3:3).

"Nicodemus," Jesus is saying, "Here's the truth. Only rebirth can set you free so you can partake of the blessings God has for you." What does Jesus mean by this? He simply means that Nicodemus must be transformed from his old nature to a new nature—from the natural man to the spiritual man. He simply means that Nicodemus is living one kind of life now that keeps him in bondage, unable to enjoy God's blessings; and he must be born into a whole new kind of life where he is released from this bondage, leaving him free to enjoy all the blessings God wants to give him.

What kind of life was Nicodemus living that bound him to the tragedies and miseries of the natural man instead of freeing him to the blessings of the spiritual man? What more could he do? He was a good man. He was religious. He was respected. He did his best to dot every "i" and cross every "t" of the scriptures. What was wrong? The record is clear—he was living a *Life of Law*. Through his own knowledge of good and evil, through his own efforts to remake his life, he thought he could live in paradise. Like Adam before him, he ignored God's warning and with the same results—deadly bondage, a distorted nature. Therefore he is no longer free to do God's will. He can only react to his bondage and to the enemies of the Spirit so prevalent in every natural man.

Into what kind of life did Jesus want Nicodemus to be born? Jesus wanted for Nicodemus the kind of life that God has always wanted for all men and women from the beginning—*a Life of Grace*. A life so totally different from the one Nicodemus was living that it was like being born all over again. Jesus wanted for Nicodemus a life that is free— free like the wind, which blows wherever God directs it—a life that moves and has its being according to God's Word alone.

Here Jesus is making it crystal clear that because our very nature has been distorted by sin, it takes nothing less than an act of re-creation by God himself to deal with our common problem of bondage and meet our basic need for freedom. We can't do it by being religious—by being good or respectable. Nor can we do it by rejecting God's law and creating our own rules to live by. Because of our distorted nature this will lead to more bondage. Nothing short of rebirth can do it, says Jesus. What does he mean by this? To understand it, we must first look at what the Bible means by a *Life of Law*.

According to the Bible, a Life of Law is basically an "I ought to" approach to life.

34

I ought to live by certain rules because the Bible says I ought to, or the church says I ought to, or someone in authority says I ought to. I ought to keep the rules, my children ought to keep the rules, and anyone who is going to be my friend ought to keep them. The rules are unending and we know them well—rules such as:

- I ought to read my Bible;
- I ought to pray;
- I ought to be humble no matter how much I humiliate others in doing it;
- I ought to love my unlovely neighbor;
- I ought not to curse or drink or commit adultery or keep my business open on Sunday.

The rules may vary according to your own background, family, and church interpretation. But when you live a *Life of Law,* you know that these are God's laws that you ought to keep, and you're going to keep them no matter how hard you have to be on yourself, or how rigid you must be in dealing with others . . . only to find yourself constantly failing in your efforts.

Did you notice that all of the laws I enumerated are admirable and good rules? In fact, there's not a bad one in the list. Both Jesus and Paul are emphatic about this. It is not the law that is bad; it's us! It's not the patch of new cloth that is bad, it's the old garment! It's not the fresh, new nectar of the grape that is bad, it's the old wineskin. It's not the wedding feast that's bad, it's the sour faces of the fasting guests that spoil the fun! It's not the *law* that's the problem with a *life of law;* it's our human nature.

This brings us to the second preliminary point we must understand before we can comprehend what Jesus means by rebirth. A great segment of people today, including most church members and most ministers, have rejected the law—at least most of the law—as a practical way to live, if not verbally, certainly by their actions. But still they do not live under grace! They simply say that those old-fashioned laws just don't apply anymore. In effect, they're saying that it's bad law. So what do they do? What do you do? What does the church do?

35

We just proceed to modernize the law to fit ourselves.

That's the history of the church in America for the past 200 years. The method stays the same, only the laws are changed. Pious rules no longer apply to this fast moving society in which we live. What the world needs now is action. So the rule is to liberate the poor, no matter how much you have to step on American business and the hard-working middle class to do it! Sexual purity is out and sexual promiscuity is in; the pill changed that law. Building beautiful sanctuaries in which to worship and church facilities in which to study is out. That's old law.

The new law is to give that money to help liberate the latest caucus, whether it be a black caucus, a women's caucus, a gay caucus, or a South African caucus. Sending missionaries to preach the gospel to those who haven't heard it is old law and it's too pious. What the world needs now is action. The job of the modern missionary is to liberate the oppressed by siding with the revolutionaries against authority—they must become peacemakers by practicing violence—which is a pretty good trick if you can do it, and about as far as you can twist the gospel without actually calling it Communism.

But again, the goals of most of these modern laws are not bad in themselves. Oh, some of them are rotten, but most of them are admirable and good, such as: eliminating poverty and working together to see that the physical needs of all human beings are met, espousing equality for all human beings regardless of color or sex, taking the Victorian wraps off sex and dealing with it frankly and openly, supporting freedom and human rights everywhere. These are all worthwhile goals for every Christian!

The point is, it is not the law that is wrong, it is us. It's not the new patch, it's the old garment. It's not the new wine, it's the old, worn-out wineskin. The trouble with living under the law is that you are pre-set. You are like a robot; you are bound; you're not free to be God's person guided by his Holy Spirit and his Holy Word. You are in the state the Bible calls death; that is, you are without the Spirit of the

Living God, so you are on your own. You are only finite. You are natural man and you are doomed.

When Jesus says, I did not come to abolish the law, but to fulfill it, he means that the law is not the culprit, we are. The problem is in us, not God's law. As legalists, we are bound and no longer free to move and have our being according to God's will, so we become hard and cold.

But let us never forget that God's world still operates according to God's law. It always has; it always will. We're just kidding ourselves—worse than that, we are actually condemning ourselves to bondage and death when we think that we can fulfill this law. I don't care what modern interpretations we put on it or under what guise we try to masquerade it—be it brotherhood, peace, personal freedom, or human rights. Jesus made this clear in his talk with Nicodemus, when he said,

> "God sent the Son into the world, not to condemn the world, but that the world might be saved through him. He who believes in him is not condemned; he who does not believe is condemned already because he has not believed in the name of the only Son of God" (Jn 3:17, 18a).

This brings us to the heart of the matter, which is this:

Although we can never fulfill the law, God can!

The good news is that God has fulfilled the law in Jesus Christ and he gives us the benefit of it in a *Life of Grace*. Rebirth is simply the change from a *Life of Law* to a *Life of Grace*. To be born again into a life where we are released from the bondage of the natural man and can enjoy the freedom of the spiritual man is, in the final analysis, simply a matter of where we put our faith.

Faith is the catalyst that brings about rebirth. The natural man puts his faith in his own knowledge of good and evil, in the law which deals with it, and in his ability to keep that law. The spiritual man puts his faith in the living Christ who already encompasses all of the law and the prophets. The moment you accept God's complete fulfillment of the law in Jesus Christ, and put your trust in

37

him and him alone for your salvation—in that very moment you are born again. And in that very moment you are transformed from a natural man to a spiritual man. From that moment on, the Bible can begin to help you with your daily problems, for his Spirit wrote it and his Spirit will interpret for you.

But the Bible can never help any person who is living under law, because that person is already pre-set. He's a robot. He knows he must do it himself, and he knows what he must do to do it himself. He's inflexible; he's bound; he can't grow; he's condemned already. God gave us the Bible as his primary means of grace, that is, as the primary instrument for channeling his grace and truth into our lives. Until we are born again and transformed from the legalism of a natural man to the openness of a spiritual man, there is no way God can channel his grace and truth into us, for we are cut off from his means of grace.

Or look at it this way. The Bible says that God has already done our work for us in Jesus Christ; and by doing it for us he has enabled us to do his work for him here on earth. He enables us to do it through his means of grace, especially his Holy Word—his Living Word in the crucified and resurrected Christ and his infallible written Word in the Bible. This is what the Bible means by living under grace instead of living under law. It means that we do God's work, not through our own efforts to keep the law, but through his living Spirit living in us, interpreting his written Word to us, and empowering us to make this Holy Word a living reality in our own lives.

This is what it means to live a *Life of Grace* instead of a *Life of Law*. It means that the living Spirit of Christ within us enables us not only to interpret the scriptures with the mind of Christ, but also to fulfill the scriptures with the love and power of Christ. Therefore, we are free like the wind, following Christ instead of law. Instead of being pre-set and rigid, we move and have our being with the mind and the Spirit of Christ himself. God's Word is a living reality for us, just as it was for him when he walked this earth.

This is why a *Life of Grace* is an absolute prerequisite if we are to receive help for our daily problems from God's Word—the Bible. And this is the message which Jesus has for the Pharisee, Nicodemus, who was a legalist, living a *Life of Law*. "Nicodemus, it all comes down to your approach to life. It comes down to whether you put your trust in your own ability to dot every 'i' and cross every 't' of the law, or you put your trust in Jesus Christ and Christ alone who has already fulfilled all of the law, and now gives his perfect life to you to be lived out in you. The legalistic approach is sure bondage and death. The faithful approach is sure freedom and life."

Let's place the picture of Nicodemus before us once again. Look at it closely one more time. Notice he is good, religious, and respectable; yet somehow life is not what it is meant to be. Look closer and you can see the worry creases around his eyes and the anxiety sealed in his face. His eyes are hard, his shoulders rigid, his mouth set. Only a cursory look and you know that here is a man who is bound to a way of life he doesn't really like down deep inside—a life which brings him no joy and fulfillment. Yet it has him in its grips, binding him. So in desperation he goes to Jesus seeking an answer to his basic need. Jesus takes the same look at him that we've just taken and says, "Unless you are born again, you cannot see the kingdom of God."

Then Jesus paints the most beautiful picture of rebirth and a *Life of Grace* ever painted as he compares it to the freedom of the wind blowing where God wills it to blow, and moving and having its being according to God's Word alone. He climaxes it with the most beautiful words ever spoken,

"For God so loved the world that he gave his only Son, that whoever believes in him should not perish but have eternal life" (Jn 3:16).

For some reason the Bible doesn't tell us what Nicodemus did about it—about Jesus' offer of a new life. I wonder why, don't you? Could it be that God wants us to slip the picture of Nicodemus out of that frame and replace it with our own picture? Could it be that God wants us to see ourselves in this picture instead of Nicodemus? Are you willing to do that? What do you see when you look at the picture now? Do you see bondage or freedom? Do you see a Life of Law or a Life of Grace?

Do you see a religious, respectable person, yet a face creased with worry, a mind filled with anxiety, fear, guilt and a legion of other problems? Do you see a heart heavy with resentment and bitterness and a spirit without joy? Do you see a natural man? Or do you see someone free as the wind, always going where God wills, truly moving and having his being according to God's word alone—a spiritual man? The good news is that our Lord is speaking to all of us today. Receive his message:

> You are born to be free. Put the right picture in the frame of your life; then you can *"continue in my word . . . and you will know the truth, and the truth will make you free!"* (Jn 8:31b, 32).

Subject: Purpose

Scripture: Romans 7:18-8:11

Text: *If the Spirit of him who raised Jesus from the dead dwells in you, he who raised Christ Jesus from the dead will give life to your mortal bodies also through his Spirit which dwells in you* (Romans 8:11).

One of the most haunting phrases I've ever read is a one-sentence prayer by William Cowper. I read it many years ago, but it has stuck in my mind, and always comes rushing back when I think of a life without purpose. Cowper prays,

> "O God, save me from dropping buckets into empty wells, and growing old in drawing nothing up."

In the opening pages of the Bible we are told that God answered this prayer, for he created us for a purpose, and it's this purpose that gives meaning to life. Dr. Viktor Frankl, an Austrian Jew, who spent World War II in a Nazi concentration camp, founded a school of psychotherapy upon this truth. He says that man's primary motivational force is his search for meaning or man's need to find genuine purpose in life. Failure to find this meaning, he says, is the root cause of our frustrations and neuroses.

Frankl goes on to point out three ways that life can take on genuine meaning and purpose:

> Through something we do,
> Through experiencing others,
> Through sacrifice and suffering.

Is it any wonder then, that most people spend their lives searching for their purpose in life in their work, or in some other person or persons, especially family, or in some particular sacrifice or suffering? But the Bible is clear that

41

none of these within themselves can ever give genuine purpose to life. For example:

- Two people can work side by side and one will be happy and the other miserable, one fulfilled and the other bored or frustrated.
- Two people in the same family and under the same circumstances can experience the other family members in totally opposite ways.
- Two people can face the same tragedy and one can be defeated by it and the other find victory through it.

So, it's not really work itself, or family itself, or suffering itself that makes life meaningful and fulfilling. Rather, it's something inside of us which determines how we see all of those things! What are we aiming at in our work, in our marriage and family, in all of our relationships and in our sacrifices? The Bible says that we must aim at two goals to fulfill God's purpose for our lives. Aiming at these two goals will give meaning to everything we do.

First, our aim must be to go into partnership with God.

You see, the Bible calls that deep well within us, which we're always trying to fill in so many varied ways, the image of God within us. The Bible opens with the message that God created us in his image so he can work in partnership with us.

Read the creation story carefully and you can't miss this working partnership between man and God. As long as this partnership exists, man prospers and thrives. Three times in this short story God reminds man of his managerial responsibility in this working partnership. Man is to take dominion over everything and manage it. But he is to do it in a working partnership with God. The trouble comes when man tries to squeeze out his Senior Partner

42

and take over the business himself. Work degenerates into drudgery, or an ego trip, or just a way to make a living. It loses its divine purpose. Love degenerates into sexual knowledge and disgusts because Love himself is no longer involved in the partnership. The pain of just living becomes almost unbearable because "the well is empty and you grow old drawing nothing up."

Turn to the Gospels. Look at the life of Jesus and you will find him saying over and over, "The pains you're suffering, the anguish you're experiencing, have one root cause—lack of purpose. Before you can find help, you must get back on the right track by going into partnership with God. You do that by following me!"

Remember the Rich Young Ruler? He had everything except the one thing he really needed: a purpose for his life. What did Jesus tell him? Not what so many try to put into the mouth of Jesus—that it's bad to succeed, to make money and to have wealth. Far from it! What Jesus really says to this foolish man is this: "Aim right! Aim to go into partnership with God by following me, and life will take on eternal significance."

Remember the woman at the well who tried to find meaning in life through sexual promiscuity, but still her well was empty? Jesus message to her was: "Aim right! Aim to go into partnership with God by following me. Then sex will become a vehicle for love that is fulfilling and lasting. Then you won't have to drop your bucket into empty wells any longer!"

Remember the first thing Jesus said to his disciples after he created his church?

"If any man would come after me, let him deny himself and take up his cross and follow me" (Mt 16:24).

That is, "Get the right aim and go into partnership with God by following me, and even your sacrifices and suffering will be transformed into victory!"

43

When Peter wanted the victory without the Cross, Jesus said to him,

"Get behind me, Satan! . . . for you are not on the side of God, but of men" (Mt 16:23).

That is, "Peter, Peter, get your head screwed on right! You can't avoid suffering and sacrifice, but you can have victory over it by going into partnership with God by taking up my cross!" When you grasp this truth, then nearly everything Jesus does and says is related to it. We find purpose in life by going into partnership with God. And we go into partnership with God by accepting Jesus Christ as God in the flesh and following him!

The second goal toward which we must aim in order to find genuine purpose in our life is this:

Make God the Boss of the partnership.

You see, we go into partnership with God by accepting Jesus Christ—God in the flesh—as our partner. But we stay in partnership with God by following the leading of the Holy Spirit—God the Spirit—as the boss of the partnership! There is only one way any person can be in business with God and that is to make the Holy Spirit the Chairman of the Board! The Bible says that when we are led by the Spirit of God we are in partnership with God, and when we are not led by the Spirit of God we are not in business with him. It's really as simple as that. According to the Bible, sin is nothing more nor less than closing our life to his Holy Spirit and trying to be the boss ourselves. That's why blasphemy against the Holy Spirit is the unforgivable sin. When we deny the Holy Spirit as boss of our life, then there is nothing left for us but sin. There is no escape from it!

Until Paul permitted the Living Christ, the Spirit of our Living God, to be the boss of his life, he kept "dropping his buckets into empty wells and growing old drawing nothing up." This is what the 7th chapter of Romans is all about. Listen to Paul:

44

"For I know that nothing good dwells within me, that is, in my flesh. (I know that deep well within me is empty!) *I can will what is right, but I cannot do it. For I do not do the good I want, but the evil I do not want is what I do.* (I'm growing old drawing nothing up!) *Wretched man that I am! Who will deliver me from this body of death?"* (Rom 7:18,19,24).

That's the Bible's picture of a person who has turned his back on God's purpose for his life. What Paul wants us to see is that no person has to stay that way. At the end of chapter 7 he almost shouts:

"Thanks be to God through Jesus Christ our Lord! . . . for the law of the Spirit of life in Christ Jesus has set me free from the law of sin and death" (Rom 7:25 & 8:2).

Paul is telling us that God sent Jesus to us to redeem us to a life led by his Spirit, so our lives will have purpose. Never again will we have to drop our buckets into empty wells. The point Paul wants all of us to grasp here is that the Christian life is not simply a matter of going into partnership with God by accepting Jesus as our Savior. It's going a step further and making his Holy Spirit the Lord of our lives—our thoughts, our words, our actions, day in and day out. It's making God, through the person of the Holy Spirit, boss of the partnership.

I received a new insight into what this means through a dramatization of the life of Father Damien, the Belgian priest who was called to be priest to the incurable lepers in Hawaii during the last century. Father Damien made a statement which, like the one by William Cowper, was indelibly imprinted upon my mind:

"You see, a man receives a call from God, but the trouble is that's not the end of it. It's the call within the call that really matters!"

That's it! Father Damien, called to be a Catholic priest, had spent most of his life going through the duties of a priest without finding any real purpose in his life. Then, one day he received that "call within the call" to minister to the incurable lepers. Responding to that call enabled him to move from mediocrity to greatness.

For the Christian, life is actually made up of a series of "calls within the call." This is the way that God gets his work done on earth, and this is the way his purpose for us becomes a living, daily reality. It's the "call within the call" that really matters! All of us are called into a partnership with God, but it's always our response to that "call within the call" which shows whether God is really the boss of our partnership.

Let me give a personal illustration that is very much a part of me right now. Harriett and I have kept our covenant with God and our commitment to you to pray about Vision I during August and to pray about what we will pledge to it. We set these ground rules: We would pray separately about it, but any time one of us felt led, we would discuss that leading with the other. Honest to God, this is exactly the way it happened. About the middle of August, I felt led to break the silence. I really felt good about it, and as I look back on it, I'm afraid I was a little proud as I said, "Honey, I think we ought to give as much to Vision I as we give to the annual budget."

She said, "You mean, make a three-year pledge to Vision I equal to our one-year pledge to the budget?"

I nodded and she asked, "How much is that?"

"Why Harriett," I said, "you know how much it is, for you put the envelope in the offering plate each week. It's $3,150."

Her face fell, and I could tell she was hurting. You see my wife is the Scotchman and real money stretcher in our family. So I quickly reminded her: "Now, you remember that our pledge to the budget is only 75% of our tithe and there's

46

still 25% in our tithe account each year to be used in other ways. We can do it!"

She said, "You don't understand, Bill. The Lord has been dealing with me too. He's been telling me that we should give twice that amount to Vision I! We should pledge twice what we pledge to the budget!"

I nearly fell out of the chair. "But Harriett, that's $6300!"

"Yes, I know," she said.

Immediately I had a great compulsion to become sole boss of that partnership and start issuing orders. Instead I stammered, "Honey, I believe we'd better spend some more time in personal prayer before we talk about it anymore." But what I thought was, "Surely the Lord will put a stop to that day-dreaming and give her some common sense."

Last Sunday, a week later, on the way to church, she suddenly said to me, "Bill, I've been praying about it, like you said, all week. I think I know God's leading. Would you like to hear it?"

I didn't really know whether I wanted to or not, but I nodded yes, so she went on, "Since Vision I is for three years and you say it is the most important step we've taken in 50 years—and I believe my pastor—I realize now I was wrong last week."

I sighed a big sigh and she went on, "I honestly believe that God wants us to pledge to Vision I three times what we give to the budget!"

I swallowed. I coughed. I choked. I opened my mouth, but nothing came out. Then, I blew out two words. The first was, "What!" And the second was, "$9,450!" Finally I was able to ask, "Harriett, do you know how much money that is?"

She smiled; a twinkle came into her eyes; and she said, "Yes, and it would mean a real sacrifice wouldn't it?"

I replied, "Not only a sacrifice. I don't know where it's going to come from."

47

"Then," she said, "it would mean real faith too, wouldn't it?"

In the light of what had already happened, I was afraid to say again, "We'd better pray about it some more," so I just kept my mouth shut, pressed down on the accelerator and drove to the church as fast as I could and got busy being a preacher. We haven't mentioned it since. But I did pray about it, and God really dealt with me. All week I kept getting two messages. The first message was simply God's way of keeping me honest, for it was simply this: "Do you really believe what you preach—that you can't out give God?"

The second message was the truth I needed to put all of the pieces together, as God said to me something like this: "Don't you realize what I've been trying to tell you through your wife? It's not only the symbol of, but also the secret to Christianity! It's the whole message of the cross. It's this: Sacrifice is the key to life! Giving is the secret to receiving! Jesus sacrificed his life on the Cross to give you life, because I was the boss of our partnership! If he'd had your attitude, there would be no gospel today. You have a choice. If you're going to be the boss, then you must do the blessing too. But if you want me to do the blessing, then first you must make me the boss and trust me!"

I got the message. Although it's a week until pledge day, I'm publicly telling Harriett I've already filled out our pledge for Vision I. Frankly, I'm afraid to turn her loose with God for another week without my supervision. You guessed it. Our pledge is $9,450—an additional $3,150 a year for the next three years.

Here's the point. It's not God's initial call to us to go into partnership with him that's the real key to finding purpose in life. It's the next step which is the real key. It's our response to the "call within the call" that really tells who's the boss of the partnership. And life is a series of one "call within the call" after another.

48

God has called all of us here at First Methodist to go into partnership with him and be his body on this spot of earth in Tulsa. All of us can nod our heads and agree that is our purpose. The trouble is, there's no real sacrifice in answering that call. There's no cross in it. In fact, most of us actually receive from that call, instead of giving. We don't really have to give up anything to do that. But it's a different story with "the call within the call!" It's a different story when God calls and says that to fulfill that purpose you must have more beds for your infants, more classrooms for your children, better teaching facilities for your youth and adults, more room for outreach into your community. And doing this will take real sacrifice for it will take gifts over and above your tithe to the budget.

You see, it's always in "the call within the call" that we actually choose between self and God as boss of the partnership. This is because such calls always call for sacrifice and are always more than we can handle ourselves. We have to fall back on God and put our trust in him by making him the boss of the partnership. It always takes complete faith in the boss to answer the call within the call. It's not something we can do once and it's over and done. No, because of our fallen nature—because the man in chapter 7 of Romans is no stranger to us. It's something we must do each time God confronts us with a new "call within the call" as a new challenge.

But the good news is, there is an eighth chapter of Romans. Fallen man can be redeemed and led by God's Spirit. God can and will fill our empty wells, when we go into partnership with him and make him the boss of that partnership, for,

> "If the Spirit of him who raised Jesus from the dead dwells in you, he who raised Christ Jesus from the dead will give life to your mortal bodies also through his Spirit which dwells in you" (Rom 8:11).

That is, he will fill that deep well within you! Then, every time you drop your bucket into that full, bubbling well, you will draw it up overflowing with abundant life. Then there's purpose in your life and that purpose is being in partnership with God as you continually answer his "call within the call!"

VI   *You Can Change!*

Subject: Resistance to Change

Scripture: Philippians 4:4-13

Text: *Whatsoever things are true . . . think on these things* (Philippians 4:8 KJV).

Do not be conformed to this world but be transformed by the renewal of your mind, that you may prove what is the will of God, what is good and acceptable and perfect (Romans 12:2).

Let this mind be in you, which was also in Christ Jesus (Philippians 2:5 KJV).

We have seen that, according to the Bible, all of us have four basic needs:

The need for the right self-image,
The need for security,
The need for freedom, and
The need for purpose.

Out of these four basic needs flow approximately a dozen other personal needs, such as our need for significance and self-worth, our need to feel competent and to feel that we belong, our need to love and to be loved and so forth. Practically all our problems and emotional upsets in life arise because we get the wrong ideas or wrong basic beliefs about how to meet our own personal basic needs. That is, our feelings, our words, and our actions flow out of these wrong basic beliefs instead of out of the revealed truth of God. Since the foundation of our life is shaky, what we build on it is bound to be insecure, resulting in all kinds of personal problems.

For example, a man's basic belief may be, "I must be a success and make money to be significant." If he fails in that goal, he will end up struggling with the problems of anxiety, guilt, insecurity, and resentment. Even if he reaches his goal, he will still struggle with these problems because his success will not fulfill his basic need to be significant—to have the right self-image.

If a woman thinks that her security depends upon her husband loving her, she is building her life on a wrong basic belief. She is setting a goal, not for herself, but for someone else—her husband. If her husband doesn't respond the way she plans, the whole foundation of her life is shattered, resulting in all kinds of problems, including insecurity and depression.

If a parent thinks that his purpose in life is for his children to "turn out right" and his self-worth depends upon accomplishing this purpose, that parent is building his life upon a wrong basic belief. He is in for all kinds of pains, hurts and emotional upsets.

All the problems I mentioned—guilt, anxiety, depression, insecurity, emotional instability, resentments— flow out of the same cause: the wrong basic beliefs. The problems arise because the mind is filled with untruth instead of truth. He is fearful, guilty, resentful and depressed because he is acting on false suppositions instead of truth. When that happens, he can work on trying to change his feelings or his behavior or his circumstances until doomsday without any positive results. Why? Because he's failed to deal with the root cause of his problem, which is his mind. His mind is filled with the wrong basic beliefs. That's why he's acting the way he is acting and feeling the way he is feeling. He will keep right on acting that way and feeling that way as long as his mind stays that way.

According to the Bible, there's only one way a human being can change, and that is by renewing his mind! The Bible agrees with modern psychology that human beings can change, but the Bible disagrees with many psychologists and therapists on how human beings do change. Freud says people change by renewing their fixations through accepting the analyst's interpretation of their difficulties. Adler says people change by renewing their goals. Carl Rogers says people change by renewing their feelings. William Glasser says that people change by renewing their behavior. Skinner says they change by renewing their circumstances. Rollo May says they change by renewing their efforts toward self-realization. But God says that people change by renewing their minds.

Of course, the Bible teaches responsible behavior. But that right behavior must flow out of right thinking, or it will be labored, hard, cold, judgmental, and hypocritical. Of course, the Bible insists upon the right goals. But goals that are not grounded in the right thinking are unrealistic, and it's almost impossible to generate any motivation to reach them. Of course, Christianity is interested in how people feel. But feelings that are not harnessed to right thinking reduce human beings to the level of animals. The Bible is clear: Changing from a problem-oriented, defeated person to a victorious, joyful person depends upon changing our minds.

Why? Because our problems, emotional upsets, feelings, behavior, and goals are all rooted in our wrong basic beliefs about how to meet our personal needs in life. In order to change we must first build a new foundation for our answers, feelings, behavior, and goals. This foundation must be God's revealed truth. In the twelfth chapter of Romans, before describing the spiritual gifts which God wants to give us, Paul tells us how we must change in order to receive these gifts. He says:

> *"Do not be conformed to this world"* (that is, do not let the world be your pattern) *"but be transformed by the renewal of your mind, that you may prove what is the will of God, what is good and acceptable and perfect"* (Rom 12:2).

Also, Paul tells us in his letter to the Philippians (4:6,7) to choose our thoughts:

"Rejoice in the Lord always,"
"Have no anxiety about anything," and
"[Allow] the peace of God, which passes all understanding, [to] keep your hearts and minds in Christ Jesus."

He concludes it by telling us what to think about:

"Finally, brethren, whatever is true, whatever is honorable, whatever is just, whatever is pure, whatever is lovely, whatever is gracious, if there is any excellence, if there is anything worthy of praise, think about these things" (Phil 4:8).

In this great letter of joy written from a prison cell in Rome, Paul tells us how to find joy and victory no matter what the circumstances or conditions. He sums it up in these dozen words:

"Let this mind be in you, which was also in Christ Jesus" (Phil 2:5 KJV).

The Bible's 3-fold formula for change is clear:

Facts
Faith
Feelings

According to the Bible, it's the only way any person can ever change. It must always be in that order: Facts first, then faith, and last, feelings. To try to change feelings, without first dealing with facts and faith is a vain act. To try to live by faith, without first getting the facts right, will simply compound the anxiety, frustrations and wrong behavior. God's formula for change is clear and man cannot alter it. It is Facts, Faith, Feelings! Let's examine this formula now and see what it means for us from a practical standpoint.

Facts

There are two things we must know about these facts. We must know first that we act the way we do, we feel the way we feel, and our goals are what they are because of the beliefs in which our behavior, our feelings, and our goals are rooted. In short, we are what we are thinking.

For example, if I think I have to have money in order to have self-worth, then making money is my goal and controls my feelings and my actions. If I fail to make money, I become anxious, consider myself a failure, and feel guilty.

If I think I must excel in everything I do in order to be significant, I may become a compulsive worker, always trying to prove myself. Or I may become so obsessed with the fear of failure that I'm afraid to try anything.

If I think I must be included in certain circles in order to belong, that becomes my goal. What other people decide and do will control my feelings and my actions.

If I think my children must turn out a certain way for me to be worthwhile or for me to fulfill my purpose in life, then I've lost control over my own emotions, feelings, and actions. I've given that control to my children.

If I think my parents must approve of me, or that my husband or wife must love me in order for me to have security, the foundation of my life will always be built on sand. The slightest wrong breeze blowing from my parents or my mate will shake that house, causing all kinds of fears, guilt, and emotional upheavals.

No matter what problem you face, if you are going to conquer it, the starting place must always be the same. You must identify the belief in which it is rooted. Sometimes that belief is so deep-seated that only a professional therapist or counselor can uncover and identify it. A man who is now a compulsive worker grew up in a home hearing his mother constantly deride his ne'er-do-well, alcoholic father for failing to make a living. "You're just no good!" She would complain. "You don't ever provide for your family.

You're worthless!" That little boy, who has now become a man, honestly and sincerely believes as a man that his significance and his family's security depend upon how hard he works. Until he identifies that root belief, nothing can be done to help him. The trouble is, that belief is so deep-seated, it will no doubt take a professional therapist to uncover and identify it.

However, most of us don't need a professional to tell us why we feel or behave like we do. We just need to be honest and ask ourselves the right question: "What's the basic belief upon which this feeling or behavior is founded?" If we're honest, when we do identify it, we shall find our problems rooted in wrong basic beliefs about meeting one or more of our personal needs.

Look at the different examples I just gave. Each one is rooted in a wrong basic belief. That's the root-cause of the resulting problems. You see, self-worth is not dependent upon making money. Excelling in everything we do is not the basis for personal significance. Acceptance by certain circles is not the answer to our need to belong. My worth does not depend upon how my children turn out; I can fulfill my purpose in life no matter what my children do. Approval by my parents or love from my mate is not the basis for genuine security. How do I know that? Because the Bible says so. That's how I know!

The other thing I want to say about our basic beliefs is obvious. You must find the revealed biblical truth which applies to your situation and accept that as the basic belief for your life, instead of the wrong basic belief you now hold.

For example, I have self-worth, not because I have money or excel in what I do, but because I am God's child who has been justified by Jesus Christ. Likewise, I belong, not because a certain circle of people accepts me, but because I am accepted by Christ and I give myself to him and to his church. Likewise, fulfilling my purpose in life does not depend upon whether my children turn out right. Rather it depends upon whether I have gone into

56

partnership with God in everything I do (including being a parent), and whether I've made God the boss of the partnership.

Faith

The second step in God's formula for change is Faith. Before you can change, you must not only know the facts of God's revealed truth, but you also must believe in God's revealed truth and make a commitment to act upon this truth. That's faith!

It's a matter of will, not feelings! You must act on it whether you feel like it or not. I can almost assure you that the first few times you won't feel like it. Your feelings have been conditioned to your old, wrong basic belief. But God's formula for change is not based upon first changing your feelings. It is based upon first changing your thinking! The formula is not, "Be ye transformed by the renewal of your feelings," but, "Be ye transformed by the renewal of your mind." Your feelings can then change too. To find God's victory over your problem, you must act upon God's truth regardless of how you feel.

The Bible says that the best way to begin is by confessing that you've built your life on the wrong foundation—the wrong basic belief. Then you must specifically confess your faith in God's word as the new foundation for your life—the new basic belief upon which you'll build. I find it helpful in doing this to use a visual aid. Many people with whom I have counseled witness that they find this helpful too. For example, if your problem is resentment, depression, guilt, or anxiety about your children, then take a 3x5 card and on one side of it write this:

WRONG BASIC BELIEF

"My worth as a person depends upon how my children turn out and how they treat me."

57

At the bottom in large red letters write:

THAT'S A LIE!

Then turn the card over and write on the other side:

GOD'S TRUTH

- Philippians 4:8 - *"Whatsoever things are true . . . think on these things."*
- John 1:12 - *"All who believe in his name, he gives power to become children of God."*
- Romans 5:1 - *"Therefore, since I am justified by faith, I have peace with God through our Lord Jesus Christ."*

Now write your new basic belief based on God's revealed word:

"I have personal worth because I am a child of God. I am a child of God because through faith, I accept Jesus as my Savior. He has justified me before God and restored my relationship with my heavenly Father. I pray for my children, and God answers my prayers, for I have an advocate with the Father in Christ. I trust God to change my children, if they need changing. They are free to live their lives and accept responsibility for their own actions. I release them to God. I love them and stand ready to help if they need me and ask for my help. I thank God he has given them free will too, and they make their own choices. Of course, I pray that they will choose to be a child of God!"

Then in large red letters write:

THAT'S THE TRUTH

Carry the card with you, and anytime you begin to feel upset, guilty, resentful, depressed or anxious about your children, take out the card and read the second side—God's Truth (ignoring the first side which is a lie you want to forget—a wrong basic belief). Then choose to build your life upon God's revealed truth. Anytime you begin to doubt God's truth, remember this: *The Bible says that the only cure for doubt is obedience.* So act upon the facts. Act upon God's truth. That's God's formula: Facts, then Faith.

Feelings

Then follows the third part of the formula: Feelings. Once your mind has been renewed with the truth of God, your feelings will be transformed by the Spirit of God. That's God's promise! That's what is meant by the phrase, "the fruit of the Spirit." The fruit of the Spirit are feelings: They are the feelings of a natural man transformed into the feelings of a child of God. They are the kind of feelings we all want. Listen to them: "Love, Joy, Peace, Patience, Kindness, Goodness, Faithfulness, Gentleness, and Self-Control."

> *"Do not be conformed to this world"* (that is, do not be conformed to the feelings of a natural man) *"but be transformed by the renewal of your mind, that you may prove what is the will of God, what is good and acceptable and perfect"* (Rom 12:2).

The transformation of your feelings is the result of your renewed mind. It's your renewed mind that opens your life to the Spirit of God. There's only one way you can open your life to God's Spirit with your mind, and that is by accepting God's Word as truth and acting upon it. This we call faith and obedience, but they really can't be separated like that. They are simply two sides of the same coin. When they're genuine, they go together. No person can have faith without obeying, and no person can obey without having faith. They must go together. When they do go together, the fruit of the Spirit will follow as surely as apples will follow apple blossoms on an apple tree.

When your mind is renewed, your feelings, words and actions will flow out of your right basic belief that you have self-worth simply because you are a child of God. With or without the approval of your parents, regardless of how your children turn out, whether or not you achieve worldly success, your life will produce the fruit of the Spirit.

You begin to feel a whole new kind of love—a love which is selfless and doesn't try to manipulate others, but accepts them as they are. Nothing can separate you from this new love, because it flows out of a new mind—the mind of Jesus.

There will well up within you a feeling of genuine joy that doesn't depend upon circumstance, but is a part of your very being.

When you think of a problem or a conflict, instead of anxiety or resentment you will experience a peace that passeth all understanding, and you will have the patience to wait upon the Lord to deal with them.

In time, all nine fruit of the Spirit will begin to blossom in your life, and you will know deep in your heart that you are changed!

How did you change? Not by working on your feelings. Not by telling yourself to be better or to stop feeling guilty or resentful or anxious. You changed because first you recognized that your mind was filled with the wrong basic beliefs. Then you renewed your mind by accepting the revealed Word of God as your truth—the right basic beliefs—and acting upon that truth through obedience to God's Word. Since your feelings are now rooted in the Word of God, they are now producing his kind of fruit—the right feelings. You changed because God's formula for change always works: Facts, Faith, Feelings. There is no other order that will work.

The application of the formula is different for different problems, because the causes of those problems are different. That's what we'll be exploring together in future sermons. But the formula is always the same: Facts, Faith,

Feelings. Write it indelibly upon your mind. Begin to use it, and you will not only know *You Can Change!—You Will Change!*

VII   *God's Plan for Marriage*

Subject: Marriage

Scripture: Mark 10:1-12

              Ephesians 6:21-33

Text: *Jesus said, "For your hardness of heart . . .*
              [Moses permitted divorce]. *But from the*
              beginning of creation, God [intended] . . . *the*
              two shall become one . . . What therefore God
              has joined together, let not man put asunder"
              (Mark 10:5-9).

The Bible says that God created the family as the basic unit of human society, and that he created marriage as the foundation on which the family must be built. Before there can be strong families, there must first be strong marriages. Is it any wonder then, in a nation where the marriage vows are regarded so lightly, that family problems are skyrocketing? Is it any wonder in a city where there are more divorces than marriages, that sincere Christians, now divorced, are struggling with guilt and untold pain and hurt, including the fear of trying it again?

It's really a paradox. On the one hand, there is the open acceptance of divorce as the solution to marital problems; on the other hand is the extreme guilt suffered by those who are divorced. As strange as it may sound on first hearing, I am confident both are rooted in the same fact—a total misunderstanding of *God's Plan for Marriage.* Both are rooted in wrong basic beliefs. The only way we can change these circumstances with their tragic consequences, is first to change our basic beliefs about marriage and divorce. That is, first we must change our minds from man's false presumptions to God's revealed truth. Then through faith, we must begin to live out that truth in our lives.

63

If you turn the coin over, you see another paradox which probably causes even more misery, pain, and hurt than the first. I'm talking about those couples whose marriages are almost unbearable, but who still refuse to get a divorce because of religious belief. In effect, they are saying that God is their reason for continuing to live in hell! What a paradox! Again, the cause is the same: wrong basic beliefs— total misunderstanding of *God's Plan for Marriage.*

Perhaps, the biggest paradox of all is found in the good marriages of Christian couples who never even consider divorce, who believe in holy matrimony and in the Bible, but still do not build their marriage on sound biblical principles. How I want to shout to them: "Oh, there is so much more! Don't settle for just a good marriage, for God wants to make your marriage a heaven here on earth." Again, the cause is the same: wrong basic beliefs—a total misunderstanding of *God's Plan for Marriage.*

In the 10th chapter of Mark Jesus reveals to us *God's Plan for Marriage.* In the 5th chapter of Ephesians Paul takes the plan which Jesus revealed and tells us the practical steps for making it a reality in our own lives. Let's examine first the plan and then the practical steps.

The Plan

The plan is really quite simple. Jesus says that from the beginning God has intended for marriage to be a three-way covenant between man, woman, and God. That is, from the beginning God created man and woman to be joined together in holy matrimony. It is God who makes marriage holy. It's God who performs the miracle of making the two become one. But, like everything else that fallen men and women touch, it doesn't always work out as God intended, because we leave God out of it. That's what it means to be a sinner. That's what Jesus means when he says that Moses provided for divorce "because of our hardness of heart"— because we are fallen creatures, because we are sinners and leave God out.

64

But the Bible says—and this is the good news—that God loves us so much that he sent his only Son, Jesus Christ, to this earth to make it possible for us to put God back into our lives where he belongs. And God belongs in our marriages! God belongs in our marriages to make them holy. The Bible says that Jesus Christ came to this earth to make that possible. That—and that alone—is *God's Plan for Marriage*.

That—and that alone—is the right basic belief about marriage. To twist that into making Jesus a law-giver instead of a grace-giver is to miss the whole point and to play right into the enemy's hand. Jesus didn't come to lay down a law either for or against divorce. He came to make it possible for God to perform the miracle of making a husband and wife "become no longer two but one." He came as our means of God's grace in all areas of our lives, not to bind us to more laws that we can't keep. He came to free us through God's grace to be what God intends for us to be, and in marriage that means holy matrimony. That's *God's Plan for Marriage*; he gives us no other alternative.

The Steps

As we turn to Ephesians and look at the practical steps husband and wife must take to make this plan a reality, we realize that Paul is writing to Christians. Ephesians was a circulatory letter, written to all of the churches Paul had founded in Asia Minor. Paul just assumes that each husband and wife who reads it will have already taken the first step. He assumes that each has put himself or herself under the authority of God by accepting Jesus Christ as Lord and Savior, personally. So, he goes on and tells them how to take the next step in this marriage in order to experience the miracle of holy matrimony.

We need to stop just a moment here and emphasize this point—that holy matrimony can become a full reality only between two Christians. Why? Simply because we are fallen creatures, and Jesus Christ is the only provision which God

65

has made for our redemption; that's why! To try to make holy matrimony out of a union between a Christian and a non-Christian is like trying to make a horse out of a cow or an apple out of an orange—it just cannot be done. This is why Paul warns us against being unequally yoked.*

So, the first step is for both husband and wife to individually put themselves under the authority of God, by accepting Jesus Christ as personal Lord and Savior. What then, are the practical steps for making that marriage a heaven here on earth?

Paul says there are two steps for the husband and two for the wife dealing with their marriage relationship. *God's Plan for Marriage* involves both a vertical and horizontal relationship. First, a relationship with God, because we are created in his image. Second, a relationship with each other, because God made us male and female and gave us different functions and different responsibilities. Paul begins his instructions to husbands and wives in the fifth chapter of Ephesians. Understanding this first statement is the key to understanding all that follows. Paul begins:

"Be subject to one another out of reverence for Christ" (Eph 5:21).

By this the Bible means that since both husband and wife already have the right personal relationship with God through Christ, they must work on the right relationship between each other. It says that the foundation principle for that relationship is this: *Be subject to one another!* In other words, there must not be a ruler-subject relationship as is taught so often. There is only one ruler and that is God, through Christ. So, as husband and wife, says Paul, you must have a subject-subject relationship, each subject to the other in a special way. Because Christ is the Ruler of your individual lives, then out of reverence for him you can

---

* I am not suggesting that if you are already married to a non-Christian, you should divorce and find a Christian mate! For a discussion of divorce see sermon, #4 in the series, "God's Word for Families," *Will God Re-Pair Marriages?*

now have a very special relationship in which each mate is subject to the other in a liberating way. Then Paul goes on to explain what this means.

Steps for the Husband

Paul says the husband's relationship to his wife is the same as the relationship of Christ to his church. He says it like this,

> "Husbands love your wives, as Christ loved the church and gave himself for her, that he might sanctify her. . . Even so husbands should love their wives as their own bodies" (Eph 5:25 and 28).

What does this mean? To understand, we must first answer the question, *How did Christ love the church?* Christ loved the church so much that he made himself subject to her in two specific ways.

First, Christ loved the church so much that he made himself subject to the church as his body on earth. The church is literally the flesh of Christ on earth. Christ and the church are truly one flesh, for the church is simply an extension of Christ on earth. Christ bound himself to the church forever, for better or for worse. He provided no other alternative. He literally made the church an extension of his own body on earth, and said that absolutely nothing could ever destroy that union. To seal it, he gave the church his name. When he did this, he said,

> "I will give you the keys to the kingdom of heaven, and whatever you bind on earth shall be bound in heaven, and whatever you loose on earth shall be loosed in heaven" (Mt 16:19).

What the Bible wants us to see is that the church is the one all-consuming love of Christ, for he gave the church his most precious gifts—his name, his Spirit, and his trust. He bequeathed to the church his most precious possession— God's kingdom on earth.

67

The Bible says that a husband must do exactly the same thing for his wife. His wife must be his one all-consuming love. The real key to marriage is right here—the husband taking the initiative, binding himself to his wife in this same indestructible way. The real key to marriage is for the husband to make himself subject to the fact that his wife is literally an extension of his own body. She is part of his very being—an extension of his flesh. She is not something to be manipulated and used, but is a part of his own body.

Like the church, a wife's needs are legion. She has many moods. She has her highs and lows. At times she is submissive and at other times she rebels. Still, a husband must be responsible and fulfill his covenant with God by being subject to her every need, just as Christ is responsible to the church under all circumstances, because she is an extension of his body.

That's the real key to marriage. Until a husband becomes subject to his wife in this way, a marriage can't even get off the ground. Just as Christ took the initiative with the church, so must the husband take the initiative in marriage in order to experience the miracle of holy matrimony.

Secondly, Christ loved the church so much that he established a trust relationship with her. That is, Jesus who is God, actually made himself subject to the faith of the church. Of course, he could have forced the church to follow his leadership in other ways, but he chose to found his relationship with the church upon trust. He trusted the church and, in return, the church put its faith in him.

Why did Jesus make himself subject to the faith of the church? Because that's the only way the church can actually be one with Christ and literally be an extension of his body on earth. Christ first proved to the church that he was worthy of her trust. He was available when she needed him. He protected her with his blood from the evil one. After his personal relationship with the Father, Christ put the church first on his list of priorities. From the beginning, the church always knew where she stood with Christ. So she could respond to him in faith. From the beginning the church and Christ have had a trust relationship, because Christ made himself subject to the faith of the church.

The same is true in marriage, says Paul. Again, it's the husband's responsibility to initiate this trust relationship by first making himself subject to the faith of his wife, just as Christ initiated it with the church by first making himself subject to the faith of his church. Until a husband subjects himself to the faith of his wife, she can only go through the motions of being a wife; her heart won't be in it. But when a husband subjects himself to the faith of his wife, he makes it possible for his wife to become one with him. How? By a faithful response, that's how! By an act of trust herself!

Steps for the Wife

Now let's turn briefly to the two steps which the wife must take to fulfill *God's Plan for Marriage.* The Bible not only says that the husband must be subject to the wife, but it also says that the wife must be subject to the husband. It says that the wife is subject to her husband "as the church is subject to Christ," which means primarily two things.

First, the church is subject to Christ as its head—as its chief cornerstone. This means that the church looks to Christ for two things—its direction and its strength. Any time a church fails to do this, that church is doomed. It will have lost direction and it will have lost its power.

The same is true in marriage. Any time a wife refuses to be subject to her husband as the head, that is, any time she refuses to look to him for her direction and her strength, the marriage is doomed for it has lost direction and power! Just as in the church there can be only one head, Jesus Christ, so in marriage can there be only one head, the husband. This doesn't mean a husband makes all the decisions, just as Christ doesn't make all the decisions for the church. But he does point the direction for the decisions. The decisions are never contrary to his leading.

Perfect coordination and unity comes in marriage when, on the one hand, a wife is subject to her husband as the head, looking to him for direction and strength, and on the other hand, the husband is subject to his wife's every need so completely that it is like an extension of his own body. These two things work together for a oneness that no human problem or outside circumstance can put asunder. But let either fail in his or her responsibility, and the marriage is headed for division, hurts, and pains that make it a living hell.

The second way in which the church subjects herself to Christ—and the second way the Bible says a wife must subject herself to her husband—is to follow him. The church is loyal to Christ. She is true to him. In everything she does she follows him. Do you get the picture? Christ first makes this possible by giving himself to the church in trust; that is, by trusting the church to be an extension of his body on earth and thus making an atmosphere of faith possible. Then the church responds by following him through faith. In this union of faith and trust a bond is made that cannot be broken. The two truly become one!

The same is true in marriage. First, the husband creates an atmosphere of faith and trust by giving himself to his wife. Then she responds by following him through faith. In this union of faith and trust a bond is created that cannot be broken.

This is God's will for husband and wife—a subject-subject relationship, in which each is subject to the other. I've set this relationship out in steps—the husband with two responsibilities and the wife with two—to make it easy to communicate. But don't make the mistake of trying to legalize these steps and make them mechanical rules to follow. It will never work that way. In fact, it works only when these steps are swallowed up in an all-consuming

70

love of one for the other. It works only when these steps are taken through grace instead of law.

I want to share with you how I discovered this truth twenty-seven years ago, and what it has meant for me and my marriage since.

Harriett and I grew up in the church and belonged to the church when we got married. But the church did nothing to prepare either of us for marriage. No minister talked to us before the wedding. After the wedding we heard nothing about it from the pulpit or the Sunday School lectern, and we were such lukewarm Christians we did nothing to dig it out for ourselves. Consequently, after about ten years, our marriage was in trouble and we began to think divorce was our only viable alternative.

Then, he touched us! We met Christ in a new, personal, vital way. We made new commitments to Christ and individually put ourselves under his authority. That was the beginning of an entirely new relationship, not only with God, but with each other too.

As I began to study the Bible, one of the first things I realized was this: In the same way that Christ initiated his trust/faith relationship with his church, he calls me, and every husband, to initiate our own trust/faith relationship with our wives. In a covenant with God, which I should have made at the time of our wedding, I committed myself to be subject to all my wife's needs, as if she were an extension of my own self. And I made a covenant with God that our future relationship would be a relationship of faith and trust, just like my relationship with him.

Her response was immediate. She began to look to me for her direction and her strength as we lived out our daily lives. She returned my faith and my trust ten-fold as we walked through life together instead of separately.

That was twenty-seven years ago. Of course we've slipped and made lots of mistakes in those twenty-seven years. We are fallible human beings who are redeemed sinners just as you are. But never in those twenty-seven years has the bond that binds us together been in danger of breaking again. It is a holy bond, growing stronger and stronger; for what God binds together no man can tear asunder. It is now a relationship of grace, not law.

For many years now, I really don't know how many—but it has been almost since the beginning—there has been no conscious awareness on my part, nor I'm sure on Harriett's either—that I'm following any kind of rules or biblical principles. There is never any conscious thought or planning or plotting—as some seem to think it must be. We don't think that this is my area and this is hers and never must the two meet. In fact this is what the marriage relationship must never become, for then it's a legalistic relationship instead of a love relationship. But once we settled that God alone is our authority, and that out of reverence for Christ we are subject to each other, then all of the rules and principles were swallowed up in one great love experience that is beyond description in words. So I beg you, don't make what I have said today into a set of legalistic rules to follow. Rather, look at it as an exciting experiment in love which you live out together.

If God can do this for Harriett and me with the mess we handed him twenty-seven years ago, I know he can do it for you. So don't doubt. Just believe him and begin to experiment. You will find that God is faithful and will keep his part of the covenant as you follow *"God's Plan for Your Marriage!"*

Subject: Guilt

Scripture: Luke 22:31-34 and 54-62

Text: *And Peter remembered the word of the Lord . . . And he went out and wept bitterly* (Luke 22:61-62).

What, in your opinion, is the hardest commandment of God for all of us to keep? Think about it. Here are a few clues:

- Adam and Eve couldn't keep it.
- The more religious we get, the harder it is for us to keep this particular commandment.
- Failure to keep this commandment is the *root* cause of most of our other problems in life.
- The breaking of this commandment is the *direct* cause for the most widespread human problem of all—our feeling of guilt.

I submit to you that the commandment of God which is hardest for every human being to keep is the commandment: Thou shalt not judge! The Bible says that setting ourselves up as the judge of right and wrong is the forbidden fruit which we must not eat. God commands that we must never judge another human being. Yet most of us do it all the time. The more religious we get, the more we judge those who fail to keep our own religious rules. Because other people do the same thing and judge us, we end up with a sense of guilt, even as they end up with a sense of guilt because we judge them. Guilt is that great chasm between the *ought* and the *is* in our lives. If we feel we *ought* to do something or we are told by someone else that we *ought* to do it, but we don't do it, then we end up with a nagging sense of guilt. Or, vice versa, if we feel we *ought not* to do it or others tell us we *ought not* to do it, but still we do it anyway, there's that nagging sense of guilt again welling up within us.

Guilt is the most common of all human problems. All of us are plagued with it. No one escapes it. Therefore, no one escapes some of its consequences which are legion, including anger, rebellion, fear, resentment, anxiety, deadening of our conscience, and aggressive behavior. Our instinct for self-preservation causes us to strike out at those who would rob us of our self-worth through judgment, just as we strike out at those who would rob us of our food and shelter.

To be alive means to encounter conflict, and to encounter conflict means guilt. There can be no life without conflict, and no conflict without guilt. Few of us spend a day without some pangs of guilt stabbing us, not so much because of the terrible things we have done, but mostly because we must choose between alternatives, neither of which is clearly good or bad. For example, our parents may need our help, but to help them, we must neglect our spouse or our children. So we feel guilty whether we help them or not. Or there's the widespread guilt resulting from the need for a wife to work. The family needs the money, but the children need their Mommy at home. No matter what decision is made, the result is the same, because there is a great chasm between the *ought* and the *is*, which means guilt!

Even if the family doesn't need the money, a woman with a good education may feel guilty if she doesn't use it in a constructive, remunerative way. On the other hand, if she does, she also feels guilty for not devoting more time to her home.

Preachers too must struggle with this strange malady called "guilt." Strange as it may sound, one of my biggest struggles is because you are such responsive Christians as a congregation, and because God has blessed our church so

74

abundantly. I don't know whether you realize it or not, but your church is, in one sense, like an oasis of life and growth in a parched desert of church stagnation and death. Open this week's church paper to the inside page showing the statistical reports of all Oklahoma Methodist churches. You will see dozens upon dozens of churches that have not received one single profession of faith during the first eight months of this year. This is a continuation of a trend that has been going on for ten years. Multiply this by fifty states and you will get the picture.

Never a week passes that I don't receive several requests from churches to come and share what they call our "secrets for church growth," so they can turn their church around. Inevitably, when I receive such requests, I feel a real need to go and help. But at the same time, I know that if I do go, I will leave many things undone here. Also, I know if I go that I will be unable to spend the time with my family I should. Oh, how easy it is to feel guilty regardless of what I do!

In one ear, I hear a voice from Macedonia crying out, "Come over and help us! We're dying!" If I don't respond, I feel guilty for not helping fellow Christians and brother preachers, and the denomination I dearly love and have chosen as my home. In the other ear, I hear you saying, "I need you too and you don't have enough time now to do all that needs to be done. Stay here and do what needs to be done." Then, in both ears, I hear my wife saying "You've got to slow down, for I want to keep you around for a while."

So, how can I make any decision without feeling guilty? The truth of the matter is I can't, because there is no life without conflict and there is no conflict without guilt. Of course, your conflicts may be different from mine and consequently your guilt will be different too; but the principle is still the same. To be alive means conflict, and conflict means guilt. All of us who live are in this thing together. Either we must learn how to handle guilt or it will continue to rob us of the abundant life which God wants for

75

us. For some it will develop into a serious neurosis and sickness. But since it is a problem which is common to man, God gives us the answer for our guilt in the Bible. Before we look at that answer, let me warn you that in one sense, God's answer for guilt is the simplest and plainest answer to all human problems; in another sense it is the most difficult of all to follow. It's easy to state, but it's hard to do.

Perhaps the clearest picture of God's answer to our guilt can be seen in the response of two of the apostles to a deep sense of guilt for denying Christ. Judas and Peter both denied their Lord, both felt remorseful and were burdened down with guilt. But the difference between them is that this guilt destroyed Judas, but it was the beginning of a whole new life for Peter. It was the end for Judas, but for Peter, it marked the time to begin! Why? Because Peter discovered God's answer and used it. Judas did not. Let's look at the answers Peter discovered so we can be victorious over our own guilt instead of being its victim.

First, Peter tested his guilt to be sure it was true guilt and not false guilt.

Many of us are burdened down with guilt. We can hardly stand ourselves because of it, but actually it is not true guilt; it is false guilt. We are carrying around a burden we don't have to carry. This too is common to man. All of us carry around a bundle of false guilt. Let me illustrate with the example I gave of myself a moment ago.

If I feel guilty because a brother preacher or fellow Christian thinks I should come and preach and teach and help his church, then my guilt is based on man's judgment. That is false guilt because Christ my Lord forbids any man to judge me! Likewise, if I do honor the request and go, but feel guilty for not staying here because you thought I should stay here, my guilt is still false guilt. Again it is based on man's judgment and man is forbidden to judge. Even if I feel guilty because I didn't do what my wife wanted me to do

76

and thought I should do, that's still based on the judgment of a fellow human being and is false guilt; no matter how much of an angel or heavenly creature I think she is.

According to the Bible, there is only one genuine basis for true guilt and that is the judgment of God. The test for whether it is true guilt or false guilt is always the same and it is this: *Is my conduct contrary to, or in accordance with, the will of God?*

To let the judgments of men, no matter how right they are, bind us to guilt is to live a life of legalism, and thus miss the amazing grace of God and the abundant life he has for us. Unfortunately, this is exactly what's happening to thousands of sincere Christians as they struggle to carry their bundle of false guilt. Here's the point: Living a Christian life is never a question of doing right as the world understands that word. Rather, it is always a question of doing what God wills for us to do! Every person must discover for himself what that is; no one else can decide it for him.

This is why I said earlier that the Bible's answer for guilt is in one sense the simplest of all answers, but at the same time the hardest to follow. It is simple to know that the answer is to follow God's will. On the other hand, discerning and knowing God's will in our everyday decisions is the hardest thing to know; for God's ways are not man's ways and the mind of God is far above our minds. No person can ever be absolutely certain that he is following God's will, when all alternatives seem good or all seem neutral or impossibly bad.

But, in spite of this, Peter does give us some specific guidance on what we must do to discern our Lord's will in our daily affairs. We are told Peter knew his guilt was true guilt and not false guilt when he remembered the Word of the Lord!

Then, we're told that he went out and wept bitterly. He wept bitterly because he knew that his conduct had been judged by the word of God and he was found wanting. He had failed to follow the will of God and thus had cause for true guilt.

This is why it is so important for all of us to discipline ourselves in the means of grace, especially in Bible study, prayer, and worship. To try to discern the will of God without knowing the mind of God in his Scriptures and without knowing the Spirit of God in prayer and public worship is like trying to find a needle in a haystack. It's almost impossible. Even when we do discipline ourselves in the means of grace, it's hard enough. Often we mistake our own human desires and egos for God's guidance and man's word for God's Word. However, if we persist we will begin to realize that it is not so hard this year as it was last year, and not nearly so hard as it was five or ten years ago.

Even more important, we find release from that damnable false guilt which is based upon the judgment of men. This will deliver us of much of the load in our bundle of guilt. But even if we discover that our guilt is true guilt, and we have truly transgressed the will of God, there's still good news for us. That's the second thing we learn from Peter.

Peter used the doorway which God has provided for forgiveness of our true guilt—the doorway of repentance.

This is the doorway Judas failed to use.

I can almost hear some of you saying, "Wait a minute, Preacher! You're all mixed up. Because the Bible says that Judas, not Peter, is the one who repented. He went back to the Jews and threw the 30 pieces of silver at their feet, but the Bible never says that Peter repents!"

Ah, but that's exactly the point. Judas was thinking of repentance as you and I so often think of it today. He was thinking of it as a *condition* for receiving God's forgiveness, when in fact, Judas had already been forgiven by Jesus, just as Peter had, and just as you and I have. Judas thought he had to make things right before the Lord would

78

accept him back, but Peter knew better. Peter knew he could never make things right. Even more important, he knew that God had already made things right for him through the death of Jesus on the Cross.

Dear friend, we don't need to repent of our transgressions against God in order to get God to forgive us! The good news is, God has already forgiven us! That's what the Cross is all about. We need to repent, because repentance is the only way we can experience this forgiveness. The word, "repentance," means "change of mind" or "turning around." According to Mark, the first words Jesus spoke were,

"Repent, and believe in the gospel" (Mk 1:15).

That is, "Change your mind and believe in the good news that you are already forgiven by an all-loving God."

Repentance is not a condition for forgiveness. Repentance is the way we accept what God has already done for us. Instead of having the mind of a Judas and thinking that what Christ does for us is first dependent upon what we do, we must have the repentant or changed mind of Peter who throws himself completely upon the mercy of Christ. How did Peter repent? How did Peter change his mind? Exactly the way all of us must repent and change our minds in order to experience God's forgiveness. Peter repented from acting on the judgment of men, when he should have been acting on the judgment of God. Peter changed his mind from thinking that the judgments of men were what mattered to knowing that the only thing which really matters is the judgment of God. That's the only kind of repentance that matters, for that's the only way we can experience genuine forgiveness. It's the only way we can be delivered from eating the "forbidden fruit" of judging what's right and wrong for others!

It was the hardest of all God's commandments for Adam and Eve to keep and it's still the hardest for us to keep; because, like them, we've never really changed our mind

79

about the amazing grace of God. We've never truly repented in spite of the words we use and the vows we take. We still think that God's grace is dependent upon what we do. We try to justify ourselves before God and men by sitting in judgment of others and dragging them down below us. There's only one way to keep from judging others like that, and that is, like Peter, to walk through the doorway of repentance into forgiveness—to actually change our minds about God's grace and accept the forgiveness which God has already given us in Christ!

But that's not the end of it. In fact, it's really just *"The Time to Begin."*

Begin what? Well, we are told in the next two encounters that Peter has with Jesus what we must begin— but this time his encounters are with the Resurrected Christ. First, in the Upper Room, Jesus appears to the disciples, greets them, and then says,

> *"'As the Father has sent me, even so I send you.' And when he had said this he breathed on them, and said to them, 'Receive the Holy Spirit. If you forgive the sins of any, they are forgiven; if you retain the sins of any, they are retained'"* (Jn 20:21b-23).

Next, on the shore of the Sea of Tiberias, Jesus asks Peter three times, "Peter, do you love me?" And three times Peter replies, "Yes, Lord, you know I love you!" Each time Jesus gives Peter the same command, "Then, feed my sheep . . . my lambs!"

Jesus makes it clear that all those to whom he has given forgiveness and deliverance from guilt are sent in turn by him to transmit it to others.

According to Jesus, the test for a Christian is not just accepting forgiveness and eternal life for himself; but the test is whether he begins to give away what he has freely received. The test is whether he transmits to others the amazing grace of God! Jesus gives us his Holy Spirit so we

80

can "set the prisoners free"—so we can pass on to others this liberating experience of forgiveness!

To be forgiven is to be awakened to our real purpose in life, which is to feed his sheep! To be forgiven is to be delivered from the spirit of judgment by which we bind others on earth, and to be endowed with his living, affirming Holy Spirit. Then we can fulfill our purpose and feed his sheep as we offer them the amazing grace of God.

One of the great modern American novels, in my opinion, is *The Winter of Our Discontent* by John Steinbeck. It's the story of an all-American boy growing up in a small town on the east coast, marrying his childhood sweetheart and having two fine children—a twelve-year-old boy and a teenage girl. Gradually, the hero, Ethan Allen Hawley, without any pangs of conscience, gives in to life's temptations to get ahead in business and provide for his family, even betraying his best friend to do it. Then one day he finds that his own son has cheated in the same way in order to win an essay contest. When he confronts him about it, the boy has no remorse, but says, "Everybody's doing it, just like you, Dad."

In that moment, Ethan Allen Hawley sees, not only what he has done to himself, but even worse, what he has done to his son. His guilt overwhelms him and, like Judas, he thinks the only answer is suicide. His teenage daughter, sensing his decision, throws her arms around him and tells him of her undying love for him, despite what's happened. As she does, she slips into his pocket a simple stone, which has long been their secret way of communicating their special love for each other.

Later, as Ethan Allen Hawley is crouched in a crevice in the rocks on the seashore, waiting for the tide to come in and take out his lifeless body, he reaches in his pocket for the razor blades he brought for the purpose of slashing his wrist. Instead, his hand encircles the special stone which says, "I love you no matter what's happened." For a long moment he sits staring at the stone, as the water gets

81

higher and higher. Then across the deep comes a life-changing revelation for Ethan Allen Hawley—a revelation of the redemptive power of unconditional love. Suddenly, he knows the most important truth of his life. Guilt is not the signal to quit, but it is the signal to begin! Struggling through the churning tide, he goes back to shore to begin again.

This is God's message to all of us, no matter how true our guilt is or what we've done in the past: This is not the time to quit, but the *Time to Begin.*

IX   *"Poor Me!"*

Subject: Self-Pity

Scripture: Luke 15:25-32

Text: *But he was angry and refused to go in. His father . . . said to him, "Son, you are always with me, and all that is mine is yours"* (Luke 15:28 and 31).

From childhood until the hour we draw our last breath, one of our worst enemies is self-pity. The temptation to say "Poor me!" is so strong at times that most of us can't handle it. What causes us to get in these "Poor me!" moods? What do they do to us? How can the Bible help us handle them?

For answers to these questions, I take you to one of the most familiar stories in the Bible, which we usually call *The Parable of the Prodigal Son*. In reality it's just as much *The Parable of the Elder Brother*. We call it *The Prodigal Son* because it's easier for us to rejoice with a boy who is saved from the far country than it is to relate to a self-centered, brooding boy who stays home. Yet, the truth of the matter is, most of us need the lesson taught by the Elder Brother because we're much more apt to commit his sins.

You remember the story in the 15th chapter of Luke. The younger brother, in a fit of rebellion, stamps off into the far country, only to find life unbearable. He comes to himself, returns home, and his father greets him with open arms, a great feast, and a joyous, hilarious homecoming. But the elder brother stands outside sulking, refusing to go in. When the father entreats him to join in the festivities and excitement, all he can do is stand outside brooding and crying, "Poor me! Poor me!"

Can you imagine a more perfect picture of self-pity? I don't know how you feel about it, but instinctively I'm

83

inclined to take his side, aren't you? This simply underlines the fact that this is a temptation which is common to man, and all of us need to find God's answer for it. Let's dig a little deeper into this parable to discover God's truth about the emotional disease of self-pity. First, let's look for the cause of it. Second, let's look for the effect of it—that is, what it does to us. And finally let's examine God's cure for it.

The Cause

The cause of self-pity can be traced directly to three wrong basic beliefs.

The first wrong basic belief is what I call "I-itis," an emotional virus of self-centeredness which attacks all of us.

Look at this sulking, brooding, elder brother. He really believes that the world is centered around himself. He's not interested in his brother. He's not interested in his father. He's not interested in the guests. He's not interested in anyone but himself. He's got *I-itis!* Listen to him when his father comes out and entreats him.

> *"Lo, these many years I have served you, and I never disobeyed your command; yet you never gave me a kid, that I might make merry with my friends"* (Lk 15:29).

Every other word is *I* or *me.* He reminds me of the little girl who said:

> I had a little tea party
> This afternoon at three.
> 'Twas very small, three guests in all
> Just I, Myself, and Me.
> Myself ate up the sandwiches.
> While I drank all the tea,
> 'Twas also I who ate the pie,
> And passed the cake to me.

This disastrous emotional virus, *I-itis*, which centers our world around ourselves, is always the culprit which sets off the disease of self-pity.

The second cause of self-pity springs from another wrong basic belief, which is common to all of us:

The belief that we really know what's best for ourselves.

Look at the elder brother. He refuses to listen to his father, because he already knows what's best for himself. He's a "Mr. Know-it-all." His mind is closed to any truth from his father's lips. All of us are tempted to be exactly the same way. Nothing separates us more from the people who are close to us than this kind of closed mind. Have you ever talked to anyone like that? All the time you're talking you know the other person is not listening, but just waiting to find an opening to set you straight. One man said to his friend, "My wife talks to herself." And the friend answered, "So does mine, but she doesn't know it; she thinks I'm listening." All of us are tempted to believe that we really know what's best for ourselves.

The third wrong basic belief which results in self-pity is what the Bible calls *legalism* or *law*.

This boy really believes that he is good enough to deserve the best. He honestly thinks he can do it himself. Listen to him again: "I have served you . . . I have obeyed you . . . I have worked hard."

"Therefore," he is saying, "I deserve better treatment than that no-good younger son of yours who hasn't done what I've done!" That's legalism! Legalism is putting our trust in what *we* do, instead of putting our trust in our loving heavenly Father. This boy was saying "Poor me!" because his trust was in the wrong place. He put his trust in his own works, instead of in the grace of God! He put his trust in the wrong place, because of the wrong basic belief that he could do it himself.

85

Well, there are the three causes of self-pity:

I-itis,
Closed-mindedness, and
Legalism.

Now let's turn to what this disease does to us.

The Effect

What does self-pity do to us? It isolates us from all that can make life full, exciting, beautiful, and joyful. It isolates us in three different ways.

First, self-pity isolates us from that which we need to keep life on an even keel, what you might call just plain old fun and happiness.

Look at the elder brother. He's missing the fun of the party, the delicacies of the banquet, the companionship of friends, the fellowship of his family, because he's too busy crying, "Poor me!" He's lost his sense of what it is to be human, his ability to laugh.

We all need to relax and be light-hearted at times. We all need to laugh. We all need to have fun. A heavy heart makes us take ourselves too seriously, and it closes our lives to the opportunities for light heartedness, fun and happiness. It causes the stress and tension within us to build. Before long most of our energy is being wasted in dealing with this stress and tension. But relaxation, fun, parties, companionship with friends, and fellowship with family are God's ways for us to vent this stress and tension. Self-pity and crying "Poor me!" will always isolate us from such fun and happiness. It will take away our sense of humor, our ability to relax and laugh and have fun. That's the first way it isolates us.

Also, self-pity isolates us from those who are sometimes called the meaningful others in our lives.

86

By "meaningful others" we mean those who can help us grow and mature—those we need most: members of our family, close friends, co-workers, and our spiritual kin in the church. One thing you can depend upon—whenever a person cannot get along with the people around him, he's suffering from self-pity. He has been infected with *I-itis*, closed-mindedness, and legalism. Nothing can so embitter life, blind us to beauty, shrivel us intellectually, warp God's image within us, fill us with hate and envy, and generally make life miserable quite so much as separation from our fellow men. This is exactly what this disease called self-pity does to us. It separates us from those close to us.

The third thing self-pity does to us, is that it isolates us from a relationship with God and shuts us off from the blessings he wants to give us.

Look at the elder brother. Physically he has stayed home, but spiritually he is a million miles away from his father. In this parable, of course, the father represents our heavenly Father. In the elder brother we see one of the clearest pictures of sin in the Bible, and one of the best definitions of sin—which is self-love instead of love for God and for others. What the Bible is telling us here is that in the final analysis, self-pity is one of the deadliest of sins. It's one of the surest ways to be separated from God and from all the blessings he wants for us.

That's what this emotional disease of self-pity does to us. It isolates us from all that can make life full, exciting, and joyful, by isolating us from the three most important things in life:

- The opportunities to relax, and have fun ourselves so we can live with the stress and tension.
- Relationship with the meaningful others in our lives,

- Relationship with Almighty God.

The Cure

What is God's cure for this deadly emotional disease of self-pity? How can the Bible help us handle the temptation to go around crying "Poor me?" God's answer is plain. We must discard those wrong basic beliefs which have given us this disease. We must accept God's revealed truth as our new basic beliefs. We must make a commitment to act on these new basic beliefs by orienting our lives around these revealed truths.

Remember, when we examined God's formula for change we saw that before we can change we must permit God to transform our minds. But we also saw that just changing our basic beliefs is not enough. We must also step out in faith and act on these new revealed truths. In short, we saw that it takes both *Facts* and *Faith* to change our *Feelings*. It takes both belief in God's revealed truth and the faith to act on that truth. Let's apply this formula to the three wrong basic beliefs which cause self-pity.

First, let's apply it to *I-itis*. There's only one cure for this infection of *I-itis*.

We must take the miracle drug of *You-itis* in order to get outside of ourselves.

Jesus reiterates this more than any other truth he reveals to us. He put it this way in his teachings: *You must lose yourself to find yourself. You must give to get. You must serve to be served. To be first you must be last.*

The trouble is, none of us can do it in our own will power. None of us can do it by just saying to ourselves, "I'm going to stop being self-centered and start being other-people-centered."

We can't do it because this tendency to center our world around ourselves is part of our very being. It's what the Bible means by the term original sin. God sent Jesus to us to defeat this sin and to make it possible for his victory to

88

be imputed to us—that is, transferred to us. Jesus accomplished this by creating his church, and promising the church his Holy Spirit—the very Spirit which defeated original sin—so we can truly be his Body upon this earth today. This means that when we honestly accept this gift, the center of our life is transformed. His Spirit is in control of the center of our life. Look at the difference between man's wrong basic belief and God's revealed truth in Christ.

Man says, "My world centers around me! Therefore, I must put myself first. I must get for myself. I must protect my rights. *I . . I . . I . . I-itis!"*

But God says in Christ, "The truth is my world centers around love, and love is giving yourself to others."

Therefore, only when you give of yourself to others can you find fulfillment. Only when you lose yourself for others can you be under the dominion of the Holy Spirit, and manifest the fruit of the Spirit: love, joy, peace, and the rest. Only when you serve instead of wanting to be served, can you be one with Jesus Christ and thus in right relationship with those around you. Only when you truly discard man's wrong basic belief of "Poor me!" for God's revealed truth of "You too!" can you be cured and made whole. That's the revealed truth of God.

The good news is, you don't have to do it yourself. All you have to do is make the decision to change your wrong basic belief, and step out in faith to live God's revealed truth. The Holy Spirit will do the rest. That's the way to let the Spirit of Christ into your life. Then it's his Spirit who transforms you; you don't have to do that. You must only make the decision to change, then step out in faith by accepting and acting on God's truth. Our life centers around love, and love is giving ourselves to others. We must lose ourselves to find ourselves!

What does this mean? We find our answer in the second and third steps in God's cure for self-pity.

Secondly, Jesus came to show us that there is only one way the closed mind of a Mr. Know-it-all can be opened:

We must establish a new relationship with the One who does know it all, Almighty God— Father, Son, and Holy Spirit!

To do that we must first discard the wrong basic belief that we actually know what's best for ourselves, and replace it with the good news of God's revealed truth—that we have a living God who continually speaks to our every need. Did you hear that good news? We have a God who speaks to us! That's the whole point of God's giving us his Word in our Bible: Our Almighty God not only knows what's best for us; he communicates that truth to us in his Holy Word. To hear that truth, we must establish a new relationship with him.

The father in the parable represents God, and continually the father tries to speak to his elder son to meet his need: "Son, listen; Son listen," is his plea. But the hardheaded boy refuses to listen. He's closed-minded. He keeps on whining, "Poor me, poor me!" His father knows what's best for him, but the boy can't know that truth because he refuses to have a *communication relationship* with his father. Before the boy can be helped, he must first listen to his father instead of shutting him out. That means an entirely new relationship with his father.

This, says Jesus, is the second step in God's cure for self-pity. Stepping out on faith not only means that we accept God's revealed truth in the Bible. It also means that we accept the truth that God's Word is a living word, because our God is a living God.

What makes the Bible the Living Word of God is not the cold print on its pages, but the fact that the Living God who gave us the Bible through the Holy Spirit is also our living Interpreter for it through the same person—the Holy Spirit. He comes to us in the person of his Holy Spirit to make his Word come alive for us as he applies it to our lives today.

God's cure for "Poor me!" is a new mind that's open to God's Word as truth and open to God's Spirit to apply that truth to our life right now. That's the second step.

The third and final step in God's cure for self-pity is to accept God's revealed truth about legalism and grace.

We must trust God's grace instead of our own works.

The Bible is clear that every person who trusts in his own works instead of God's grace must eventually end up crying "Poor me! Poor me!" Paul leaves no doubt about this in the seventh chapter of Romans, when the natural man within him cries out,

> *"Wretched man that I am! Who will deliver me from this body of death?"* (Rom 7:24).

What body of death? Why, the death that legalism causes, of course—the suicide we commit when we put our trust in our ability to be good and do right, instead of trusting God's grace to bless us with the goodness and righteousness of Christ Jesus our Lord. This was the root of the elder boy's problem in our parable. He put his trust in himself and what he had done, and in his ability to continue to do it. Listen to him as he brags about himself: "I stayed home. I never disobeyed you. I worked hard. I didn't get drunk and live with harlots like he did. But now you're blessing him, not me; and I'm the one who deserves it. Poor me!"

He's a Pharisee, not a Christian. He's a legalist, not a repentant sinner who is open to God's amazing grace. He doesn't even know that he needs help. God can't bless him because he won't accept the blessings. Outwardly the boy has been moral by worldly standards, but inwardly he is eaten up with hate, envy, jealousy, bitterness, and resentment. In fact, he's so eaten up that all of his thoughts and vocabulary have been reduced to one common denominator: "Poor me!"

As Henry Drummond says in his classic book, *The Greatest Thing in the World*, there are two great classes of

91

sins—sins of the body and sins of the disposition. The Prodigal Son represents the first and the Elder Brother the second. In our human weakness we often think the sins of the body are most damnable, "But," writes Drummond, "to the eye of God who is Love, a sin against Love may seem a hundred times more base."

The good news is, it really doesn't matter which is the more base. The answer for both is the same. It is the amazing grace of God. It is a life of grace, instead of a life of law. It is a life lived out under the holy and perfect Spirit of our living Christ, instead of in our own power. All this elder brother has to do in order to start singing "Blessed me!" instead of whining "Poor me!" is exactly what his younger brother has done: throw himself totally upon the mercy of his father. All he has to do is to trust in the grace of God, instead of in his own good works.

That's God's cure for the disease of self-pity, and no one has ever said it more beautifully than a little blind woman who had every reason by worldly standards to go through life saying, "Poor me! Poor me!" Instead she wrote over six thousand hymns, all of them singing praises to God for his many blessings to her. Fanny Crosby in her inspired hymn, *I Am Thine, O Lord*, shows us how the wrong basic beliefs of man can be transformed by our Living God into the three eternal truths that bring us the *Blessed Assurance* which she writes about in another great hymn. Here are those three truths:

God's world centers around love, not us. We must lose ourselves in love in his service to find ourselves.

Anytime we open our minds to him and step out on faith we can "commune with him as friend with friend" and his Living Word will become our Word for life.

"By the power of grace divine" we can stop trying to do it ourselves and discard this body of death—legalism.

Then, we can sing with Fanny Crosby,

"Let my soul look up with steadfast hope,
and my will be lost in Thine." *

---

*
I Am Thine, O Lord, Cokesbury Hymnal #139.

Subject: Anxiety

Scripture: Matthew 6:25-34

Text: *But seek first his kingdom and his righteousness, and all these things shall be yours as well. Therefore, do not be anxious about tomorrow, for tomorrow will be anxious for itself. Let the day's own trouble be sufficient for the day* (Matthew 6:33-34).

From the time we are born until we die, life is a struggle to be a whole, integrated person—to be an individual in our own right. It is the universal struggle to reach our potential in life. This struggle becomes especially noticeable around age two, when the child begins to recognize that he's no longer bound to his mother, but is a separate individual from her, and that he can say "No!" This struggle intensifies each year thereafter, until at adolescence, it is an almost constant battle between dependence and independence. The outcome of this battle is crucial for every person.

During his first two years, the child is totally dependent upon his parents, and all of his needs are met by them. They give him his significance and his security, which are his two basic needs at this time. Around two years of age, two other needs begin to surface: the need for freedom, and the need for purpose or meaning.

So, from two years of age on, the battle lines are drawn. Will the individual break the infantile ties of dependency and become a whole, integrated person on his own? This he must do in order to meet his own four basic needs:

Significance,
Security,
Freedom, and
Purpose

95

Or, will he continue to be dependent upon his parents or parent substitutes to meet these needs for him? This is the basic battle in life for every person born upon this earth, and it's this battle that generates the painful emotion we call anxiety.

What is anxiety? Anxiety is that feeling within us resulting from conflict, when we think that conflict threatens our basic needs. It strikes at the core of our being. It is not just a fear of something unpleasant happening to us. Rather, it is a life and death struggle deep within us to keep from losing our whole personhood. It comes when we think we are in danger of losing our significance, our security, our freedom, or our purpose in life. You can see why psychiatrists say,

> "In its full-blown intensity, anxiety is the most
> painful emotion of all for human beings, because it
> is a threat to everything we hold dear in life." [*]

Perhaps a simpler definition is this: Anxiety is the conflict within us which results when we think what we are seeking is essential to our being, and we think this essential which we are seeking is being threatened or is lost.

Notice that anxiety may be provoked by a threat or event outside of ourselves. Almost anything, in fact, will do it, such as war, inflation, business failure, drop in the stock market, divorce, argument with a loved one, final exam, loss of job, unfinished work, not enough money to pay bills, etc. But these outside things are not the real problem. The real problem is inside of us; anxiety is the battle or conflict within us.

Therefore, the answer for anxiety is not to be found in trying to eliminate the outside events which trigger it nor in rebelling against them. Eliminating all of them is impossible, except through total withdrawal. (Incidentally,

---

[*] Rollo May, *Man's Search for Himself*, p. 35

belief that this is the only answer causes some people to withdraw into psychosis or become suicidal.) Because anxiety is a conflict within us, the answer for anxiety must be found within us too. It's also apparent that, because anxiety is a life or death struggle to keep from losing our personhood, the answer must be found in breaking our infantile ties of dependency upon our parents. This must be done in a mature way, so we can become whole, integrated persons in our own right. In short, both the psychological and the logical answer for anxiety is to discover the source of strength and integrity within ourselves which can handle our anxiety.

This is exactly the answer which Jesus gives us in his great Sermon on the Mount in the 5th, 6th and 7th chapters of Matthew. In this teaching, Jesus describes for us what life is like when it is lived out inside God's kingdom. At the end of chapter 6, he gives us God's answer for anxiety. He makes it clear that life lived out inside the kingdom of God is a life "beyond anxiety." Beginning with verse 25, after telling us that we need not be anxious about life, or food, or clothing or shelter, or length of life, or death, or tomorrow, Jesus concludes with:

> "But seek first his kingdom and his righteousness, and all these things shall be yours as well. Therefore, do not be anxious about tomorrow, for tomorrow will be anxious for itself. Let the day's own trouble be sufficient for the day" (Mt 6:33-34).

That is God's answer for anxiety, and it contains three very important points. The Bible says if we will orient our lives around these three points we can live beyond anxiety.

Jesus says that whether we are anxious or not hinges upon what we seek first in life.

Remember the definition for anxiety which I gave earlier? Anxiety is the conflict within us which results when we think what we are seeking in life is essential to our being, and we think this essential we are seeking is being threatened or is lost.

This is Jesus' first point. Our anxiety is always directly related to what we are seeking. It is always related to what, in our own opinion, should have priority in our life. Paul Tillich, one of the outstanding theologians of this century, calls this our "ultimate concern." Whatever we make our ultimate concern, Tillich says, is really our god, no matter what we call it; for it is what actually controls our life day by day. For example, if being successful in our work or business is our ultimate concern, then this is what we seek first and any threat to this will cause us our greatest anxiety. If our marriage and family are our ultimate concern, then any threat to them will cause us our greatest anxiety, and so forth.

Although, that is certainly true, life is not quite that simple. Since the Bible shows us that we have four basic needs, and all of these needs must be met before we can be whole, integrated persons, it just naturally follows that each of us has a number of ultimate concerns under each of these four headings. A threat to any of them can trigger anxiety.

Consider our basic need for the right self-image or for significance. In the second sermon in this series, *"I'm OK—You're OK,"* we saw that this need can be met only through

> A feeling of worthiness
> A feeling of competence and
> A feeling of belonging.

No matter how much our work means to us, it takes more than just a feeling of competence in our work to meet this basic need. It also takes a feeling of competence in our other relationships. It takes a feeling of worthiness and of belonging, too. We must also feel worthy as a husband or wife or parent. We must feel significant as a member of society and in our peer groups.

98

Or, consider our basic need for security. Just thinking we will be secure if we make so much money or have a certain bank balance, doesn't make it so. It takes more than feeding and clothing our bodies to meet this basic need for security. For instance, to feel secure, we must also feel secure in our love relationship with our mate, and secure in our eternal relationship with God. (See sermon *III, God's Cure for Insecurity*.)

The point is this. There are many ultimate concerns in all of our lives that must be met to fulfill our basic needs. If we go through life putting each one of these first when it is threatened, or we think it is threatened, we are automatically condemning ourselves to a life of painful anxiety.

Jesus says the one way to integrate and consolidate all of these concerns is to seek first the one truly ultimate concern. This brings us to the second point in God's answer for anxiety.

"But seek first God's kingdom and his righteousness," says Jesus, "and then all of these other concerns will be integrated into this one truly ultimate concern."   Jesus says to seek first two things, and they go together; they cannot be separated. You see, it takes both for any individual to become a whole, integrated person. It takes what we saw earlier was both the psychological and logical answer for anxiety, and now we see it is also our Lord's answer for anxiety. It is this:

We must discover that source of strength and integrity within ourselves which can handle our anxiety.

This is exactly what Jesus means when he says, "Seek first God's kingdom and his righteousness." He means, "Seek first God's power and God's integrity."

First, seek God's kingdom. That is, make your ultimate concern or your first priority citizenship in the kingdom of God. Jesus is saying we must do whatever has to be done to

99

permit God to rule our lives. That's what it means to live in the kingdom of God. It's apparent what that involves. We must give God's Living Spirit dominion over our minds, bodies, and wills. We must give him control over our thoughts, our emotions, and our actions. This is what Jesus means when he says,

"The kingdom of God is within you" (Lk 17:21 KJV).

This is what it means to be baptized with the Holy Spirit. This is what he was telling his disciples, when before his Ascension, he told to them to go back to Jerusalem and wait for the promise:

"You shall receive power when the Holy Spirit has come upon you" (Acts 1:8).

Jesus means we are, first of all, to seek the power of the Holy Spirit—of our living God—not so we can become "super-spooks"; but so we can become whole, integrated persons and live beyond anxiety. We can live beyond anxiety, because no matter what our concern or need is, it will be under the control and power of God's Holy Spirit, the ultimate creating force for all life. Jesus came to this earth to give us God's power from on high, to dwell within us, not just an outer form of religion. He came to give us inner strength to become whole persons!

Not only must we seek first his kingdom, we must also seek first his righteousness. The two must always go together: power and integrity, strength and responsibility. Lack of both is what keeps us from becoming whole, integrated persons; lack of both is what causes our anxiety. On our own, we lack the power to break infantile ties to our parents or parent-substitutes, and the integrity to do it in a mature way. We lack the strength to honestly be ourselves and take responsibility for our own actions, rather than simply reacting to others and blaming them for our mistakes.

100

Now, to "seek first his righteousness" is exactly what the Bible means by a life of grace as opposed to a life of law, for the Bible is clear that Christ and Christ alone is our righteousness. The truth is that practically all of our anxiety can be traced directly to living, in one way or another, a life of law instead of a life of grace. That is, our anxiety can be traced directly to tying ourselves to a set of rules to live by instead of yoking ourselves to our Living Christ, who is our righteousness.

What makes us choose such a life of law when the Bible is clear that as Christians, we are to live by grace? Paradoxically, it is our anxiety which is the culprit. The very thing which only a life of grace can cure is the cause for our choosing a life of law. Our thinking goes something like this: A life of law is secure. That way, I can always know what to do, and what not to do. It makes me acceptable to my peers. (They also live by law instead of grace, and it's their approval upon which most of us base our self-worth.) A life of grace is so uncertain. It's apt to make others think I'm different.

We ignore the fact that a life of law causes us to live a lie. We choose the anxiety of a life of law, rather than risk the uncertainty of a life of grace. Does it sound familiar? It should, for it's the normal pattern for most 20th century Christians. The most important truth any person can learn is this: Christ and Christ alone is our righteousness!

There is no way we can be righteous on our own. Only as he lives in us, and we live in him, can we have the integrity to be a whole, integrated person. Otherwise we will go through life putting on the outer cloak of righteousness—saying the right words, going to the right meetings, objecting to the right things—while on the inside the excruciating pain of anxiety will be almost more than we can bear.

You see, becoming a whole, integrated person is a process, not an accomplishment. It is a process which breaks our infantile ties to rules, and enables us to freely

101

live and move and have our being in the stream of God's Holy Spirit. It is God's process for our maturing. It's a process which begins when these four things happen in our life:

1. When we recognize our self-worth in being a child of God;
2. When we find our security in a personal relationship with our eternal God;
3. When we experience our freedom in a life of grace; and
4. When we get about our purpose of being a co-worker with God on earth.

In short, it's a process which begins when we "seek first God's kingdom and God's righteousness." It's a process which begins when we truly seek God's power and God's integrity as our own inner resource by seeking the Living Christ himself to live in us!

This brings us to this final point which Jesus is telling us about God's answer for anxiety:

We can continue to live beyond anxiety only as long as we live our lives according to God's timing; that is, as long as we actually live out our lives in the eternal moment.

Jesus concludes like this:

"Therefore, do not be anxious about tomorrow, for tomorrow will be anxious for itself. Let the day's own trouble be sufficient for the day" (Mt 6:34).

God does not intend for us to waste our todays by being anxious about our tomorrows. God intends for us to spend our todays beyond anxiety and he provides the way for us to do this in Jesus Christ our Lord.

The Bible says that Jesus came to this earth to relate us to a whole new kind of life, a kind of life which he calls eternal life. By this, the Bible doesn't mean that Jesus came to earth simply for Christians to delay living until our earthly lives are over and we can begin to really "live it up" in heaven. By the way some Christians act, you would think that is what eternal life means. But the Bible says,

"Jesus came into Galilee preaching the gospel of God, and saying 'The time is fulfilled, and the kingdom of God is at hand . . .'" (Mk 1:14-15).

That is, "The Eternal Moment is here and now. Eternal Life is available right now. So, begin to live it now." There are two things we know for certain about eternity: eternity transcends all time as we understand it; and eternity is God's timing.

There is no yesterday and no tomorrow in eternity, because eternity transcends time. God's timing is the Eternal Now—The Eternal Moment.

Jesus came to show us that our real problem is our failure to relate our lives to the new life he brought us. Instead of relating to eternal life—which is God's timing—and experiencing the reality of the present, we go right on living in the past or in the future. Any time we do that, we can be sure of one result: anxiety, because anxiety is a creation of time. There is no anxiety in the eternal now, because God is in control. It is God's timing. Anxiety always results when we confront the reality of our present with the resentments and guilts of our past, or with the fears and worries of our future. The Bible says it is our ties to our past or our fears of the future that keep us from being free to live in the present moment. We all know that's true.

When we think of eternal life as just some time in the future, instead of the eternal moment right now, we are trying to relate God to man's timing instead of relating ourselves to God's eternity.

To live beyond anxiety, we must begin now— today—to relate to an entirely new kind of life—eternal life—the God-life where the when of the future and the then of the past all merge together in the reality of the present moment in

103

Jesus Christ our Lord. That's the life Jesus came to give all of us—a life where our past has been cleansed by his Cross, our future has been assured by his Resurrection, and now we are free to live according to God's timing in the blessed eternal now. That's really what it means to live and move and have our being in God's Spirit. It's a life of faith. It's a life of trust. It's a life beyond anxiety!

XI   Temptations Are Common to Man

Subject: Temptation

Scripture: Matthew 4:1-11

Text: *No temptation has overtaken you that is not common to man. God is faithful, and he will not let you be tempted beyond your strength, but with the temptation will also provide the way of escape, that you may be able to endure it* (I Corinthians 10:13).

But he [Jesus] answered, "It is written..." Jesus said to him, "Again, it is written..." Then Jesus said to him, "Begone, Satan! for it is written . . ." (Matthew 4:4, 7 & 10).

I want to begin with a rather unusual request. I want you to suppose for just a moment that you have been employed as the Devil's Advocate. That is, your responsibility is to advise the devil on how he can best thwart God's plan for men. What is the one sure way the devil can keep us on his side, instead of on God's side? I want to suggest that the best way is for him to tempt us to try to meet our basic needs in the wrong way. If Satan can get us to turn our back on God's way and accept his lies as the way to meet these basic needs, then he's got us! Then we belong to him, not to God. We have seen in this series of sermons that we encounter all kinds of painful problems when our lives are founded upon wrong basic beliefs, instead of upon God's revealed truth. This is why Jesus calls Satan "the Tempter" and "the Evil One." The Holy Spirit drove Jesus into the wilderness to be tempted by the devil, so that Jesus could reveal to us both the nature of Satan's temptations and God's answer for these temptations. Jesus was tempted so we can know both Satan's ways and God's ways—both the way to death and the way to life. Let's look first at the nature of our temptations so we can recognize them when they come, and then we'll look at God's answer for these temptations.

I. The Nature of our Temptations

In one sense there are really only four basic temptations in life, although they take hundreds of different forms. The four basic temptations are the temptations to meet our four basic needs in the wrong way. In fact, the best definition of temptation that I can think of is this:

Temptation is the urge or enticement to meet our basic needs in life by violating God's principles and following Satan's principles.

Therefore, these two things are always present in every temptation: an urge to violate God's principles and an enticement to follow a destructive principle. To understand this let's look now at Jesus' three temptations in the wilderness, and analyze them. We shall see other truths about the nature of our temptations too. Jesus was tempted first to turn the stones to bread and win people's allegiance by meeting their physical needs alone.

Perhaps, the most basic need for every living creature is the need for security in the physical realm. Dr. Abraham Maslow places it as the basic need for all of us. Without it we cannot have peace of mind. Without it we lose hope. Without it human beings will turn into the lowest form of animal.

One thing you can write indelibly upon your mind is this: Satan is not going to waste his time with temptations that don't go to the very basis of life. He's not interested in our just being bad little boys and girls now and then. He's interested in getting our priorities in life so confused that we miss eternal life altogether. He does this by striking at our most vulnerable spots. Where was Jesus most vulnerable at this time? There was his hunger, because he had been fasting for forty days. And there was his compassion for the needs of men. So, that's exactly where

Satan struck. But Jesus wouldn't let him stop there. Jesus was looking beneath the surface temptation to the real temptation when he said, "Man does not live by bread alone."

There's more to human life than the material things of this world. When God created us in his image, he set a bit of eternity in our hearts. He gave us an eternal value system. Jesus saw that the real temptation here was to violate one of God's basic principles for living. What was this temptation?

It was the temptation to make temporary things ultimate, instead of a means to the truly ultimate values.

It's the temptation to try to satisfy our basic need for security with mere material things. Of course, we all must have physical things—food, clothing, and shelter. These are basic needs and essential for all of us. Jesus is not ignoring such physical needs, but he is saying that they alone can never meet our basic need for security. The image of God within us can only be secure in God. Jesus came to earth to make man right with God, not to start a welfare agency. But the Tempter says, "That's not where it's at! You've got to forget that relationship stuff and be realistic. Fill their bellies, that's the important thing. That's what they want. That's what they really need."

Have you heard the Tempter speaking to you in a similar way recently? Such as, "Hurry up! Get up! Get to work! You don't have time for a prayer with your mate. You're too busy; you've got to make a living. Forget that relationship stuff. Be realistic!"

Or, do you ever hear him say on Sunday morning, "You work so hard all week and you have an especially hard week coming up. Stay in bed. You need the rest more than worship. Forget that relationship stuff. Be realistic!"

The devil's no fool. He doesn't deal in theory. His temptations are always real and concrete, and they are always aimed at our most vulnerable spots. He's not going to tempt you to go fishing or play golf on Sunday morning when it's snowing. No, he'll wait until the sun's shining and the conditions are right. He's not going to tempt you to commit adultery when you return from a delightful second honeymoon with your mate. No, he'll wait until after an argument when your mate doesn't understand you and you need the soothing security of understanding arms.

That's the first side of the nature of temptation. It strikes at our basic need for security. It urges us to violate God's principle for meeting this basic need, which is eternal security in Christ, and to substitute Satan's lie that our security is to be found in the temporary things of this earth. It is the temptation to make the temporary things of this earth ultimate instead of eternal life in Christ—to settle for full stomachs, instead of transformed minds and hearts.

Secondly, Jesus was tempted to throw himself down from the pinnacle of the Temple and be saved by the angels of God in order to win people. Here, Satan is appealing to the basic need in all of us for personal worth, the need to be accepted by others. All of us are tempted to put ourselves in the limelight to win the approval of others. Certainly, preachers are. Preachers are tempted to preach to win the approval of the congregation instead of to proclaim the Word of God. It's a temptation not only of preachers, but a temptation which is common to man.

It's the temptation to make what others think of us ultimate—to make the opinion of others our god. The real temptation here was to center life around self instead of God.

Note another side of the nature of this temptation. Not only does it undermine God's answer for our basic need for self-worth; it also glosses over the real temptation with something that looks good and that we can rationalize as good, but which is very destructive. Why shouldn't Jesus win people with miracles? Why shouldn't he attract

108

attention this way? It's the surest way to get a crowd. Well, the Bible is clear why not: It undermines our part in the salvation process—the only way any person can discover he is a child of God and actually know his self-worth. It undermines faith. You see, the real temptation was for Jesus to live by signs and wonders instead of by faith, but that is glossed over here. It always is.

Have you noticed how your temptations are always glossed over too? The temptation for young people to have sex before marriage is never to cheapen one of life's most precious experiences, or to defy parental authority. No, it's to find fulfillment, to express "true love," to be realistic. The real temptation is always glossed over.

The temptation to gossip is never to build ourselves up by tearing someone else down, or to harden our hearts to the weaknesses of others. No, it is to be truthful and tell it like it is. It is to stand up for what's right. The real temptation is always glossed over.

The temptation to neglect our family in order to work harder and make more money is never to satisfy our own ego or to escape from family responsibilities. No, it's to provide better for our family, so they can have the good things of life. The real temptation is always glossed over.

The point is, we must learn to look beneath the surface of life's temptations, as Jesus did, in order to spot the real temptations of life—the destructive temptations.

This brings us to the third temptation of Jesus. Satan takes him to the top of a high mountain, shows him all of the kingdoms of the world and offers them to him. Here Satan pulls out all of the stops, and attacks Jesus on two fronts. There are only two basic needs left, so Satan decides to strike at both of them: our need for freedom and our need for purpose.

- All of us need to be free from bondage to anyone or anything. It's a basic need.

- All of us need to find meaning for our lives through a useful and worthwhile purpose to live for.

Satan offers Jesus one answer for both of these needs. Satan's answer is power—physical power. Satan says that power over others is what really frees us—power to direct others in what they do is the way we find meaning for our own lives.

It sounds reasonable, doesn't it? If we exercise power over others, then it stands to reason they can't control us; we are free. If we direct other people in what they do, then it stands to reason that we can decide what is really meaningful and purposeful for life. Yes, power over others sounds like the perfect way to fulfill both our need for freedom and our need for purpose, doesn't it? But let's go beneath the surface of this last temptation and see what the real temptation is. Notice what Satan said to Jesus:

"All these I will give you, if you will fall down and worship me!" (Mt 4:9).

The temptation to power is always the temptation to compromise our covenant with God and try to play God ourselves. It's the temptation to make our own will ultimate, instead of God's will. It is the temptation to live under self-will, instead of God's will. Have you heard Satan whispering to you lately? "Preacher, lord it over your people! Mother, lord it over your children! Husband, lord it over your wife! Employer, lord it over your employees! Supervisor, lord it over the ones under you! Young man, lord it over your girl friend! Young woman, lord it over your friends!"

Each of us is tempted to play God—to seek to fulfill our basic need for freedom and purpose by exercising power over others.

Daily, all of us are tempted to compromise, and here is a truth you can depend upon: temptation always demands that we compromise. Compromise your marital vows, compromise your business ethics, compromise truth, compromise justice, compromise the personhood of others. We must learn to recognize this demand for compromise before we can successfully deal with this temptation.

Well, that's the nature of temptation. It's the urge to look for the answer to life's basic needs in self instead of in God. It's an appeal to our own physical appetites, to our own egos, and to our own willfulness in order to exercise dominion over the Spirit of God within us. It's the urging to compromise eternal values for temporal values. It's the enticement to build our lives upon Satan's lies; that is, to build our lives on the wrong basic beliefs, instead of upon God's eternal revealed truth.

II. God's Answer For Our Temptations

The Bible gives us God's answer for our temptations. Jesus demonstrates God's answer for temptations in showing us how he answered temptation in the wilderness. Paul tells us God's answer in I Corinthians where he writes:

"No temptation has overtaken you that is not common to man. God is faithful, and will not let you be tempted beyond your strength, but with the temptation will also provide the way of escape, that you may be able to endure it" (I Cor 10:13).

Listen to Jesus each time he is tempted. When Satan tempts him to turn the stones to bread:

"It is written, 'Man shall not live by bread alone, but by every word that proceeds from the mouth of God'" (Mt 4:4).

When the devil tempts him to jump from the pinnacle of the Temple:

111

"Again it is written, 'You shall not tempt the Lord your God'" (Mt 4:7).

Finally, when the devil tempts Jesus with power over the whole world, if he will bow down and worship Satan:

"Begone, Satan! for it is written, 'You shall worship the Lord your God and him only shall you serve'" (Mt 4:10).

Paul says in I Corinthians 10:13 that God gives us a way to escape every temptation, and Jesus demonstrates that way for us in the wilderness. What is that way? It is God's Word. It is God's revealed truth to us. God has already given us all of the truth we need for our life's foundation. He has given us this truth in his Word.

Once Jesus compared the human mind to a house (Mt 12:43-45). He said that when temptation enters our mind, it is like a house with a demon turned loose in it. The answer, says Jesus, is not simply to track down that one demon, catch him and throw him out of the house, for worse demons would come and take his place. What then should we do?

Jesus says we should fill our house so full of the right thing that there is no room for the demons to live there. Oh, they'll knock on the door; they'll keep probing to get in, because temptations are common to man. But they can't take up residence there and become sin, which separates us from God, if our mind is fully occupied by the right thing, which is the Word of God.

So, God's answer for temptation is to fill our mind with his eternal truth, which is his Holy Word. This means we must do three things to handle the temptations in our life.

First, we must fill our mind with God's Written Word.

We must read, internalize, and memorize Scripture, so it is available to us when Satan strikes with temptation.

Like Jesus, we must be able to test every temptation against God's Written Word. The Bible shows us that is the one test the Tempter cannot withstand. Why don't you start today by memorizing this great promise of God against temptation, Corinthians 10:13? I memorized it many years ago in the King James Version, and Oh how many times I have said to Satan since:

> "*Begone Satan! It is written! "There hath no temptation taken you but such as is common to man: but God is faithful, who will not suffer you to be tempted above that ye are able; but will with the temptation also make a way to escape, that ye may be able to bear it."*"

"Get out of here, Satan," I say to the Tempter. "The Bible says that down through the ages, other people have resisted this same temptation. God is faithful, and he won't let me be tempted beyond my ability to resist. Every time you tempt me, God gives me a way out. I can stand up against anything you throw my way!"

God's way for us to escape is through his Holy Word, hidden in our minds and hearts.

Next, you must let the Incarnate Word of God take up permanent residence in the house of your mind.

Get to know Jesus so well that you live with him. Get to know his thoughts, his actions, his words, so well that he is always there with you to confront temptation when it enters your house. He and he alone is the Victor over Satan. The good news is, he wants to share that victory with you. That is why he came to earth. That is why he died on the Cross. That is why he rose from the dead. His victory can become your victory too.

Finally, open the house of your mind to the Living Word of God—God's Holy Spirit.

113

Without the Holy Spirit to interpret God's Written Word there is no way we can understand it and apply it to our own lives today. Without the Holy Spirit to roll back the stone of the entombed Jesus, the Incarnate Word cannot come to life again within us. Only the Living Word of God, giving life to God's Written Word within us, witnessing to the reality of God's saving act in his Incarnate Word is any match for the Tempter of this world. Begin today to fill the house of your mind with the Word of God—the Written Word, the Incarnate Word and the Living Word of God—and you will have God's answer for your temptations. *"For all the promises of God find their Yes in him"*—who is God's Perfect Word to us.

XII How to Get Up When You're Down

Subject: Depression

Scripture: Matthew 14:22-23

Text: *When Peter saw the wind, he was afraid,*
            and beginning to sink he cried out, "Lord,
            save me." Jesus immediately reached out his
            hand and caught him, saying to him, "O man
            of little faith, why did you doubt?" (Matthew
            14:30-31).

TOday, I want us to look at *How the Bible Can Help You*
with the problem of depression. What is depression?
Ancient writers in Greece at the time of Plato called it
melancholia. The Psalmist in the Bible speaks of it as being
forsaken by God.

> *"My God, my God, why hast thou forsaken me? Why*
> *art thou so far from helping me . . .*
> *O my God, I cry by day, but thou dost not answer;*
> *and by night, but find no rest"* (Ps 22:1-2).

Over 400 years ago, a Spanish mystic named St. John
of the Cross wrote a book about this experience and called
it *The Dark Night of the Soul.* It's like groping in the dark,
unable to find the light.

A modern day psychologist, who calls it emotional
depression, says it's the most common emotional problem
in our country today, and has risen to the level of a national
epidemic. He points out that one out of eight Americans
require treatment for depression in their lifetime; and in
any one year, between 4 and 8 million Americans are
depressed to the extent that they cannot effectively function
at their jobs or must seek some kind of treatment. (*An
Answer to Depression,* p. 6 by Norman Wright).

What are the symptoms of depression? You don't want to get out of bed in the morning, but, no matter how much you sleep, you're still exhausted. It's hard to concentrate; you become indecisive. You don't feel like laughing, food loses its taste and sex loses its appeal. You begin to withdraw and don't want to be bothered by family or friends. You try to avoid talking on the phone or attending social gatherings. You feel hopeless and think no one cares about you and certainly you don't like yourself. You begin to get new aches and pains and wonder if you've got some serious disease. There are many more symptoms, but that's enough for all of us to identify it; for none of us is immune to depression. In short, depression is getting down emotionally and being unable to get up!

Perhaps a modern Jewish songwriter came close to describing it when he wrote:

"When you're weary, feelin' small,
When tears are in your eyes,
When time gets rough, and friends just can't be found,
When you're down and out,
When evening falls so hard,
When darkness comes and pain is all around,
Like a Bridge over Troubled Water,
I will lay me down,
I will ease your mind!" *

Jesus chose the same metaphor to reveal to us God's answer for depression. He says that it is like the hopelessness of sinking in dark, deep, troubled water, unable to do anything about it.

You remember the story in the 14th chapter of Matthew. We are told that while Jesus is up in the hills praying, the disciples get in a boat and go out to sea. Darkness overtakes them and a violent wind blows up. The waters are troubled and so are the disciples. When Jesus

---

* Paul Simon, *Bridge Over Troubled Waters*, 1969

comes to them walking on the water, they think he is a ghost and are frightened. But when he speaks, they recognize him. Peter gets out of the boat and starts walking on the water toward Jesus, but as the wind blows and swirls around him, Peter turns toward the wind and fear grips his heart. He begins to sink and cries out, "Lord, save me!" Jesus reaches out his hand saying, "O man of little faith, why did you doubt?" Jesus lifts Peter up; they get in the boat and the wind ceases.

Before examining what Jesus is revealing to us here, we need to be clear about one more preliminary fact. There are three primary causes for depression.

First, there are physical causes for depression, ranging from such simple things as not eating properly or not getting enough sleep, to toxic depression from medicine and drugs and serious diseases. For example, infection of the nervous system or certain body organs can cause depression and so can glandular disorders such as low thyroid condition, or hormones, or imbalance of secretions from adrenal glands.

The list of physical causes for depression is lengthy, and of course, this is a wholly different matter than what we are considering. If depression strikes, a wise person will see his doctor for a check-up and make certain the cause is not physical.

A second primary cause for depression can be in the subconscious. In her book, *Behold Your God*, Agnes Sanford tells about a German woman who had been driven out of Germany before World War II because of her Jewish ancestry. Before her escape as a young girl, she suffered many hardships, pains, and indignities. After coming to America, she became a Christian, forgave her persecutors, and began living a vibrant Christian life. Periodically, however, she would fall into unaccountable periods of depression and brooding anger, which no amount of logic or reason could reach. Her conscious beliefs and actions were beyond reproach. Even prayer did not help. Finally, God

117

revealed to Agnes Sanford that the trouble was in the woman's subconscious. The little girl, still alive within the grown woman, was the real cause of her depression. She had never received the comfort she needed when her parents were taken to a concentration camp nor when she was molested as a child. The little girl had repressed her feelings of helpless resentment in order to survive. When some experience caused this "child within" to start hurting all over again, it brought on these feelings of depression; but the memories were repressed at much too deep a level for her to recognize them.

Obviously, this required specialized treatment of either deep psychiatric therapy or prayer counseling and prayer therapy. This type of depression is also beyond the scope of this sermon. But let me make it clear that such depression is not beyond the scope of the Christian faith. In recent years, such Christian leaders as Agnes Sanford, Ann White, and Ruth Carter Stapleton have been used by God to show us how the Living Christ, who is timeless, can go back into our memories and our subconscious minds and heal these old hurts and pains and deliver us from such depression. This is not something to be done on the spur of the moment by the untrained, but should be practiced only by those who have been properly equipped.

For several years now we have been seeking to equip some of our ministers and laymen for this specialized ministry. A number of us have attended Ann White's Prayer Counseling clinics and Ruth Carter Stapleton's training sessions here at our church and Agnes Sanford's School of Pastoral Care in California. Such prayer counseling is tremendously effective, but it requires considerably more time than any minister with all of his other duties can do alone.

My vision is to equip those dedicated laymen in our church who are called of God and who have the gifts for this special ministry, so they can work closely with our Heritage Services Counseling Center and bring God's

118

healing love to bear upon such subconscious depression. I will be telling you much more about this in the weeks and months ahead.

The third primary cause for depression is in our conscious thoughts, or what might best be called negative thinking. It was this type of depression that Peter faced in this unusual experience on the Sea of Galilee. In this event, Jesus is revealing to us four very important eternal truths about depression.

First, Jesus is showing us that such depression is a signal, not a sin.

To accuse yourself or another person of being a sinner when depressed is the surest way to sink deeper into depression or to cause another to sink deeper. Of course, unforgiven sin can be the cause of depression, but so can many other things. Sin and depression are not synonymous.

Notice Peter here. Certainly, he's not a sinner. He starts off full of faith, confident. He knew who Jesus was. He trusted Jesus. He wasn't a sinner; he was a faithful believer.

Notice, too, what Jesus says to Peter: "O man of little faith, why did you doubt?" Jesus doesn't call Peter a sinner, rather he signals Peter why his faith is failing and the reason is negative thinking—doubting. Jesus is saying that negative thinking is not compatible with great faith. He is saying that doubting eats away at our faith. Negative thinking and doubting changed Peter's great faith to little faith and it will do the same to any of us. This is an eternal truth: Negative thinking and great faith are incompatible!

Symptoms of depression should not be a time for condemning yourself or anyone else, for that simply adds more negative thinking to what's already started. It's not a time to tell someone else to "snap out of it" or "start being yourself again," for that simply proves you don't understand the real problem. Depression is not a sin nor a willful fault

119

that someone can snap out of, but depression is a signal. It's a signal that negative thinking is eating away our faith. That's the first truth about depression.

Next, depression signals us to identify the underlying trouble that is causing our negative thinking.

Negative thinking is always brought on by something. Before you can do anything about it, you need to identify the basic cause.

The basic trouble with Peter was physical danger—the storm, the strong wind, the high waves, the turbulent sea. His underlying trouble was that he was facing a physical danger he could do nothing about. Depression is always caused by some underlying trouble. A recent survey by *Science Digest*[*] lists in order of importance the distressing events which induce depression in present-day Americans:

death of a child or spouse
a jail sentence
being fired
a miscarriage
divorce
marital separation
a court appearance
unwanted pregnancy
major illness in your family
unemployment
death of a friend
demotion
major personal illness
an extramarital affair
loss of valued objects
a lawsuit
academic failure

---

[*]For another more detailed approach to this issue see Holmes/Rahe *Social Readjustment Rating Scale,* Journal of Psychosomatic Research, 1967, 11, 213-18

a child married without family approval
a broken engagement
taking out a large loan
  a son drafted in time of war

Notice that many of them are things over which we have no control. Some are inevitable. The point is, just as the waters of the Sea of Galilee were not always smooth, neither will the waters of life always be smooth. Storms are bound to come to all of us, and when they do, just as they did for Peter, they almost always generate negative thinking. If we let such depression or negative thinking become a signal for us to get busy identifying the underlying trouble causing it, we're well on our way of getting up instead of sinking deeper!

Most people in depression will say to you, "I don't know why I feel this way." But when you talk with them, you discover there has been a death or serious illness in the family, or perhaps a divorce, marital problems, financial trouble, or one of the other things on the list. Here's a truth you can depend on: There is always some underlying trouble causing negative thinking, and when you discover it you are ready to move on to the third step in God's answer for depression.

Depression signals us to identify our specific negative thoughts about this trouble.

Our scripture tells us that Peter's negative thoughts were thoughts of fear. It says:

"When he [Peter] saw the wind, he was afraid and beginning to sink, he cried out, 'Lord, save me'" (Mt 14:30).

Peter's trouble, coupled with his negative thinking about that trouble, was causing him to sink deeper and deeper. It always does! These are the two ingredients making up all depression—trouble coupled with negative thinking about that trouble. We must identify these negative thoughts before we can do anything about them.

A loved one dies, and our thinking begins to center on all kinds of negative things, such as our great loss, our loneliness, our hopelessness, the new problems we must face because of our loss. Negative thinking always generates more negative thinking, as the negative thoughts begin to reproduce and multiply. Unless we recognize these negative thoughts for what they are, they will get completely out of hand and exercise total mastery over us.

One psychiatrist told a patient to carry a stop watch with him and each time he had a negative thought to start the watch and let it run until a positive thought replaced it. Then, he told him to keep a record of each negative thought and how long it mastered him. It proved to be good therapy because, first, it gave the patient a handle for identifying his negative thinking, and second, it gave him a method for controlling his negative thoughts.

Finally, depression should signal us to take our eyes off our trouble and our negative thinking about it, and look at Jesus.

As Christians, we believe that Jesus is God's answer for all of man's trouble. In fact, the Bible says this is exactly why God sent Jesus to us—to be the answer for our trouble. But he can't be our personal answer until we lift up our eyes and look to him as our answer. When we do, we will see the same three things that Peter saw in Jesus.

First, we will see that Jesus will cross all troubled waters to come to us and meet our needs.

There are no troubles we have that are too big, or too rough, to keep Jesus away. This is the heart of the gospel, because this is the meaning of the Incarnation itself. Everything else in the Christian faith depends upon our acceptance of this basic truth: God has come to us in

Christ, across the most difficult obstacles, to rescue us from the troubled waters of life!

The second thing we will see when we lift up our eyes and look at Jesus is that he is real, not a ghost or a myth.

Our scripture says that when the disciples first saw Jesus coming to them, they thought he was a ghost. They thought it was some kind of magic, instead of the most down-to-earth reality in life.

This is still the mind set of many church members today, and why they are unable to deal with depression and other problems. They think that Christianity is some kind of magic, instead of the most realistic, down-to-earth way to live. Consequently Jesus Christ cannot be their answer for depression nor for any other problems.

This is the whole point of the rest of the New Testament after the four Gospels. The Gospels tell us the good news of God becoming man in Jesus Christ and crossing the obstacle of time and space to come to us and save us from sinking. The remaining twenty-three books of the New Testament tell us how Jesus is still doing this for us today. All of these books agree that there is only one way it can become a reality for you and me, and that is through the ministry and work of the Holy Spirit! Anything else, except the reality of the ministry of the Holy Spirit, makes Christianity into magic or a ghost story. It's the reality of the Holy Spirit that makes our Lord's victory on the Cross a victorious reality for us! It means that our Risen Christ sends us his own Holy Spirit, who has already won the victory over all of life's problems, to abide in us and be our Victor over these problems. This, and this alone, takes Christianity out of the realm of magic and ghost stories, and makes it the most down-to-earth reality in all of life! The Holy Spirit is real. He is our real power for life. He is our real living God, living in us!

This brings us to this final thing we see in Jesus when we lift up our eyes and look at him:

He will help us when we are down!

The Bible says that God's answer for our depression is for us to accept the help which Jesus offers us—to let him lift us up when we're down! This is what saved Peter when he was sinking. He cried out, "Lord, save me!" Jesus immediately reached out his hand, caught him, and lifted him up. Notice that Peter asked and Jesus answered.

The same formula still applies to us today. But how can we ask, when our thinking is all haywire and our emotional stability is gone? Norman Wright, a Christian psychologist, suggests one way we can do it. He says he doesn't remember where he first heard about it, but he has tried it many times and it works. He calls it "The STOP-THINK method." Here it is:

On one side of a card write in large red letters the word
STOP!
On the other side write
THINK
Below that write out the scripture,

Have no anxiety about anything, but in everything by prayer and supplication with thanksgiving let your requests be made known to God. And the peace of God, which passes all understanding, will keep your hearts and your minds in Christ Jesus.

Finally, brethren, whatever is true, whatever is honorable, whatever is just, whatever is pure, whatever is lovely, whatever is gracious, if there is any excellence, if there is anything worthy of praise, think about these things. (Phil 4:6-8).

Carry this card with you, and anytime a negative or worrisome thought comes into your mind, take out the card. If you are alone, look at the card and say the word

"STOP" out loud. Turn the card over and say out loud, "Think God's thoughts." Then read the scripture. If you are not alone, you can still do it silently.

We can change our feelings only by first changing our wrong basic beliefs—our negative thought patterns—and accepting God's revealed truths. Use this "STOP-THINK" tool regularly to help you defeat depression. Take your eyes off of your own trouble and look to Jesus who is God's answer for depression.

Subject: Worry

Scripture: Matthew 25:14-30

Text: *He also who had received the one talent*
came forward, saying, "Master, . . . I was
afraid, and I went and hid your talent in the
ground" . . . But his Master answered, . . .
"Take the talent from him, and give it to him
who has the ten talents. For to every one who
has will more be given, and he will have
abundance; but from him who has not, even
what has will be taken away" (Matthew
25:24-26,28-29).

Last Thanksgiving most of us gathered around our tables and gave thanks for our blessings, which, of course, are many. Yet, I wonder if any of us gave thanks for what could be God's greatest gift to us as human beings? I wonder if any of us even thought about it. I know I didn't. It wasn't until Friday—the day after Thanksgiving and the day I reserve for final sermon preparation—that I began to think about that which best illustrates our being created in the image of God. I did it because of the subject I'm preaching on today—the problem of worry. It so happens that the name of this great gift comes from the same root word as "image." I'm talking about imagination— our gift of imagination! In many ways, our gift of imagination best illustrates what the Bible means when it says we are created in the image of God.

One of the most ambitious publishing events of our day ties *The Great Books of Our Western World* to the *100 Great Ideas of Human Thought*. It is interesting and enlightening that in this outstanding work, memory and imagination are joined together as one great idea, because in one sense they do the same thing: they keep us from being confined to the present moment. They enable us to use both the experiences of our past and the possibilities of the future. Through memory we can go back into the past and through imagination we can go forward into the future. Without memory and imagination man could be neither poet nor historian, doctor nor lawyer, teacher nor researcher. Without them there could be neither science nor literature, mathematics nor creativity. In fact, without memory and imagination man could not be man. Every work of creativity and every invention since the beginning of time, as well as every advancement experienced by mankind have found both their beginning and end in this great gift of God! Yes, it is in the memory of experience and in the imagination of possibilities that man finds his greatness—or his downfall!

This brings us to the problem of worry. What is worry? Here is my own personal definition: Worry is the misuse of God's gift of imagination.

It sounds almost paradoxical, doesn't it, that one of God's most precious gifts could be the cause of some of our most terrifying and miserable times. Yet, it is true. It is true because everything in God's creation, including all of his personal gifts to us, can be used either right or wrong—for good or for bad. This truth applies to the gift of imagination and its misuse through worry.

Jesus gives us a clear picture of this misuse in one of his most familiar parables, *The Parable of the Talents*. You remember the story. A master goes on a long journey, but before leaving he calls his three servants and gives one servant five talents, another two talents, and the third one talent. A talent at that time was worth approximately $1,000 in our money. When the master returns he discovers that the servant with five talents invested it and made five talents more. The one with two talents made two talents more. But the one with one talent was afraid and hid his one talent in the ground. The master commends the first two servants, but calls the third servant "a wicked and slothful servant," and takes the one talent away from him, giving it to the servant with ten talents. Jesus concludes by stating the universal truth:

"For to everyone who has will more be given, and he will have abundance; but from him who has not, even what he has will be taken away" (Mt 25:29).

Since this parable is almost always used to point up our responsibility as Christian stewards—and certainly it does that—we are apt to miss an even more fundamental truth which Jesus is revealing to us about the importance of our memories and our imaginations, and the right use and misuse of them! Here is one of the clearest pictures in the Bible of what worry is, what it does to us, and how we are supposed to handle it.

I. What is worry?

Look at the third servant—the one Jesus calls "wicked and slothful" and you will see. We are told that this servant knew that his master was a hard, demanding man, so he was afraid and hid his talent in the ground. Here we see the relationship between his memory and his imagination—between his worry and his memory of his master. As we look at his actions and hear his words, we also see that worry is closely related to three other emotions: fear, anxiety, and concern. They are closely related, but there is a distinct difference between worry and these other emotions.

Concern is being legitimately bothered or troubled about a specific situation or condition because of the known facts.

Worry is conjuring up threatening "facts" of the situation in our own imagination.

For example, the families of the members of the Peoples Temple religious sect in Guyana, when they heard the grim

129

news of the mass suicide, had every right to be concerned about their loved ones. Such concern would be the reaction of every normal human being, and such concern should result in concrete action to find out about the situation and to do whatever they could. But such concern turns into worry the moment they let their own imaginations begin to conjure up horrible, imagined "facts" about their loved ones.

Worry is different from fear, too, although fearfulness is always involved in worry.

Fear is a legitimate, protective response to danger.

We need to experience fear, because it protects us from harm. We shall examine both the right and wrong use of fear later on in this series of sermons, but for now let's just distinguish fear from worry. It was the response of fear to the danger of certain death by either poisoning or shooting that motivated a few of the sect members in Guyana to take to the jungle. But that fear turns to worry the moment those members, still in the jungle, let their imaginations take over and begin to conjure up imagined "facts" about what the American soldiers and Guyana police will do to them if they come out of the jungle.

Anxiety and worry are even more closely related, because apprehension, uneasiness, and dread are always present in both anxiety and worry. But there is one big difference. When it's anxiety, you can't quite put your finger on why you feel that way. But when it's worry you know what's causing it, for your imagination keeps painting specific, make-believe pictures upon the walls of your mind.

What is worry?

Worry is the misuse of God's gift of imagination.

Isn't this exactly what happened to the third servant in our parable? He says he did what he did because he was afraid, but he is not talking about legitimate fear. He is talking about the "fearfulness of worry." First, in his

130

memory he sees his master as a firm, strict, demanding man. No doubt, his master had previously dealt with him about failure or irresponsibility and these pictures still hang on the walls of his memory. As he gazes at these old pictures on the walls of his memory, he begins to use this amazing gift of God to jump time and see into the future— the gift of imagination! He uses this gift to hang similar pictures on the walls of his imagination. The trouble is, he misuses this great gift! Instead of using the facts as they actually are, he begins to conjure up new, imagined, make-believe "facts" such as: "What would happen if I lost the money? What if the money were stolen? What if the business deal fell through? What if my master returned too soon? What if—What if—What if!" There's the danger sign! There's the question to always watch out for: "What if . . . ?" That's the way we always begin when we misuse our imaginations and turn genuine concern into worry. What is worry? Worry is the misuse of our gift of imagination!

What does worry do to us?

Look at this slothful servant and you can see what it does to us.

Worry undermines our sense of responsibility.

The master gave this servant one talent in trust and the servant's responsibility was to use the talent for his master. But his worry kept him from being responsible in this trust. As I look back on it, I think the greatest lesson I learned during 3 1/2 years in combat in World War II, is that the most important character trait a person can have is a sense of responsibility. Thirty-five years later I am more certain than ever that this is true. That's the first trait a wise employer will look for in hiring a new employee or in promoting an old one. That's the first trait a wise girl will look for before saying "yes" to a proposal, or a young man should look for in choosing a wife. That's the most important character trait any person can have: a sense of

131

responsibility. And nothing undermines it more than worry, the misuse of our imaginations!

Worry stifles creativity and initiative.

This irresponsible servant was so worried that all he could think to do was to bury his one talent in the ground. Why did God give us the gift of imagination? He gave it to us because, being created in his image, we are meant to be creative as God is creative. This is the right use of our imagination. We are supposed to use it to find new ways to serve God and man, to come up with new insights and new opportunities. We are supposed to use it to motivate us to take the initiative and to be creative. Nothing stifles that quite so much as worry—because worry is a misuse of our imagination.

Worry drains us of our courage.

This "wicked and slothful servant" was afraid to take a chance and make himself vulnerable. Do you see what this means? It means that worry keeps us from being able to love, for the first step in genuine love is always a willingness to make yourself vulnerable for another.

Over and over I talk with people who are afraid to get married because they are worried about what might happen. What has happened is that their worry has drained them of the courage they need to make themselves vulnerable, which must always be the first step in love. I see the same thing in couples who are afraid to have children. They miss life's highest experience, the experience of love, because they have permitted worry to drain them of the courage they need to make themselves vulnerable.

It's easy to see how this happens when we understand how our memory and our imagination work together. A person begins gazing at the bad memories from his childhood or at the bad memories of a first marriage. As he looks at the ugly pictures on the walls of his memory, he uses this amazing gift of God to jump time and see similar pictures in the future hanging on the walls of his imagination. Misusing his imagination in this way, he becomes the victim of worry, with all of its bad effects.

There are many more harmful effects of worry, such as making us indecisive and stymieing our productivity, to say nothing of what it does to our health and our peace of mind. But certainly that's enough to show that it is one of the most destructive and debilitating of all emotions.

What is God's answer for our worry?

If worry is the misuse of our imagination, God's answer must be the right use of our gift of imagination!

This is exactly the answer which Jesus shows us in our parable. The first two servants used their imagination right. They used their imagination in order to be responsible, to take the initiative, to be creative, to be courageous, and to make themselves vulnerable for their master. In short, they used their imagination to live a life of love for their master!

What is love? Love is taking the initiative to give yourself responsibly, creatively, and courageously to another. Love is taking the initiative to make yourself vulnerable for another.

The Bible says that God created us to live in love with him and with other people, and only when we do, can we be complete and fulfilled. God gave us both our memory and our imagination so we can find this life of love. He gave us memory so we can store up the right facts and experiences and then use these facts and experiences in our imaginations to motivate us to take the initiative in responsible, creative, courageous behavior as we make ourselves vulnerable for others. The trouble is, sin enters our world and keeps us from using our memory and our imagination right. That's where sin does most of its diabolical work. Sin comes in and hangs the wrong pictures on both the walls of our memories and the walls of our imaginations.

But the good news is, God sent Jesus Christ to us to take those wrong pictures down and hang up the right ones. God sent Jesus so we can stop misusing these precious gifts and start using them right! God sent Jesus to bridge this gap between our memories and our imaginations with perfect love—with the very image of God himself!

If we try to go from the experiences and facts of our memories to the uncertainties and possibilities of our imaginations without Jesus, the result will always be distorted by sin. The result will always be tension, anxiety, and worry. This is because both the facts and experiences of our memories and the pictures of our imaginations are always distorted by sin! And there is absolutely nothing we can do to correct this distortion. Only Jesus Christ, the Son of God, who has already won the victory over sin, can correct this distortion. Only Jesus Christ, who is perfect love, can be the perfect bridge between our memories and our imaginations and enable us to live in love.

How does Jesus do this for us?

The Bible is clear:

He enables us to live in love by both cleansing our memories and purifying our imaginations with his perfect love!

Do you want your memory cleansed? According to the Bible there is only one way it can ever be done, and that is through faith in Jesus Christ as your Savior! This is why faith always looks back to what Christ has already done for us on the Cross. The reason why faith always deals with the past—the work of Christ which has already been accomplished—is because it is also dealing with our past— our memories! When through faith, you accept Christ's death on the Cross as God's saving act for you personally, you are, in fact, permitting Christ himself to take all of those ugly, grotesque pictures off the walls of your memories, and cleanse them of all the filth and cobwebs they've gathered across the years. You are permitting Christ to re-paint those past experiences in your life into beautiful images of his perfect love. You are permitting him to paint the new you! The cleansed you! The significant you! The secure you! The free you! The responsible you! The courageous you! That's what faith in Jesus Christ as Savior means for you: It means cleansed memories.

Do you want your imagination purified? According to the Bible there is only one way it can be done, and that is through hope, through hope in Christ as your Living, All Powerful and Life-giving Lord! This is why hope always looks forward to the future, because it is God's way of dealing with our future—our imaginations! When through hope you accept the reality of the Living Spirit of Christ, the Holy Spirit, coming to you to assure you, to enlighten you, and to empower you, you are actually permitting Christ to purify your imagination. Then, no longer can sin misuse your imagination by conjuring up false "facts" and images; because through hope your imagination is now grounded in Truth himself! And this Truth will make you free! Free from worry! Free to be yourself! Free to be responsible! Free to be creative! Free to take the initiative! Free to be vulnerable! Yes, free to love!

This is why Paul says in I Corinthians 13 that there are three eternal verities: faith, hope, and love. Faith finds its eternal significance in the past work of the Crucified Christ—the cleansing of our memories. Hope finds its eternal significance in the future work of the Living Christ, in the purifying of our imaginations. But Love finds its eternal significance in the present moment!

Love is the Spirit of Jesus Christ living in us right now! Love is Love himself living in us right now! This is why Paul says that Love is the greatest! All three are essential, but Love is the greatest because it is what faith and hope are all about. Faith appropriates what Christ has already done for

135

us in the past. Hope looks forward to what Christ will do for us later. But Love is experiencing the presence of Christ right now.

Faith is essential in order to free us from bondage to our past by cleansing our memories.

Hope is essential in order to free us from worry about the future by purifying our imaginations.

Love is the bridge which Christ builds in the present between our memories and our imaginations!

Love is life as God intends for it to be. That's why it is the greatest! Love is being in Christ and Christ being in us; that's why it is the greatest! But such a life of love is possible only through faith and hope—only through the cleansing of our memories and the purifying of our imaginations. My prayer is that God will bless you with Faith, Hope, and Love; that is, bless your past by cleansing your memories, bless your future by purifying your imaginations, and bless your present moment with his Holy Presence, so you may have life and have it abundantly!

XIV   STOP! THINK!

Subject: Impulsiveness

Scripture: Hebrews 12:1-17

Text: *God disciplines us for our good, that we may share his holiness. For the moment all discipline seems painful rather than pleasant; later it yields the peaceful fruit of righteousness to those who have been trained by it* (Hebrews 12:10b-11).

What is impulsiveness? The author of the Book of Hebrews gives us our best picture of impulsiveness when in the 12th chapter he speaks about the sin of Esau.

What is the sin of Esau? Let's refresh our memory about the story of Esau in the book of Genesis. Isaac, the only son of Abraham and Sarah, married Rebekah. Isaac and Rebekah became the parents of twin sons, Esau the first born and Jacob, the younger. Esau's birthright as the eldest son was to inherit God's covenant blessing made with Abraham. He was to carry on this covenant as the head of the tribe and the heir of God's promise.

As Esau grew up we are told he became a "cunning hunter, a man of the field." He delighted to roam the desert free as the wind, uninhibited by the restraints of settled, civilized life; yet God's call upon his people was a call into community. Life as God intended was possible only in such community. We are told that Isaac loved Esau, the loner, despite his shunning of community life, and still intended for him to become the heir of God's covenant and promise One day Esau came in from the chase ravenously hungry. On the spur of the moment he traded his birthright for the food he saw his younger brother enjoying. He gave up his inheritance just to satisfy his momentary desire.

Later, while Esau was out roaming the desert again and hunting for food, Rebekah and Jacob tricked the elderly, blind Isaac into blessing the younger son, Jacob, as the heir. The Bible says that after such blessing was given, it was irrevocable. The writer of Hebrews tells us that even though Esau regretted selling his birthright for a "mess of pottage" and "sought it back with tears" he could not repent and was rejected. What does this mean?

What was the sin of Esau? According to the Bible there can be no doubt about what it was. The sin of Esau was substituting sensual satisfaction for his birthright. It was substituting feeling for his rightful inheritance. Esau's sin was living by *feeling* instead of by *fact*. He lived by emotion instead of by reason. He acted on impulse instead of on faith. The sin of Esau is the height of idolatry. It is breaking the first commandments of Moses and the Great Commandment of Jesus. It is making our own feelings into our god. It is being feeling-oriented instead of God-oriented!

Since Esau was sorry that he had lost his birthright, why couldn't he repent and change? Why was he still rejected? The author of Hebrews says it is because Esau failed to deal with the "root of bitterness" deep within himself. Certainly, it wasn't that God or his parents did not want to forgive him and restore him to his rightful place. It was because he was concerned only with the symptom, not the root cause!

My friend, we are dealing with an eternal truth here. The one common trait I have observed in all impulsive people is that they want to deal only with the symptom, never the root cause.

Let me illustrate. One common symptom of impulsiveness that is especially commonplace during December is compulsive buying—that is, being motivated by feeling instead of by reason in our Christmas shopping. After Christmas when the bills start coming in, the impulsive person, like Esau, is always sorry for the mess he's in. As he tries to figure a way out of his financial trouble, he resolves to never do it again. Like Esau he's concerned only with the symptom, not the root cause!

Here's another illustration. Because an impulsive person lives by feeling instead of by reason or by faith, he almost always has a stormy marriage. Invariably, such "feeling-living" will lead to extra-marital affairs and adultery, for sex is one of our strong, basic feelings like hunger. When such unfaithfulness causes a breakup of the home with all of its tragic consequences, as inevitably it must, the impulsive person is, of course, sorry and begins to make new resolutions: "I'll never do that again! From now on I'll be faithful." The trouble is, like Esau, he/she is dealing with only the symptom, not the root cause.

No matter how many symptoms you get under control, as long as that corrupt "root of bitterness" is untouched, a dozen more symptoms will break out to take the place of each one you eliminate. In fact, the sin of Esau—impulsiveness—is the root of more of our modern problems than possibly any other single cause. The list of such problems is endless, such as: guilt, insecurity, nervousness, depression, poor self-image, lack of real purpose, anxiety, worry, self-pity, a critical spirit, immaturity, financial problems, job changing, and worst of all, spiritual stagnation.

In the first 11 verses of Chapter 12 of Hebrews, the Word of God tells us God's answer for the sin of Esau before even mentioning it in verses 12 to 17. In fact, all of the preceding chapter, chapter 11, is simply one illustration after another of the godly men and women who triumphed because they found this answer. God's answer for the sin of Esau is to live by faith instead of by feeling. Over and over in Chapter 11 we are told: "Stop! Think!" Think about Enoch, Noah, and Abraham. "Stop! Think!" Think about Isaac, Jacob, Joseph, Moses, David, Samuel, and the prophets. Always, God's answer to keep men from falling victim to the sin of Esau is faith—live by faith instead of feeling! Then in the first 11 verses of Chapter 12 we are told exactly what faith is and how we can live by faith instead of by feeling.

What is faith?

What is the faith we must live by rather than feeling? The writer of Hebrews uses the metaphor of a race to tell us what faith is, dividing it into three parts. I call them "the three P's" to help me remember them: Presence, Perseverance, and Power.

Presence

Faith is the conviction of an unseen presence. We can't be loners like Esau and have genuine faith. People of faith are surrounded by a "great cloud of witnesses" and live out their lives in the presence of a great community of believers which began with Abraham. The saints named in Hebrews 11 are not mere examples; they are not just witnesses to what has already happened. They are actually fellow participants with us in the race we are running today. Through faith they are present with us even now in a real way! They are fellow participants because they are part of our own preparation for this race of life. We are yoked with them by faith. These heroes of our faith are still witnessing to us about faith.

As we look back at the heroes of our faith, we see that the greatest hero of all is the object of our faith himself— Jesus Christ Our Lord. He has already defeated the enemies who would destroy us, and he has bequeathed us his victory. We are his heirs. Through him we have the victory! Through his victory over our enemies he is truly present with us right now. That is the substance of faith.

No person can be strong when he is alone. Nothing is so disheartening as a lonely struggle, when no one else sees or cares, when no human friend helps bear the burden. Then our own feelings begin to plague us. We begin to live by feelings. We become impulsive. Then we commit the sin of

Esau and trade our birthright—our inheritance—for sensual satisfaction.

But the good news is: A person of faith is never alone, for all the men and women of faith who have gone before us are present as our fellow participants in the race. A person of faith can never lose his birthright nor be cut off from his inheritance, because he is a continuation of that great family of God. He is an heir of Christ. He is part of the "community of believers" which goes all the way back to God's first covenant with man. He's a part of the "community of believers" which reached out and adopted him, the person of faith, as a member of God's family in the New Covenant. Because of Christ we don't have to run this race alone. Because of Christ we have "a conviction of a Presence not seen."

I want to suggest a formula, which really is God's formula, and which I guarantee will cure the disease of impulsiveness if you will follow it. You can put it all on a small card to carry with you. On one side of the card write in large red letters the word: "STOP!" On the other side of the card print at the top in block letters the word "THINK!" Underneath write the number 1, followed by a paraphrase of Hebrews 12:1, like this:

1. I am not alone! I have a conviction of a Presence not seen. I am surrounded by a great cloud of witnesses, who run with me the race of life. I am a part of the Family of God. I am an heir of Christ and he bequeaths me his victory. Through his victory over my enemies he is present with me now!

Leave the card right there and we'll come back to it, but for now let's move on to the second "P."

Perseverance

Our Scripture says, *"Let us run with perseverance the race that is set before us"* (Heb 12:1).

Faith requires perseverance. Faith *is* perseverance! Faith is staying with it! The way to run a successful race, we are told here in Hebrews, is to have a goal, to have a definite objective, and then stay with it until we reach that goal! Without a goal toward which we direct all of our energy, we tend to go off in all directions, guided only by our own feelings and impulses! So, Stop! Think! What is your goal in life? What is your objective? That's the subject we looked at in the fifth sermon in this series, *What Are You Aiming At?* All of us have a basic need for genuine purpose, and, according to the Bible, God's purpose for each one of us is to go into partnership with God and make him the Boss of the partnership!

Of course, your partnership with God is different from mine, just as a partnership of lawyers is different from a partnership of engineers. But, God's call to all of us is: "Go into partnership with me." Then God's call within that call is different for each one of us.

In order to live by faith instead of by feeling, we must have the right goal and we must stay with it until we reach that goal. We must persevere! So, now write on your card a second statement:

2. I am not alone! I am in partnership with God and he is boss of the partnership. That's my goal in life. That's the race set before me, and I run it with perseverance!

Now, lay the card aside again while we look at the third "P".

Power

The author of Hebrews says next that we don't have to run this race of life in our own human power alone, but we also have the power of him who is Life as God intends it to be. He says it like this:

142

"And let us run with perseverance the race that is set before us, looking to Jesus the pioneer and perfecter of our faith" (Heb 12:1b-2a).

In other words, not only do we look back to Jesus as the object of our faith, but we also trust the living Christ to perfect our faith! We trust him to give us the power to live by faith instead of by feeling! That is, not only do we have "the conviction of his Presence" because of his past victory over our enemies, but we also have the assurance of his power so we can live victoriously too! That's what faith is all about, says the author of Hebrews. It is

". . . the assurance of things hoped for, the conviction of things not seen" (Heb 11:1).

So, now it's time to put a third statement on your card:

3. I am not alone! I have the assurance of things hoped for. Christ is alive and he is my power! He perfects my faith. He is my power to live by faith instead of by feeling!

That's the substance of faith, says the author of Hebrews. It is the Presence, Perseverance, and Power!

> It is the conviction of a Presence not seen.
> It is Perseverance in our divine purpose.
> It is assurance of a Power hoped for.
> It is life as it is meant to be.

It is a God-directed life, instead of a feeling-directed life! This brings us to the most important question of all:

How can I live this life of faith, instead of living by my feelings?

The Book of Hebrews answers this question in verses 3-11 of chapter 12. The answer can be given in one word. Nowhere in the Bible is more emphasis put upon one single word. In these nine verses this word is mentioned nine different times. This key word is "Discipline!" The Bible is clear and there can be no misunderstanding about this. The only way any person can live a life of faith is through discipline!

What does this mean? It means that God has provided ways or means by which we can experience the Presence, Perseverance, and Power to live by faith. In order to experience this, we must discipline ourselves in the use of these *Means of Grace,* says the Bible. God's part is grace; our part is discipline!

The Bible says that discipline in the Means of Grace is the only way a person can live by faith instead of by feeling! This is God's answer for our impulsiveness.

Then, what are these Means of Grace? Although God can use anything as a means of grace, the Bible teaches us that God has chosen five specific things as his primary means for making himself known to us:

Prayer
Bible Study
Worship
The Lord's Supper
Christian Fellowship

Without discipline in these five Means of Grace the sin of Esau is every person's destiny. But through this discipline we can make the Lord's victory our own victory. Through discipline in these five Means of Grace God will purify us with his presence, strengthen us by his love, and sanctify us with his perfecting power. Only when we discipline ourselves in these five ways can God bless us as he wants to bless us. Yet, we are living in a day when this word "discipline" is shunned as an enemy, instead of sought as a friend. Superficial psychology has hoodwinked many modern parents and many modern educators into believing that impulses should be given free rein instead of being disciplined, and that growth comes through some form of osmosis instead of through hard work.

In one issue of our daily paper last week, there were two articles that deserve mentioning here. One points up what happens in public schools when there is lack of discipline and the other points up what happens when there is discipline. The first was a report given by Admiral Hyman Rickover to the Foreign Policy Association, concluding with this: "Both the destiny of individual Americans and the destiny of our country are in jeopardy unless we return to the philosophy that education is possible only through discipline and hard work."

After pointing out the 10-year dip in test scores and basic skills, he says it is due to the notion that learning must be easy and entertaining. This idea is cruel to the child and dangerous to society. Rickover concludes, "No learning takes place, just as no ditch gets dug, without discipline and hard work." We'd better realize this before it's too late.

The other article was a report of a nationwide survey conducted among the 21,000 juniors and seniors in the new edition of *Who's Who of American High School Students*, showing by overwhelming statistics that they are where they are primarily because of one thing: *Discipline!* For example: 98% of them have never smoked pot, 76% have never participated in pre-marital sex, 81% are religious and adhere to high moral standards. In short, they were able to keep from "living by feeling" because of one thing: *Discipline!* They have disciplined themselves for the race.

This is a universal truth. There is really only one thing we can do to avoid the sin of Esau, which is impulsiveness or living by feeling, and that is to discipline ourselves! The Bible says, if we discipline ourselves in the means of grace, then God's grace will do the rest. That's the good news! God's part is grace, our part is discipline. That is the way we'll begin our fourth statement:

4. My part is discipline. God's part is grace. God does his transforming work in me, as I discipline myself in these five means of grace:

> Prayer
> Bible Study
> Worship
> The Lord's Supper
> Christian Fellowship

Thank God I'm not alone!

When you complete this card, carry it with you, and when your feelings try to usurp God's rightful place in your life, take it out and use it. First, heed the red flag:

STOP!

Stop living by feeling! Then, turn the card over and

THINK!

Think on these four things:

> Presence,
> Perseverance,
> Power, and
> Discipline.

This is God's formula for living by faith instead of by feeling. Let this card be the beginning of discipline. "STOP! THINK!" And you will win the battle with impulsiveness!

Subject: Wrong Priorities

Scripture: Luke 14:12-24

Text: *These things I have spoken to you, that my joy may be in you, and that your joy may be full* (John 15:11).

             He sent his servant to say . . . "Come; for all is now ready." But they all alike began to make excuses (Luke 14:17-18).

One of the biggest problems for all of us is deciding how we should spend our time, talents, and money. When should we say yes and when should we say no? How can we know God's will in living out our daily lives? How can we have the right priorities in life?

Fortunately, Jesus answers these questions for us in one of his most penetrating illustrations, *The Parable of The Great Feast*, found in both Matthew and Luke. A man gave a great feast and sent his servants out to tell the guests, "Come, for all is now ready." But the guests began to make excuses:

- One had invested in a piece of land and had to go see it.
- Another had acquired some new oxen and had to examine them.
- The third simply said, "I have married a wife and cannot come."

When these excuses were reported to the master, we are told that he was angry and sent his servants out into the streets to invite everyone to the great feast. When the servants had done this, the master gave them one final command:

"Go out to the highways and hedges, and compel people to come in, that my house may be filled. For I tell you, none of those men who were invited shall taste my banquet" (Lk 14:23-24).

This is where Jesus leaves it. He leaves it here because he wants us to grasp three basic truths.

The first truth is that Jesus came to invite us to live a life of joy!

He expressly says this in his last talk with his disciples in the Upper Room:

"These things I have spoken to you, that my joy may be in you, and that your joy may be full" (Jn 15:11).

Over and over in the Gospels, Jesus compares the Christian life to the experience of being at a joyful feast. The Prodigal Son returns to a joyful feast. The five wise bridesmaids go with the bridegroom to a joyful feast, while the foolish ones miss the festivities. Jesus performs his first miracle at a joyful wedding feast, and he concludes his earthly ministry by commanding his followers in the Upper Room to celebrate in remembrance of him with a Eucharistic meal, which literally means "joyfully giving thanks!"

One of the most popular novels ever written was *The Robe* by Lloyd C. Douglas. When someone asked him how he came to write the novel about Christ, he said it was because he was never satisfied with the wording of the Apostle's Creed that skipped from the birth of Jesus to his death with nothing but a comma in between:

". . . born of the Virgin Mary [comma] *suffered under Pontius Pilate . . ."*

Douglas said that he wanted people to know what happened in that comma; that's why he wrote *The Robe*. He said he wanted to put the emphasis where Jesus put it—on the beauty and joy that Christ brings to life!

I would have to say the same thing if someone were to ask me why I entered the ministry. I entered the ministry to help others find and experience the genuine joy which Christ brings to life! I wanted to help others see that there is more to the Christian life than just conversion, comma, then heaven in the sweet bye-and-bye. There is something tremendously important in that comma! Jesus came "that his joy might be in us, and that our joy might be full!" Jesus came to put joy into our lives on every level: in our marriage and family life, in our work, in our social life. Jesus came to touch all of our living with his joy! Then, why don't more Christians actually experience this joy?

The answer to this question is the second truth which Jesus reveals to us in this parable, and it's this:

We miss the joy that Jesus came to give us because of our wrong priorities!

Let's put ourselves in the place of the invited guests who send their regrets, and we can see what Jesus means. All of us are familiar with the three excuses they give, aren't we? In essence they are still the same excuses we are using today. Listen to them again. The first man had invested in land. He could just as easily have invested in an apartment house, a shopping center, a new product, a business, or in stocks or bonds. Land is the oldest and most common form of investment and, of course, represents all kinds of investments here. This first man couldn't attend the joyful feast because his investments came first!

Have you ever been so preoccupied with your own investments that you've missed the joy of the feast? Show me a man who says he hasn't and I'll show you either a liar or a drone on society.

Charles Darwin confessed that after years of concentrating on science he no longer could appreciate listening to music. Sir Robert Walpole picked up a book one time in his library and cried out, "My God, I can't read!" He hadn't lost his sight, he'd lost his sensitivity and his appreciation of the best in life. He had been involved with politicians for so long, to the exclusion of everything else, that he'd lost his taste for the best. In the final analysis, when we talk about America becoming a secular society this is what we are really talking about. We Americans have been so preoccupied with our investments that we miss the real joy in life—the joy Jesus came to bring us!

The second man was expanding his business. He was in the midst of his own "industrial revolution," for he was adding ten new oxen-power to his operation and he was preoccupied with that. Of course he had to send his regrets and miss the joyful feast, because his expansion program demanded all of his time. It usually does, doesn't it?

Nothing can be quite so absorbing or exciting as your own industrial revolution, whether you manage a fruit stand or a giant corporation or a church. I know, for I've been absorbed with my own expansion program right here in our church. We've already added seven or eight new "minister-power"—one more this week—and need to add more. We've already added many new modern machines to turn out the material faster and better, and have plans for adding more. We've already added new classes, new services, new parking, new baby beds; but most exciting of all are our plans for Vision I—a building for our mushrooming children's department. Oh, how exciting and absorbing it is to be involved in your own industrial revolution! I've seen it on your faces and in your spirits as hundreds of our members have been involved in committee work for Vision I during the past two months!

There is just one trouble with it, says Jesus, when you get so absorbed with it that you give it priority over the joy of the feast. You miss the real point in life—you miss what Jesus came to earth to give us. And you miss it for the same reason this second man missed it: because of wrong priorities!

150

The third man, we are told, had gotten married so he had to send his regrets. He had taken a wife. Notice the difference in the attitude of this man and the other two. The other two asked to be excused, but this man just flatly said, "I cannot come! I've taken a wife and I cannot come!" Period! In other words, the first two felt some pangs of conscience about sending their regrets; but this man was so sure that he was doing right that he didn't even ask to be excused. He was staying away because of his family and that made it right!

Don't most of us feel the same way? If it is done in the name of the family, then it must be right. Why shouldn't we believe that way? Hucksters on TV, magazines, radio, newspapers, and billboards have indoctrinated us with this half-truth so they can peddle their merchandise to us. We have heard so often: "The home comes first!" that most of us really believe it without ever giving it a second thought. The truth is that it comes so close to being true, that it is tragically false!

Oh, how often I see it happen! Boy meets girl and they fall madly in love, get married, and like the man in our parable, life is so exciting and full that they only have eyes for each other. Then, after a few years they are jolted with the realization that something is lacking in their lives and in their marriage. They have each other, yes; but somehow that is no longer enough. Somehow there is no genuine joy in the marriage anymore!

Isn't this exactly the condition in countless homes right now? The honeymoon is over and the joy has disappeared. We've tried so hard to put family first and we've taught our children to put family first. Now we can't understand how things could be so fouled up! But we think, as Christians we're supposed to be joyful and happy, so we put up a good front and grin and bear it!

Jesus pulls no punches in telling us exactly why things are so fouled up in such families. They are fouled up, he says, because of wrong priorities. If you always put the family first, he says, you are bound to lose the very thing you want most in life, which is real joy in your home and in your family relationships. In fact, says Jesus, if you are missing this joy on any level of life, you are missing it because you are living out your life according to the wrong priorities.

How can we live out our lives according to the right priorities and experience the joy Jesus offers us? The answer to this question is the third and most important truth Jesus reveals to us in this parable.

When the servants returned and told their master that the invited guests had sent their regrets and were not coming to the feast because they had something more important to do, we are told that the master got angry. When I first read this, I was shocked that the master was actually angry about it, because like you, I had been brainwashed with "gentle Jesus meek and mild." A Christian wasn't supposed to get angry. Then I began to think about it this way: Have you ever tried to give your child something very special that was essential for his or her own well-being; but out of sheer stubbornness the child refuses it and then suffers untold misery and pain as a consequence? Doesn't it get you so upset that you want to just take him or her by the shoulders and shake and shake until you shake some sense into that thick head? Weren't you angry then? Well, I think that is the kind of anger which Jesus is talking about here—a loving anger! An anger motivated by love. An anger that wants to shake some sense into our thick heads! An anger that wants to compel us to come to the joyful feast for it knows that otherwise we shall be miserable and waste our lives!

What kind of sense is Jesus trying to shake into our thick heads? What truth is he revealing to us who have our priorities all mixed up, and consequently our world turned upside down? He's telling us how we can turn our world right side up. He's giving us the only formula that will work

152

for keeping our priorities right. He's giving us his own formula for having the right priorities in life!

But let's get one thing clear. Jesus never says what some who purport to preach his gospel would have you think he says about priorities; for Jesus never lays down a law that says you must always put this first and that second and something else third. Jesus doesn't say that, because life is not that simple. Jesus doesn't say that, because he knows there are times when your work must come first, and other times when your family must come first. There are times when your worship must come first and other times when Christian service must come first, and so on. No preacher who is true to the gospel and realistic about life can stand in a pulpit and tell others what they must put first, second, third and so forth each day. Furthermore, this is trying to legalize the gospel, which is the very thing Jesus says we must never do if we are to experience the joy he came to bring us. The joy our Lord wants for us is possible only through a life of grace, says the Bible, never through a life of law.

Then, what is Jesus' formula for keeping our priorities right each day? Look again at the illustration he uses to teach us about right priorities and the formula is clear. What keeps the invited guests from participating in the joyful feast? Two things: first, they fail to trust the master's plan for them, and second, they refuse to obey him.

Jesus didn't come to this earth to lay down more rules for us to try to follow in order to participate in the joyful feast of life. He came to be our Lord—our Master—and participate in it with us!

Usually I keep my car radio set to KRMG and I enjoy at times listening to the strange things people say when they call the talk-show host on the telephone. I remember back at the time of the last election, a woman called in to complain about all of the crooks in government who were candidates and the host asked her if she was going to vote.

She said, "Nope, I'm not going to vote!"

153

He asked why, and she replied, "Because I don't want to encourage 'em!"

Well, a lot of people are that way about getting personally involved with Jesus. They want to stand off and observe from a distance, and follow a set of man-made religious rules. But they don't want to encourage Jesus with their own personal involvement. They are afraid to actually let themselves go and make him Lord of their minds, hearts, bodies, and souls. They are actually afraid to obey him because they don't really trust him with these important areas of their lives! Yet, Jesus specifically says that before his joy can be in us and our joy can be full, we must abide in him, and he must abide in us. This is what Paul means when he says in Galatians:

"I have been crucified with Christ; it is no longer I who live, but Christ who lives in me" (Gal 2:20).

He means that his own will has been crucified—put to death—and now the will of Christ—the resurrected Christ—lives in him and controls his thoughts, his words, and his actions. He means that he has actually surrendered his mind, heart, soul, and body to the dominion of the living Christ. His one goal in life now is to trust Christ and to obey him! This is our Lord's formula for having the right priorities in life. It is a life of grace under his lordship! It is trusting him with our lives—our work, our marriage, our family, our fun, our church—and obeying him day-by-day!

Trust and obey. That's the formula for right priorities! That's the third and most important truth Jesus is telling us in this parable.

In order to live according to the right priorities and experience the joy Jesus offers, we must trust the Lord Jesus Christ and obey him as the Lord of our life.

Jesus is not telling us that in order to experience the joy he has for us we must neglect or ignore our opportunities for investments, or sacrifice our own exciting personal industrial revolution, or ignore our family responsibilities. Far from it! In fact, just the opposite. What Jesus is revealing to us is the way to bring genuine joy into all of these areas of our lives! That's why we say Christianity is a way of life and not a religion. He is showing us the only way our joy can be full in all areas of life, including our investments, our work, and our families. That way is to be completely Christ controlled, and to live a life of grace, which is possible only by trusting and obeying him as our living Lord.

Write these two words—Trust and Obey—indelibly upon your mind, and then open your life to the living Spirit of Christ and you will begin to turn your world right side up.

"Trust and Obey, for there's no other way to be happy in Jesus, but to trust and obey!"

XV   The Price We Must Pay for Love

Subject: Grief

Scripture: John 11:17-44

Text: *Jesus wept* (John 11:35).

All who are born on this earth must deal with grief. Not only do we need to learn how to handle this problem of grief ourselves, but as the Church—the Body of Christ on earth—we also need to learn how to help others who grieve. Fortunately, Jesus shows us exactly how to do this as he ministers to Martha and Mary after the death of their brother, Lazarus.

Three important books deal with this subject from different perspectives:

- The first by an M.D. and psychiatrist, Dr Elizabeth Kubler-Ross, *On Death & Dying*, gives the scientific approach.
- The second is a book by an outstanding English scholar and professor, who at one time set out to debunk Christianity and in the process became a converted Christian. Dr. C. S. Lewis, in a little book entitled *A Grief Observed*, actually chronicles his own grief when his wife died, giving a personal approach.
- The last book is the Gospel of John, where we are told how Jesus deals with the grief of Martha and Mary over the death of Lazarus. Here, in chapter 11, we are given the biblical approach.

Although stated in different terms, all three of these books agree that there are generally five stages that people go through in grief:

1. The first stage is shock or denial. C. S. Lewis says this stage feels like being mildly drunk or concussed.
2. Anger or hostility. Lewis calls it wanting to hit back at God.
3. Bargaining or seeking the presence of the dead.
4. Depression. C. S. Lewis describes it like this: "Up to now, I always had too little time. Now there is nothing but time. Almost pure time, empty successiveness." (A Grief Observed, p. 29)
5. Finally, acceptance or genuine identification with the deceased.

Now, don't misunderstand me. Jesus doesn't name these five stages in the Bible, but better still he shows us what they are like as they affect Martha and Mary at the death of Lazarus. In verse 35 of chapter 11 we are told that Jesus himself wept. Why? Jesus Christ, the Resurrection and the Life—why did he weep? Not because he was grieving for Lazarus who had died (and not even so we can say that we know the shortest verse in the Bible). Jesus wept because Martha and Mary and the others present misunderstood the meaning of the death of Lazarus. Jesus wept for them—the bereaved. This is clear when you set this 35th verse in context. In verse 33 we are told,

> "When Jesus saw Mary weeping, and the Jews who came with her also weeping, he was deeply moved in spirit and troubled."

Then, when he asked where the tomb was, we are told "Jesus wept." Jesus wept because they misunderstood the meaning of death. Jesus wept because they were not ready to carry on his ministry to the bereaved, although the time of his death was near.

I wonder what would happen if Jesus were standing in our midst today, observing our response to death and watching us—his church—minister to the bereaved? I'm confident scripture would record the same two words: "Jesus wept!" Here Jesus is permitting us to see into the greatest mystery on this earth—death. Also, he is showing us how to minister to the bereaved. As we examine this truth, I hope you will begin to use your sanctified imagination creatively to discover how Christ wants us to use this truth in the healing ministry in our church today.

First we must recognize that the underlying truth is this: Jesus wept because he truly loved! Jesus wept because he saw those he truly loved in grief. What is grief? Grief is the pain, suffering, and anguish we experience when we lose someone we love. In this discussion we'll speak of grief primarily when the loss is through death, but it's just as real when the loss is caused by divorce or some other form of alienation. Grief is suffering and hurting because the love so essential to our fulfillment has been terminated.

When that love is terminated, there are several other emotions we experience which we sometimes confuse with grief—such as guilt, fear, or self-pity. But these emotions are different from grief, and therefore, the answer for them is different.

Guilt is self-condemnation for failure to love. Grief is pain suffered because of the loss of opportunity to love.

Fear is dreading the future because of a feeling of insecurity. Grief is the anguish you experience because you are deprived of an opportunity to love in the future.

Self-pity is feeling sorry for yourself because you center your world around yourself. Grief is the suffering you experience when your life is centered around love and you are deprived of that love.

God's answer for guilt, fear, and self-pity is not the same as his answer for grief. We must understand that, before we can handle these problems. God's answer for guilt is forgiveness—forgiveness through the crucified Christ! God's answer for fear is assurance—assurance of the living Christ living in us. God's answer for self-pity is service—

159

getting outside yourself to serve others in the name of Christ! But God's answer for grief is love—love personified in Jesus Christ as the Resurrection and the Life! God's answer for our grief is his gift of love to us in Christ.

Jesus wept because he truly loved the grieving Mary and Martha. Jesus wept because he saw in them pain and agony because of their loss. Jesus wept because Mary and Martha were suffering and hurting and no one was doing anything to alleviate their hurt. When Jesus arrived in Bethany, he saw Mary and Martha experiencing the first four characteristics of grief:

- *Shock.* (They couldn't believe it was true.)
- *Anger.* (They were angry because Jesus hadn't come sooner.)
- *Bargaining.* (Martha told him he could still do something if he would.)
- *Depression.* (They were down emotionally and they could not get up).

What did Jesus do about it? He loved them; that's what he did about it! That is, he met their immediate need. What was this need? It was to work through their grief to a victory, and this is exactly what Jesus helped them do. How? By showing them the three truths they needed in order to work through their grief.

First, grief is the price we must always pay for love.

Anytime you give your love to another or accept love from another you make yourself vulnerable to grief; for remember that grief is the pain, suffering, and anguish we experience when we lose someone we love. In his book, *A Grief Observed*, C. S. Lewis describes it like this, after the death of his wife:

160

[We love] *and then one or the other dies. And we think of this as love cut short; like a dance stopped in mid career or a flower with its head unluckily snapped off. . . I wonder. If, as I can't help suspecting, the dead also feel the pains of separation, . . . then for both lovers, and all pairs of lovers without exception, bereavement is a universal and integral part of our experience of love. It follows marriage as normally as autumn follows summer. It's not a truncation [cutting short] of the process but one of its phases; not the interruption of the dance, but simply the next figure* (p. 41).

Marjorie Kinnan Rawlings has a little backwoods boy named Jody describe grief for us in her great novel, *The Yearling*. Upon the death of his little playmate, Fodder-Wing, who was mentally retarded and crippled, and the only playmate Jody had in the swamplands of Florida, she describes it in these words:

Jody's throat worked. No words came. . . Fodder-Wing's silence was intolerable. Now he understood. This was death. Death was a silence that gave back no answer. Fodder-Wing could never speak to him again. He buried his face against Buck's chest.[*]

We are told that he saw all of Fodder-Wing's pets—the wild animals Fodder-Wing had tamed. Then the author goes on:

. . . he longed so painfully for Fodder-Wing that he had to lie on his belly and beat his feet in the sand. The ache turned into a longing for his own pet fawn. . . He sat down under a live oak and held the fawn close to him. There was a comfort in it . . .[*]

---

[*]Marjorie Kinnan Rawlings, *The Yearling*, p.192-194.
Marjorie Kinnan Rawlings, *The Yearling*, p.192-194.

Helen Keller captured the very heart of true grief in one sentence, when she said,

With every friend I love who has been taken into the brown bosom of the earth a part of me has been buried there too.

That's the first truth which Jesus wants us to see: Grief is the price we must always pay for love. The second truth is this:

True love is always worth the price.

A husband and wife, the parents of several children, buy just the right house in which to rear their family, arranging to pay for the house over a period of 30 years. Even after the patter of little feet and the babble of little voices are no longer heard in the house, still they must continue to sacrifice and pay for the house. But the joy which they have shared across the years is worth the payment! It's like that with love and grief too: Love is worth the price of grief!

It is understanding this that reveals one of God's best answers for grief: Only by giving thanks and by praising God for the love we have experienced can we be victorious over grief. This is what Jesus means when he tells Martha to stop focusing on grief and look to him who is love personified. He says it like this:

"I am the resurrection and the life; he who believes in me, though he die, yet shall he live, and whoever lives and believes in me shall never die" (Jn 11:25-26).

C. S. Lewis says it like this in chronicling his grief, when he realizes that, like Martha, he is focusing on the wrong thing:

The notes have been about myself, about H. [his wife], and about God. In that order. The order and the proportions exactly what they ought not to have been.

162

And I see that I have nowhere fallen into that mode of thinking about either which we call praising them. Yet that would have been best for me. Praise is the mode of love which always has some element of joy in it. Praise in due order; of Him as the giver, of her as the gift. Don't we in praise somehow enjoy what we praise, however far we are from it? I must do more of this. (A Grief Observed p. 29)

This is what Paul means when he says,

"In everything give thanks" (I Th 5:18).

Instead of focusing on grief, focus on the love out of which the grief flows. How ridiculous it would be for the parents who are still making house payments after the children are grown to spend their years begrudging the money. How much wiser to give thanks and praise for the happy hours they have had there with their precious children.

This same truth applies when we want to help a friend at the time of the death of a loved one. We should focus on the love, instead of the grief. Instead of sending a card that says "In Sympathy" and a note about the friend's great loss, how much wiser it would be to write a brief note and say something like this:

"I will always remember your husband's contagious laugh and friendly spirit. They don't come like that very often. Both you and your children have been greatly blessed to be able to live with such a loving example of our Lord's love."

The best thing we can do for a friend at such a time is to give thanks and praise for the love of the deceased. This brings us to the third and final truth that Jesus reveals to us here, and it is this:

Love is stronger than grief.

That's the good news. Love is stronger than grief! Earlier I quoted a sentence by Helen Keller concerning grief:

With every friend I love who has been taken into the brown bosom of the earth a part of me has been buried there;

Well, Helen Keller doesn't stop there. Instead she just put a semi-colon and goes on to say,

*but their contribution to my happiness, my strength and my understanding remains to sustain me in an altered world.**

That's it! Love is stronger than grief! The love we have received, the contributions to our experiences, to our character, to our memories, can never be taken away from us. Death cannot destroy this love. In fact, it only makes this love more vivid and more precious. This is what Paul means when he says in I Corinthians 13 that "love never ends." All other things pass away, but love never ends. This is what he means in the 8th chapter of Romans when he says:

"For I am sure that neither death, nor life, nor angels, nor principalities, nor things present, nor things to come, nor powers, nor height, nor depth, nor anything else in all creation, will be able to separate us from the love of God in Christ Jesus our Lord" (Rom 8:38-39).

Paul is telling us that death and grief are temporary, but love is eternal. He is telling us that the love which begins here on earth shall continue throughout all eternity. So, the best preparation we can make for dealing with grief is to learn how to truly love! Because God's answer for grief is love!

---

*Helen Keller, *The Open Door*, p.14

This brings us to the key question: Why did Jesus raise Lazarus from the dead? Certainly, it was not for Lazarus' sake, for Lazarus already had the best; he had already reached the goal for which he had been preparing. Again, C. S. Lewis recognizes this as he chronicles his own grief. When he enters the stage of seeking some sign of her presence, he says:

> *What sort of lover am I to think so much about my needs, and so little about hers? . . . I never even raised the question whether such a return, if it were possible, would be good for her. I want her back as an ingredient in the restoration of my past. Could I have wished her anything worse? Having got once through death, to come back and then, at some later date, have all her dying to do over again? They call Stephen the first martyr. Hadn't Lazarus the rawer deal? (A Grief Observed p. 34)*

Why did Jesus raise Lazarus from the dead? Certainly not for Lazarus' sake. No! He raised Lazarus for the sake of Martha and Mary and for our sake! He raised Lazarus so we can know once and for all that love is stronger than grief! He raised Lazarus so we can know that he – Jesus—is the Resurrection and the Life, and all who believe in him shall never die. He raised Lazarus to give us God's answer for our grief, and that answer is love—eternal love!

Love is the answer for our grief because it is the love of God which gives us life after death, that enables us to work through our grief to victory. It is the love of Christ which enables us, as it did Martha and Mary, to see beyond the grave to eternal life, even while we grieve. It is the love of Christ, who resurrects us and our loved ones into an eternal life of love, that gives us a lasting victory over grief. Yes, God's answer for grief is love—love personified in Jesus Christ as the Resurrection and the Life!

Norman Vincent Peale says that the day his mother died, he went to church and stood in the pulpit, for she had

165

always said to him, "Anytime you are in your pulpit, I will be there with you." He said that as he stood there,

> *"Suddenly and distinctly I felt two cupped hands, soft as eiderdown, resting very gently on my head. It was an inexpressible joy . . . and I knew from that moment on that God's answer for death is life and love!"*

Yes, God's answer for grief is love—love that brings new life! A love which resurrects us and our loved ones into a life of eternal love! A love which even raised Lazarus from the dead, so we can know that love is stronger than death and grief. Grief is the price all of us must pay for love, yes. But the good news is,

Love is stronger than grief and will see us through to victory!

XVII   God's Answer for Emotional Cancer

Subject: Resentment

Scripture: Ephesians 4:17-32

Text: *Put off your old nature which belong to your former manner of life... and be renewed in the spirit of your minds, and put on the new nature, created after the likeness of God in true righteousness and holiness"* (Ephesians 4:22-24).

Let all bitterness . . . be put away from you . . . forgiving one another, as God in Christ forgave you" (Ephesians 4:31-32).

What would you do if after a physical examination, your doctor told you there was evidence of cancer in one of your organs and prescribed the treatment you needed to rid yourself of it? Anyone in his right mind would do whatever he had to do to stop the spread of this deadly disease, wouldn't he? All of us would, because we know that otherwise, the cancer would destroy us.

Yet many of us—the same people who would act so quickly and logically under such circumstances—react just the opposite way when we are stricken with "emotional cancer."

Instead of doing what needs to be done to get rid of it as quickly as possible, we begin to nurture it and feed it and relish it until it spreads throughout our being, contaminating and ultimately destroying everything good within us!

The generic name for this emotional cancer is *resentment,* sometimes called "holding a grudge" against another or "a feeling of bitterness" because of what someone else has done. This emotional cancer does to our minds, our spirits, and our emotions exactly what physical cancer does to our bodies.

One of the most fertile fields for resentment and bitterness is in families where there is divorce. I see it almost daily. I not only see it; I have also struggled with it myself when members of my own family have been involved in divorce. Perhaps your husband or wife wrongs you and there is divorce. Or, a divorced mate offends you in some way, perhaps uses the children to get back at you. Your natural reaction, of course, is bitterness and resentment. But when you react this way, it immediately constructs a barrier between you and the offender, making any further genuine communication impossible. Then, the offender tells his or her family and friends about your bitter reaction and naturally they also react to you with the same bitterness and resentments, causing you to react in kind. This constructs the same kind of communication barrier with them. Then, you tell your family and friends your side of the story, and the same chain of events happens all over again.

Are you beginning to get the picture? Just as the cancer cells in our body divide and spread and conquer, so do the emotional cancer cells in our minds and in our hearts, unless we take the necessary steps to stop them.

How strange we human beings are! We will stop at nothing to rid ourselves of physical cancer, but we pride ourselves on the tenacious way we hold onto our emotional cancer, even refusing to see the deadly work it is doing to us as we treasure it. I want to describe for you briefly how this emotional malignancy works.

First, it begins to show itself in physical fatigue and loss of sleep, as it begins to drain us of needed energy. Still, we refuse to turn loose of it. Instead, we give it deeper root as we shove it further down into the recesses of our mind. But it refuses to stay there and begins to show up in that cold stare in our eyes and the etched hardness in our face. Gradually, it works its way into most of our physical organs, calling forth certain hormones from the pituitary, adrenal, thyroid, and other glands. Eventually it causes illness, such as ulcerated colitis, toxic goiters, high blood pressure, and scores of other diseases; some authorities say on good evidence, even physical cancer itself.

At the same time it is spreading physically, it is also spreading spiritually, emotionally, and mentally, causing us to doubt our own salvation and severing our personal relationship with God. Prayer and worship become harder for us, and we begin to find excuses for our spiritual dryness. As we exhaust more and more of our emotional energy to maintain this grudge, we find ourselves falling deeper and deeper into depression, self-pity, and worry. The doctor can't help us, and drugs bring only temporary relief.

Worst of all, as we focus more of our bitter thoughts upon the person we resent, we put more of ourselves directly under that person's control. Instead of being free to act as God would have us act, we become enslaved to that person's tyrannical grasp upon our mind, until finally we are only reacting to him or her. We have actually condemned ourselves to the last thing on earth we would wish for ourselves, by refusing to deal properly with our resentments and bitterness. We become like the very person we resent—a mere pawn in that person's hand.

But the good news is Jesus has given us a sure cure for this emotional cancer! Not only has Jesus shown us this sure cure, his Holy Spirit has recorded this cure for us on the pages of the Bible. If you will use it, the Bible can help you get rid of this deadly disease and help you find the overall health God wants for you!

Jesus spoke of this cure often while he was here on earth, perhaps most extensively in the Sermon on the Mount, where he gives us the Lord's Prayer and teaches us to pray:

"Father . . . forgive us our debts as we also have forgiven our debtors" (Mt 6:12).

Certainly, he spoke most clearly about forgiveness in his great Parable of the Unmerciful Servant, who was forgiven of an astronomical debt of ten million dollars. Do you remember the story found in the 18th chapter of Matthew? This man, having been forgiven, is still so bitter toward his fellow servant that he refuses to forgive him of a debt of less than twenty dollars. For this, he is condemned to hell! Jesus concludes the parable by warning us that this is exactly what will happen to all of us who refuse to forgive!

It was Paul, the great interpreter of the gospel for the gentiles, who explains to posterity how this miraculous cure of forgiveness really works. No place does he do it better than in the concluding half of the 4th chapter of Ephesians. In the first half of this great chapter, Paul explains how the Holy Spirit equips us with specific gifts for ministry. Then, in the last half, he explains how many of us, who claim to be Christians, actually grieve the Holy Spirit and keep him from doing his great work in our lives because of our bitterness and our failure to forgive as God in Christ has forgiven us. Here are his concluding words:

"And do not grieve the Holy Spirit of God, in whom you were sealed for the day of redemption. Let all bitterness . . . be put away from you . . . forgiving one another, as God in Christ forgave you" (Eph 4:30-32).

Both Paul and Jesus want us to see that there are two sides to forgiveness, and we can't experience one without the other. Jesus says,

"Forgive us our debts, as we also have forgiven our debtors" (Mt 6:12).

"Blessed are the merciful, for they shall obtain mercy" (Mt 5:7).

"If you forgive men their trespasses, your heavenly Father also will forgive you; but if you do not forgive men their trespasses, neither will your heavenly Father forgive your trespasses" (Mt 6:14-15).

Let's get at it this way: Every experience in life, where God's law is transgressed and we are wronged or we wrong another, we deal with in one of two ways. Either we think that we did wrong and feel guilty about it, or we think others did wrong and we blame them for it. In one real sense, our life is like a delicate scale we keep trying to balance. Either we are pouring our guilt on one side of the scale , or we are pouring blame on the other, heaping up resentments and bitterness. The Bible says there is only one way we can balance this scale in our lives. That is to take the weight off both sides of the scale through forgiveness.

First, we accept the forgiveness of God for our own guilt.

Jesus says that in living life, all of us are put into a debtor-creditor relationship. We both owe debts and are owed debts. We give to others and they owe us. They give to us and we owe them. That's part of living. But the shocking thing Jesus says is that the ratio of what we owe to what is owed us is about five hundred thousand to one! The Unmerciful Servant owed approximately ten million dollars and he was owed approximately twenty. That is, he owed five hundred thousand times what he was worth, so he was bankrupt! Jesus wants us to see that we all are bankrupt! We all owe astronomical debts we can never pay—astronomical debts to God, to Christ, to our parents, our friends, our fellow Americans, and our fellow Christians. How can we ever pay our debt to God for life and this wonderful earth on which we live? Or to Christ for dying that we might not perish? Or to parents who nurtured us and reared us, to patriotic Americans who have died that

171

we might be free, to Christian martyrs who died to preserve our faith, to friends who have encouraged us?

Yet, who among us has not failed to pay his astronomical debts, misused what his creditor has let him have, and even wronged or betrayed the creditor with selfish acts and lack of love? Each time the weight on the guilt side of the scale gets heavier and heavier. Still, there's no way we can pay because we are bankrupt!

Jesus came to let us know that God has provided a way to lift this terrible weight of guilt, and that way the Bible calls "Forgiveness." *Forgiveness!* It's the most beautiful and most meaningful word in the Bible. Also, it's the most costly word in the Bible. *Forgiveness!* God has provided a way to handle all the debts which we cannot pay, and that way is this: He pays them himself. God pays our debts himself and sets us free. That's why it's the most costly word in the Bible. Because it cost God the death of his only Son to pay our debts and set us free. It's on the Cross that God shows us Jesus as the surety for our debts. It's on the Cross that Christ co-signs our notes and stands good for our debts. It's on the Cross that God pays your debt in full—your entire ten million dollar debt!

This brings us to the whole crux of the matter and the all-inclusive healing power of this miraculous divine process called forgiveness. According to the Bible, forgiveness not only means that Christ died to forgive us of our guilt, but

Christ also died to forgive those we blame—the people we resent!

Until we acknowledge this, we cannot really participate in his great redeeming act on the Cross, because we cannot fathom the meaning of his selfless love.

Here's the point. Until you acknowledge that the death of Jesus on the Cross is for all people, even those you resent, you cannot participate in that part of it which is for you. On the Cross, God not only pays your entire ten

172

million dollar debt in full; he pays the twenty dollar debt of your debtor in full too! It's impossible for any person to honestly acknowledge the payment of one debt—his own—without accepting the payment of the other—his debtor's. Both debts are paid with the same price. Both are paid by the death of Christ on the Cross!

When the Bible speaks about your *being forgiven,* it means you actually accept the payment that Christ has made *for* you. But when it speaks of you *being forgiving,* it means that you actually accept the payment that Christ has made *to* you—his selfless love—for someone else. It's impossible to have one without the other, because the cost for both is made with the same payment: Jesus' death on the Cross!

This brings us to the all-important question: How can I forgive the debts of those who owe me? How can I get rid of my bitterness and resentment toward them? How can I actually eradicate this emotional cancer once and for all? Thank God the Bible is clear in answering these questions. Paul spells it out specifically for us, not only in the 4th chapter of Ephesians; but in many other places too. Here's his answer in two steps.

First, you must change the focus of your life!

Heretofore, you've been focusing on the person you resent; you can't keep from it. As long as you keep your focus there and relive that person's offenses and wrongs against you, the more bitter you will become—the more weight you will add to the "blame side" of your scale of life—and the more unbalanced your life will become. Worst of all, the more you will take on yourself the very faults you detest in that person, for that is where your mind is focused. The Bible says,

"As a man thinketh in his heart so is he!" (Prov 23:7, KJV).

Paul says,

173

"Put off your old nature which belongs to your former manner of life and is corrupt . . . and put on the new nature, created in the likeness of God in true righteousness and holiness" (Eph 4:22-24).

That is, you must begin to focus on him who alone is righteous—Christ Jesus! Set your focus on Jesus. See him in all of his glory, as he leaves his heavenly home to come to earth for you. See him in all of his love, as he dies on the Cross for you. See him in all of his power, as he rises for you and sends his Holy Spirit to cleanse you, heal you, and empower you. Focus on Jesus.

"Set your minds on things that are above" (Col 3:2), and you will begin to *"Let this mind be in you, which was also in Christ Jesus"* (Phil 2:5 KJV).

Focus on Jesus, and you will *"be renewed in the spirit of your minds"* (Eph 4:23).

You will begin to become like him, for *"as a man thinketh in his heart so is he!"* (Prov 23:7).

You will begin to take on his characteristics of love, joy, peace, patience, kindness, goodness, faithfulness, gentleness, and self-control. Then, and only then, are you ready for the second step, which is the step that assures you of a complete healing of emotional cancer.

The second step is to forgive your offender.

That is, you completely empty all of the weight on the blame side of your scale of life! Pour it out! Get rid of it! The moment you do, your life begins to move back into balance. Note again how Paul says it in concluding the 4th chapter of Ephesians:

"Let all bitterness and wrath and anger . . . be put away from you, . . . forgiving one another, as God in Christ forgave you" (Eph 4:31-32).

Note that order again: First, put away all bitterness and resentment by focusing on Christ, says Paul. That's the only way anyone can ever put away bitterness. Once you have changed your focus and have begun to take on the mind of Christ, then forgiveness for your offender just naturally follows, as it did for Christ. But if you try it the other way, that is, try telling yourself that you must forgive and you must not be bitter or resentful, you can try for a lifetime and never do it. For only Christ can ever lift the gigantic weights of guilt and blame. Only the grace of God is big enough to handle them. We can never do it by simply trying harder. We can do it only by permitting the living Christ to live in us. And that's grace!

What's impossible for you is possible with God! I know, because when I began thinking about this sermon, I was focusing on the wrong thing. I felt I had been especially wronged by someone I had befriended; consequently, I was getting more and more resentful. Everything in me said, "Strike back!" In my mind, I knew what I should do, but I couldn't do it. The only sermon I could find in my heart was a sermon of law: "An eye for an eye, and a tooth for a tooth!"

I had committed myself to prepare this sermon on God's answer for resentment, but I couldn't even find that answer for myself. One thing is certain, you can't give away something you don't have! Then, I began to read in the Bible such passages as this—and there are many of them:

"Do not be conformed to this world but be transformed by the renewal of your mind, that you may prove what is the will of God, what is good and acceptable and perfect" (Rom 12:2).

And this: *"To set the mind on the flesh is death, but to set the mind on the Spirit is life and peace"* (Rom 8:6).

As I read, suddenly I knew what it means to shift the focus of my mind to Christ Jesus and to "let that mind be in

175

me which was also in Christ Jesus." For when I did, I began to "put away all bitterness . . ." and to forgive the other person "as God in Christ had forgiven me."

It was then that God's Word became my own Word for living. It was then I could share God's truth in a sermon, for it was then I realized I had been healed of emotional cancer!

Do you want to receive that same healing right now? Then begin now to change the focus of your life from the person you resent to the only Person in all heaven and earth who can heal all. Focus on Christ Jesus, and you'll receive it! That's God's promise in the Bible, and that's *How the Bible Can Help You* to be healed of emotional cancer!

XVIII   Your Most Diabolical Enemy

Subject: Critical Spirit

Scripture: Luke 15:25-32

Text: *But he was angry and refused to go in* (Luke 15:28).

In the 15th chapter of Luke we find Jesus' famous parable about the father and two sons. One son is lost and the other son is saved. The strange thing about this parable is that the son you expect to be lost is actually the one who is saved, and the son you expect to be saved is actually the one who is lost.

The young son who has character traits we normally think of as bad—such as being a spendthrift, a carouser, irresponsible, lazy, and running with the wrong crowd, ends up being saved because he comes to himself, repents, and returns home with "a servant's heart." But the elder brother who stayed home and has admirable character traits—such as being moral, hard working, thrifty, temperate, and obedient, ends up being lost!

Why? Because of only one dark blot on an otherwise spotless character; he has a critical spirit and this critical spirit eventually contaminates all of the good within him! He's got a devil in him, so to speak, and doesn't know it. And that devil will not stop until everything good is destroyed. He's got an internal enemy—a diabolical enemy—who is more powerful than all of his good human character traits combined. That diabolical enemy is his critical spirit!

Why is a critical spirit so destructive? What is God's answer for such a critical spirit? Jesus specifically answers these two questions for us in this great parable which has been called *The Greatest Story Ever Told.*

177

Why is a critical spirit so destructive? Jesus says it is because it separates us from the three important and meaningful things in life.

First, a critical spirit separates us from our heavenly Father.

That, my friend, is what the Bible means by *sin*. Of course, in this, the greatest story ever told, the father in the parable represents God, and the two sons represent the two ways that men rebel against God and separate themselves from him. Some rebel like the Prodigal Son; that is, they openly defy God's authority. Physically, mentally, morally, spiritually, and emotionally they openly and purposefully separate themselves from God's authority. Many others rebel like the elder brother. Outwardly they stay home and acknowledge God's authority, but inwardly they separate themselves from him by trying to take over his judgment seat and sit in judgment of both themselves and others.

No matter which way we do it, the result is the same; we are cut off from God and his blessings for us! The younger son deliberately and openly defied his Father and struck out on his own to "live it up" in the far country, so he was cut off from his father and the father's blessings. The elder brother openly acknowledged his father, but inwardly tried to usurp his father's authority by playing God and sitting in judgment of both his father and his brother. So, he too was cut off from his father and his father's blessings! The difference is that the younger boy realized his predicament, came to himself, repented, returned home, and accepted his father's authority and blessings. The older boy did not!

This is why a critical spirit is our most diabolical enemy: because it's the vice of the virtuous! It's the spirit of the devil himself controlling us, even though we claim obedience to God. What makes it so diabolical is that we feel most righteous when we are most dominated by this evil, critical spirit and sitting in judgment of others. This is why the Bible shouts from the beginning to the end: "Leave all judgment to God!" We must leave all judgment to God because we don't have his eternal perspective; we don't have his grace; we don't have his love and mercy; we don't have his knowledge and wisdom. We must leave all judgment to God because we can never know all of the facts. We must leave all judgment to God because we are not God and such judgment is reserved for God alone. Because we are not God, our judgment of others must always be justified by building ourselves up and tearing others down, as the elder brother did here. Of course, such justification of ourselves causes us to close our eyes to our own sin and prevents us from seeking and receiving forgiveness. Our critical spirit has separated us from our Heavenly Father! But that's only the beginning!

A critical spirit also separates us from the meaningful people around us: our family, friends, fellow church members, and co-workers.

Look at this elder brother. What a lonely, pathetic person he is! Look at him standing outside by himself, pouting, eaten up with anger, bitterness, resentment, and hostility. Only two people even speak to him: the servant he calls to him, who has no choice and can't help himself, and his father, who represents God and never gives up on anyone. Everyone else ignores him. Why? Because his critical spirit has cut him off from them! It always does.

Think of the critical-spirited people you know—those who are always correcting faults in you and in other people around them or in the way things are done. Do you really like to be with them? Don't you avoid them when you can? Doesn't their heavy, critical spirit put a dark blot on everything else? Don't they always pollute the atmosphere with their judgmental heart and critical spirit?

A judgmental heart and a critical spirit always separate us from the meaningful others around us: our family, friends, fellow churchmen, and co-workers. Both the Bible

179

and personal experience illustrate it endlessly! But as bad as this is, there is still more!

A critical spirit separates us from the truth which God has revealed to us in the gospel—the Good News.

In order to justify ourselves for our own critical spirit and our harsh judgments of others, we must twist this good news of the gospel into the bad news of humanism. Look at the elder brother and note what his judgmental heart and critical spirit have done to him. First, note how he changes morality into moralism. That is, instead of knowing the joy of clean living through grace, he has set himself up as the norm for everyone else as he creates his own set of arbitrary rules to live by.

Also, he substitutes legalism for genuine service. That is, instead of serving in order to give, now he serves in order to get. He has made service into a system of rewards which he earns, instead of a way to work with his father to meet the needs of others.

His critical spirit has also changed his faith and faithfulness into doubt and distrust. (Remember, we can receive the gospel only through faith!) Paul continually tells us there are two stumbling blocks to faith and we see both of them in the elder brother. One Paul calls the law and uses the Jews as the best example. By law Paul means trying to justify ourselves by what we do, substituting both moralism and legalism for faith.

The other stumbling block to faith Paul calls knowledge, and uses the Greeks as the best example. By knowledge, Paul means trying to justify ourselves by what we know, substituting what we have learned for trust in God. The elder brother's faith is tainted by both law and knowledge, so he is distrustful of his father instead of faithful to him. Now, because of his lack of faith, he has shut himself off from the truth of the gospel.

Also, his critical spirit has changed what was once genuine obedience into dull duty. Obedience is eagerly aligning your life with God's will as revealed in Christ, by giving the Spirit of the living Christ—the Spirit of Love—dominion over your body, mind, and will. But duty is forcing yourself to try to give in to what Christ says without sharing the power and love of his Spirit. It's drudgery. It's impossible.

Step-by-step the elder brother has separated himself from the truth of the gospel as revealed in Christ, until now he is living a lie and missing the abundant life altogether! Jesus wants us to see that this must always be the end for those who are in bondage to this diabolical enemy named a "Critical Spirit!" Like the elder brother we become separated from the truth of the gospel, but we don't know it, because we've twisted it into humanism. We've taken the good news out of it! The diabolical thing about it is this: the more lost the elder brother becomes, the more self-righteous he feels. The more separated he becomes from his father, from his brother, and from the truth, the more critical he also becomes, which results in more separation. It is a vicious and devilish circle!

The good news is, although the elder brother didn't see it, there is a way out of this vicious trap! In this, *The Greatest Story Ever Told*, Jesus reveals to us God's three-fold answer for a critical spirit. This answer comes from the very heart and the lips of the father in the story, who, of course, represents God himself.

Notice the first encounter of the father and the elder brother in verse 28. We're told in the first half of this verse that the elder brother "was angry and refused to go in." That's the problem. Then, in the last half of it we are told this: "His father came out and entreated him."

That's God's answer; God takes the initiative to save us! The word which is translated "entreated" is used often in the New Testament, but most of the other places it is translated as "exhorted," "beseeched," or even "begged." A

181

person with the spiritual gift of exhortation is one who "strongly urges others to live by faith and earnestly advises them how to do it." This is exactly what the father is doing here! He is strongly urging his eldest son to change from a "do-it-yourself religion" to a life of faith, and earnestly advising him exactly how to do it. He is telling him, and all of us, that the first step is "to come to ourselves" and see ourselves as we really are.

The first step is to honestly look at ourselves!

The father pleads with or "entreats" his eldest son to look at himself honestly and see what his critical spirit is doing to him. He wants all of us to do the same thing. How? Perhaps the best way is to turn some of the symptoms of a critical spirit into questions that we ask ourselves. Test yourself as you answer these questions honestly.

- What is your first reaction to a new idea? Are you automatically against it? Are you really open, or are you critical?
- What is your reaction when someone else is honored or gets a promotion, and you don't?
- Can you rejoice with a child who is honored when your child is not?
- How do you feel about people who worship differently from you? What if the person next to you wants to praise God by raising his hands to heaven or by saying "Amen!" or "Alleluia!"? Does your spirit accept him or reject him?
- Or, how do you feel about the person who will have nothing to do with your way of open demonstration when you worship? Are you critical of him? Is he not as "spiritual" as you are?
- How do you listen to a sermon, or to a Sunday School lesson, or better still to a talk by someone in your own profession? Do you listen

182

with a critical spirit or with a mind open to receive?

- What is your reaction when someone who hasn't lived by your strict moral standards joins the church and begins to receive the honors and acclaim you feel you deserve as a longtime member? Do you rejoice for him or do you begin to justify yourself with a critical spirit?
- Do you live by a standard of morality or by a standard of moralism? That is, do you set up moralistic standards for everyone else to try to live by, or do you say, "Except for the grace of God there go I, for Christ alone is my morality and my righteousness?"
- Is obedience for you a life of grace and joy, or is it a life of law and dull duty?

Well, that's enough questions to help us see ourselves honestly and recognize whether we have a critical spirit. And the truth is none of us comes out one hundred per cent clean, do we? If we're honest, all of us must admit that this diabolical enemy is always close at hand trying to put us in bondage even though, like the elder brother, we have stayed home. Recognizing this, says the Bible, is the first step toward victory over this vicious enemy.

Let's move to the second step we see in the heart and hear on the lips of the father in our parable. After the father entreats the elder brother to come to himself, and the son finishes justifying himself and criticizing his younger brother (vs 29 and 30), we are told that the father says this to him: "Son . . . all that is mine is yours" (vs 31).

The second step we must take, says the Bible, to defeat this vicious enemy is to see what the grace of God means for us.

The second step is to see that God wants to give us all that we need in order to be released from this terrible bondage.

183

"All that is mine is yours!" is God's promise to all of us. That's God's grace. These first two steps define what the Bible means when it says "the prodigal came to himself." First, he saw himself honestly as being separated from God, from those meaningful persons in his life, and from truth. Second, he saw that only God's grace—God's eternal, redeeming love in Christ—could end that separation and make him the person he was supposed to be. These two things are the very things that the elder brother refused to see. Still the father continues to the third and final step.

When you do take these first two steps the third step comes naturally and this is the final thing the father tries to help the elder brother see. We are told about it in the final verse of this great story as the father says this:

> "[Son, you must see,] *it was fitting to make merry and be glad, for this your brother was dead, and is alive; he was lost and is found"* (Lk 15:32).

The third step, says the Bible, is to begin to see others through the eyes of God, but only after you have taken the first two steps:

First, you must honestly see yourself separated from God by sin, that is, by that critical spirit within you which makes you try to usurp the place of God and "play God" over the lives of others as you sit in judgment of them and their actions. Second, you must truly see the grace of God and what it means for you, as God comes to you in Christ to redeem you and set you free. Then, the third step just naturally follows as you give the Spirit of the living Christ dominion over your thoughts, your decisions, your words, and your actions. Then, and only then, can you begin to see others through the eyes of God—that is: through the Spirit of Jesus Christ himself! This is what Paul means when he exhorts all Christians:

> "Let this mind be in you, which was also in Christ Jesus" (Phil 2:5 KJV).

184

That is, see others through the mind of Christ—who is God in the flesh. This is what Paul is telling us 172 different times in the New Testament as he uses the terms "in Christ" and "Christ in us." In fact, the Bible says this is why God sent Jesus Christ to us: so his Spirit can replace all those evil spirits within us which separate us from God, from other people, and from the eternal truth we need to live by.

This is what Christianity is all about. This story is called *The Greatest Story Ever Told* because it so clearly illustrates these basics of our faith, and so clearly shows us:

- How to be moral, instead of moralistic!
- How to genuinely and joyfully serve God and his kingdom on earth, instead of being legalistic with our own system of rewards!
- How to truly trust God and his amazing grace, instead of feeling that we must justify ourselves by tearing others down.
- How to joyfully obey Christ, instead of being bound by the demon duty.

The only way we can defeat our most diabolical enemy and begin to participate in the blessings God has for us is to:

Honestly look at ourselves and see ourselves as we try to "play God" over the lives of others, and acknowledge how this separates us from all that is meaningful in our lives.

Truly see the grace of God in Christ and how this grace alone can redeem us and set us free.

Genuinely begin to see others through the eyes of Christ by giving his living Spirit dominion

over our thoughts, our decisions, our words, and our actions.

When this happens to any of us, I am confident that Christ truly rejoices in heaven. Then he can give this *Greatest Story Ever Told* its proper ending. Then, the Father can say of his elder son exactly what he said of the Prodigal:

> *"Bring quickly the best . . .* [blessings] *. . . and let us eat and make merry; for this my son was dead, and now is alive again; he was lost, and is found"* (Lk 15:22-24).

Then all of the angels in heaven will join with Christ in the merrymaking to celebrate your victory over your most diabolical enemy!

Subject: Fear

Scripture: Romans 8:1-17

Text: *For God has not given us a spirit of fear, but*
                a spirit of power and love and a sound mind
                (II Timothy 1:7 J. B. Phillips).

                For you did not receive the spirit of slavery to
                fall back into fear, but you have received the
                spirit of sonship (Romans 8:15).

Some months ago in a cover story, *Time Magazine* said that America had become "A Nation of Fear." By this it meant that a spirit of fear permeates our nation and the hearts of our people. Now, the editors of *Time* didn't know at the time they published this cover story that they were being prophetic; this was probably the very last thing in their minds. But they were! The Bible says that when God's people fall away from God, fear will become a way of life for them—that they will be absorbed and controlled by a spirit of fear. In fact, the Bible says that it is impossible to be God's people and to live in such fear.

What does this mean? It means that God has given us an answer for our fear, and recorded this answer in the Bible! It means that the Bible can help you and me overcome this spirit of fear, if we will let it! God's gives us his answer for fear in the 3-fold formula Paul sets out in his letter to Timothy:

"God has not given us a spirit of fear, but a spirit of power, and love, and a sound mind" (II Tim 1:7 J. B. Phillips).

For better understanding and for emphasis sake, I want to reverse the order as we look at these three things.

"God has not given us a spirit of fear, but a spirit of . . . a sound mind."

By this Paul means that God has endowed us with the great gift of a mind which is capable of reasoning and making right decisions. All other animals are controlled by a spirit of fear, which is their means of self-preservation, but not human beings. We are created in the image of God and have the potential to rise above the spirit of fear. The first resource we have for rising above fear is a sound mind—our ability to think and to reason.

To understand what the Bible is saying, we must first understand the difference between what the Bible means by a spirit of fear, and fear as a legitimate, protective response to danger. Fear is a good emotion when properly understood as a danger signal of approaching harm. When I made this point in a previous sermon, I received a very indignant letter from TV viewer, who said, "How can you say that any fear is good, when the Bible says that all fear is bad. I prefer to believe the Bible, which says that all fear is sin!"

Now, I rejoice that this listener prefers to believe the Bible rather than man (even when I am that man). But the trouble is, this listener didn't really know what the Bible says. The Bible does not say that all fear is sin, rather it says that a *spirit* of fear is sin! And that is a big difference! Paul says that God has given us a sound mind, so we can distinguish between fear which is healthy and a spirit of fear which is destructive.

In Herman Melville's great novel of the sea, *Moby Dick*, Captain Ahab says to his crew: "I won't have a man on my ship who does not fear a whale." By this he means that he doesn't want foolhardy men; he wants men who respect the truth about whales. A mother is teaching her child the same thing when she warns him to fear the hot stove or playing in the street; she is teaching her child to respect the truth about fire or about automobiles. The Bible means exactly the same thing when it admonishes us to fear the Lord. It means we must respect the truth about God or we shall destroy ourselves.

But that's different from a spirit of fear which permeates your whole being and everything you do! When the Bible speaks of a spirit of fear, it's talking about a whole way of life, not isolated danger signals. It's talking about an evil spirit that keeps you from living life to the fullest, and from reaching your potential in life by tainting everything with fear. It's talking about a spirit that pushes your heart up into your throat when the boss calls on the telephone, or a spirit that keeps you from taking an airplane although the occasion demands it. It's talking about a spirit that denies you the fulfillment, joy, and excitement of getting married because you are afraid you are not up to it or it won't turn out right. It's talking about the fear of taking a new job because you fear you will fail, or a fear of teaching a Sunday School class or visiting in evangelism or getting involved in the healing ministry, because you are bound by a spirit of fear. This spirit of fear makes us jealous without reason, irritable without cause, and distrustful without a sound mind!

A good description of this spirit of fear is found in an old Indian fable. A mouse lived in mortal fear of a cat, so the medicine man turned the mouse into a cat. Immediately he was fearful of the dogs; so the medicine man turned him into a dog. Then the new dog began to fear the wolf, so the medicine man turned him into a wolf, but the wolf feared the hunter. The wise Indian looked at him and said, "I can do nothing for you, because you have the heart and mentality of a mouse." So he turned him back into a mouse. When we have the spirit of fear it follows us no matter what we do. The Bible says,

"Know the truth, and the truth will make you free!"
(Jn 8:31-32).

189

Before we can know the truth, we must first use the sound mind God has given us. This is the first part of God's answer to fear—A Sound Mind. The second part of God's answer to fear is love.

"God has not given us a spirit of fear, but a spirit of . . . love "

"There is no fear in love, but perfect love casts our fear" (I Jn 4:18a).

The Bible is telling us, not only here but throughout its pages, that the opposite of fear is love! The Bible is telling us that the weapon God gave us to deal with fear is love, and the way to get rid of fear is to put on love! Look at love and fear side-by-side and you can't keep from seeing that this is true.

Love is self-giving; fear is self-protecting.
Love reaches out for others; fear shrinks from them.
Love makes itself vulnerable; fear hides.
Love is trustful; fear is wary.
Love relates honestly; fear wears a mask.
Love believes in others; fear is distrustful of others.
Love is open to God; fear hides from God.
Love builds others up; fear tears others down.

Love and fear are opposites: the more fear, the less love; the more love, the less fear. The good news is that love is more powerful than fear, and "perfect love casts out fear!" Notice that the Bible never says that Jesus is afraid. Why? Because his love was perfect and "perfect love casts out fear!" So, the question is: How can we put on this perfect love that casts out fear? The truth is you can never put it on in order to cast out fear! That is, you can't seek perfect love just to get rid of fear. Perfect love is always self-giving; seeking it just to help yourself is "self-getting." When you seek perfect love to get something for yourself, it immediately ceases to be perfect love and becomes selfishness; and selfishness creates more fear.

The Christian seeks perfect love because that is God's will for him—that is God's way for the Christian to live. Then—serendipity! The result of putting on such love is the total disappearance of the spirit of fear! The Christian seeks love out of obedience to Christ. Then serendipity!—Christ honors that obedience with a whole new way of life that is without a spirit of fear!

How can the Christian be obedient to Christ and put on this perfect love that casts out fear? How does a Christian follow God's will and live a life of love? Well, that's what the 8th chapter of Romans is all about. Here Paul tells us exactly how to do it. In the 15th verse of this great chapter Paul is referring to destructive fear when he says,

> *"For you did not receive the spirit of slavery to fall back into fear, but you have received the spirit of sonship"* (Rom 8:15).

As Christians we are entitled to, and God wants to give us, the perfect love of Christ that casts out fear. This is God's will for all of us! He gives it to us through what the Bible calls "the power of the Holy Spirit." This brings us to our final point.

"For God has not given us a spirit of fear but a spirit of power . . ."

What is power? Power is simply the ability to accomplish purpose or will, and we have already seen that God's will for all of us is the perfect life of Christ, which casts out fear. Thumb through the New Testament and you can't miss the fact that there is a dynamic spirit of power available to all persons who accept Jesus Christ as Lord and Savior. God accomplishes his will in the lives of Christians—his people—by giving them extraordinary, new, supernatural power. Some receive it the moment they are baptized with water, others realize this power months and even years after water baptism! But whenever they do accept it, this new spirit of power casts out the spirit of fear. Then, we see unlearned, awkward men like Peter stand up and speak so winsomely and so convincingly that thousands of people are moved to give their lives to Christ.

This new spirit of power even opened prison doors, first for Peter and John, and then for Paul and Silas. It's also this new spirit of power that encouraged them to pray for the sick and open blind eyes and even raise the dead! Study Paul's missionary journeys and you will see that it is this new Holy Spirit of power which directed him from place to place, watched over and protected him. No person can honestly and seriously read the New Testament without concluding that there is a Holy Spirit of power, available to every baptized Christian, who will guide him into the right paths, will deliver him from the jaws of evil, will heal him and keep him safe and sound until his purpose on earth is fulfilled.

The real problem is that many people confess Christ as Savior, but never take the necessary steps to make him the Lord of their life by accepting the power of his Holy Spirit! Oh, they are Christians, yes, for they confess Christ; but they are not Spirit-filled Christians—what Paul calls "spiritual men" in Romans 8. Consequently, these Christians try to live up to the law of God in their own power and are always being defeated and falling back into the slavery of a spirit of fear.

Consider the disciples. They all confessed Christ and left everything to follow him for three years, as he lived with them and taught them. Even so, Jesus knew the disciples were not ready to deal with fear. He told them in John 16 that he must go away so he could send them his Spirit of power. Right before he ascended, after telling them to stay in Jerusalem and wait for the promise of the Father, Jesus promised them:

". . . you shall receive power when the Holy Spirit has come upon you; and you shall be my witnesses in Jerusalem and in all Judea and Samaria and to the end of the earth" (Acts 1:8).

That is, "You shall be equipped to do the work I've called you to do and be the people God created you to be."

The disciples were obedient. They did go back and wait, but they waited in a very special way. The Bible says they waited "in prayer and one accord." They waited in prayer— that is, looking to God in faith and expecting God to keep his promise to empower them. They waited in one accord— that is, they got right with each other and accepted each other as they were. They waited in faith and in obedience to Christ. Then on the Day of Pentecost it happened! Like a mighty wind and tongues of fire, this new power came to them. Then serendipity! New life followed as surely as fruit follows blossoms on a tree.

No one could say that these first disciples were not Christians before the Day of Pentecost. Of course, they were. They accepted Christ. They followed Christ. But they were powerless Christians! They were operating on their own just as many of us are.

Do you want this new power that they found? Do you want this ability to accomplish purpose and fulfill God's will in your own life? The good news is, you can have it right now, if you honestly want it, if you will be obedient to Christ, and if you will open your life in faith.

If you have not accepted Christ and received water baptism, then just like Cornelius, the Roman Centurion in Acts 10, you too can receive this power when you are obedient and are baptized. That is, you can if you fulfill the two requirements. Or, if you have already been baptized with water, but didn't accept this power at that time, then God will give it to you right now, as he did the Christians in Samaria (Acts 8) and the Christians in Ephesus (Acts 19). But, again, you must first fulfill the two requirements and be obedient to Christ. That is, you must get right with God through faith, and you must get right with other people through a giving love.

Get right with God. Acknowledge that he is all powerful and he is your only true source of love and power and wisdom; look to him for this power and expect to receive it. Love God; that is, give yourself to him totally by accepting Christ as your source—as your Lord and Savior—and earnestly desire his Holy Spirit to control your life! Then,

Get right with other people. Don't seek this new power selfishly, but let this love of Christ flow through you to others by accepting them just as they are and willing the best for them.

According to the Bible, the true sign of the Holy Spirit is not the gift of tongues or prophecy or healing or discernment, or any other manifestation, for all of these can be faked. But the one true sign that you are now the spiritual person God wants you to be is "a spirit of power, and love and a sound mind!" A new and supernatural spirit permeates your whole being ---a spirit which casts out fear--a spirit which leaves no room for any evil spirit such as jealousy, envy, hate, vengeance and all the rest ---a spirit which reaches up for God in faith as its source and reaches out to man in giving love---a spirit of "prayer and one accord"---a spirit of a sound mind, which does not claim to be a "Mr. Know-It-All," but rather looks to him who does know it all!—the Spirit of Christ himself—nothing less than the Holy Spirit of Almighty God! This is your inheritance as an heir of Christ—the spirit of sonship! And you can claim this inheritance this very moment. Jesus told us,

> *"If you then, who are evil, know how to give good gifts to your children, how much more will the heavenly Father give the Holy Spirit to those who ask him!"* (Lk 11:13).

If you honestly want this new "spirit of power, of love and a sound mind" today, then obey Christ—come to your

194

own Upper Room and wait "in prayer and in one accord." Ask the Father to give you his Holy Spirit and you shall receive it. For God is the same yesterday, today, and forever. He is saying today what he has always said to his people:

> "Fear not, I am with thee;
> O be not dismayed
> For I am thy God
> And will still give thee aid.
> "I'll strengthen thee, help thee,
> And cause thee to stand,
> Upheld by my righteous,
> omnipotent hand."[*]

How Firm a Foundation, The Methodist Hymnal #48, (1964)

Subject: Selfishness

Scripture: Luke 14:1-11

Text: *For everyone who exalts himself will be humbled, and he who humbles himself will be exalted* (Luke 14:11).

So faith, hope, love abide, these three; but the greatest of these is love (I Corinthians 13:13).

Now the works of the flesh are . . . selfishness . . . But the fruit of the Spirit is love . . . (Galatians 5: 19,20,22).

Each of us is born with the characteristic of selfishness. By "characteristic" I mean that this selfishness shows up in our character, and it shows up from the beginning. It is built into us; it is part of us and it's going to come out regardless of the environment we live in or what others around us do and say. This means that it is "natural" for us to be selfish, and when we are selfish, we are simply "doing what comes naturally." Or, to say it another way: This selfishness has its "seat" in our inner being, in the inclination of our will, and therefore applies to every person born upon this earth.

Those who are trained for such things can see it in the tiniest babies, and all of us notice it when the child begins to walk and talk. I have a two-year-old grandson, Timmy, and two granddaughters: Sarah who is four, and Laurelin who is seven. I purposefully observed some of their actions this week and recorded them. There is not a mother listening who could not tell me Timmy's favorite word at the age of two. Why, of course, it is "Mine!" No matter what new thing he encounters, there is an inner compulsion to possess it, and this compulsion comes out in the word "Mine!" Now, the world has conditioned four-year-old Sarah to the point that she knows she can't possess everything she sees—at least she knows she can't just walk up and grab it and say "Mine!" like Timmy. Still, the world can't eliminate that deep desire for it, so, this characteristic expresses itself differently in Sarah. She waits until she's sure it is possessable, like being in the hands of her seven-year-old sister; then comes her favorite phrase: "Me too!" All mothers of four-year-olds know that is their favorite phase: "Me too!"

Since Laurelin has had three or four years of conditioning in the sophistication and finesse of the ways of the world, her "Me too!" takes a different form. But believe me, it's always there and always comes out! It comes out in ways no grandfather or grandmother can resist—in the eyes, or a hug, or kiss—all adding up to "Don't forget—Me too!"

The point is: As we grow older, we may change our tactics, but we don't change our selfish nature. We don't change it, because it is built in and is part of us. We can camouflage it, but we can't eliminate it. Each of us is born with the characteristic of selfishness, and it stays with us all of our lives! It's like a shadow. You can stomp on it, you can curse it, you can cover it up; but you can't get rid of it. It follows you everywhere you go!

Have you guessed what I am really talking about this morning? I am talking about what the Bible calls "original sin." Now, don't misunderstand me, for I am not saying that selfishness *is* original sin; but I am saying it is this characteristic of selfishness that caused man's fall and is still causing our fall today. It is this deep-seated characteristic which caused Adam and Eve to rebel and disobey God. It is still what causes us to disobey and rebel against God. It's the root of original sin.

Oh, I wish there were a better common word for it than the word "selfishness," because of its limited connotation.

Now, there is a word which describes it much better, but it is one of those "two-bit words" which is too cumbersome for common usage. I'm talking about the word egocentricity. "Ego" meaning self, and "centric" meaning center. Egocentric—self-centered. "Mine!" "Me too!" That is the origin of all sin. All sin is based there. It is the home place of all sin. That's the place where sin was born, and that's where it grows up and manifests itself in so many ugly ways. That is where all sin originates; thus, the name original sin. Sin does not refer to something external or peripheral or something accidental. It refers to that inner throne or inner seat in our being that keeps us in bondage. It rules us, it controls us as grown-ups as surely as it rules and controls two-year-old Timmy, four-year-old Sarah and seven-year-old Laurelin.

This is what the Bible means when it declares that it is hell to live in bondage—to be tied up with ourselves! It means that, even though you now have the body and mind of an adult, you still have the will of a child and you still act like a child. It means that this inner "characteristic of egocentricity" sits on the throne of your life and calls all of the shots, even though most of us are usually able to hide it from others with our sophistication and finesse. Still we know, for we can't hide it from ourselves! We know that our egocentricity has corrupted our will, so that now practically all of our decisions are made with one thought in mind, the childish thought of "Mine!" or "Me too!" It is so deep-seated and so much a part of us that it even taints and corrupts the things we do for God and his church. Often the things we do—such as teaching, preaching, singing, serving and even praying, are done to feed the voracious appetite of this ruthless dictator deep within us ---our own ego! Can you see why the Bible calls it original sin, and says it is the origin of all misery and incompleteness in life? It is what so often causes us "to miss the mark."

Yet, all of us tend to treat this selfishness superficially, don't we? Even after we accept Christ and join the church,

199

most of us still try to deal with it by sewing a new patch of love now and then onto our old garment of selfishness, honestly thinking we are making progress.

No doubt, we preachers are the worst offenders. I seriously doubt if there has ever been a better "patch sewer" than I was for many years. I knew what the Bible said. I knew that God's answer for selfishness was love. Every Christian knows that! Selfishness is wanting to get for yourself. Love is giving to others. The essence of selfishness is seeking for itself, but the Bible says that "love seeketh not its own." So naturally, God's answer for selfishness is love. And, oh, how I used to preach it and teach it. "Now, Christian," I'd say, "You ought to be more loving! Christian, you ought to do this and you ought to do that! You ought to love!"

The congregation would always nod their heads in agreement, because they knew what they ought to do, and they would tell me what a wonderful sermon I preached, because I agreed with what they knew. But the trouble is, those skimpy, legalistic patches never could hold their rotten garments together for even a week. I knew that, because I'd been living in the same patched clothes too long not to know it. I would counsel with a couple having marital problems, and before we barely got started I'd spot a half-dozen selfish splits in their marital garments. Immediately, I'd get busy with my patch sewing: "You ought to cover up that hole with a little patch of love." "You ought to be more loving!" Always with the same results: They hardly got out of the office before they were back in the same old, tattered selfish rags! My counseling record was really phenomenal—almost 100% failure!

Thank God, I don't waste my time and yours anymore telling people what "they ought to do!" The reason people don't love is not because they don't know that they ought to love! We all know that! Every husband and wife knows they ought to love each other! Every parent knows he ought to love his child, and every child knows he ought to love his parent. The reason we don't love is not because we don't know we ought to; the reason we don't love is because we can't love. And the reason we can't love is because we are in bondage! We can't love because we are under the dominion of selfishness, we are ruled by egocentricity! We can't love because we are all victims of original sin! We can't love because even though we are grown-ups, we are still thinking, talking, and reasoning like a child. Paul tells us this in the great 13th chapter of I Corinthians, where he describes all of the attributes of love. He says:

"When I was a child, I spoke like a child, I thought like a child, I reasoned like a child; when I became a man I gave up childish ways" (I Cor 13:11).

By this, he means that only spiritual maturity can deal with this ingrained, original characteristic of selfishness! Why are we still selfish, even though we are adults? Simply because we are incomplete; because we have not permitted God to complete the work he started in us with Christ; because we are spiritually immature! We know what we ought to do—that's not our problem—but we can't do it. We can't do it because there is a limit to all human love. Our human love is always limited by that ingrained, original characteristic of selfishness within all of us.

Think back to the time you met that certain person who became—or will become—your wife or husband. Remember the excitement? Why were you excited? Because you knew that person had something special which would fill the vacuum in you. Because you suddenly realized there was something lacking in you that only your beloved could supply. You realized that to be complete you needed him or her; and just the thought of this completion really turned you on.

Now, that's human love. We love because the object of our love has something worth our love, such as beauty, character, or charm. The other one has something we need for our own completion. And that's good! Human love is

201

very precious love, and we shouldn't speak disparagingly about it; it is absolutely essential for our completion! But if we stop there, we'll miss the best of all and even lose the excitement of our human love, because all human love is necessarily egocentric. It is rooted in self. It gives to get! We must go on to a much deeper kind of love for our real completion. Let's call it divine love, for it begins with God. It is the way that God loves us. You see, God is already complete. God is already perfect. God doesn't love us because of our worth to him or because we are attractive or beautiful or lovable. God doesn't love us to get for himself. God loves us to give himself to us, because we are incomplete without him and we need his love to be whole!

God doesn't love us because of ourselves, but he loves us in spite of ourselves! God loves us like this, the Bible says, because "God is love!" That's God's nature. Divine love is different from human love in this basic respect: God's love is not simply an attitude toward another, like ours; his love is the very character of God himself—for God is love!

As human beings, it is impossible for us to love in any other way than in a human way—an egocentric way. That is, our love is always based on the worth of the object of our love. For that is our basic human character. That's our nature, a nature that is tainted by selfishness, a nature that is basically egocentric. But the good news is, that in creating us in his image, God has made it possible to change our character so we can love others the way that God loves us—we can love others with "divine love." God has made it possible for us to love, not just to get for ourselves, but to meet the need of the other person. He has made it possible for us to love that other person in spite of himself. The Bible says that God sent Jesus to release us from the bondage of our egocentricity, so we can accept divine love and be instruments of this divine love to others. In fact, this is the way that God intends for his kingdom to come upon this earth as it is in heaven!

Perhaps our imagination, coupled with a human illustration, can explain what this means. I remember a picture I took in the Holy Land a few years ago. It was the picture of a pathetic, blind beggar on the streets of Jerusalem—dressed in rags, covered with patches, groping through the filth of the street with his tapping cane. I took this picture in front of the Jerusalem bus station. From there I walked around the corner and entered the site of the garden tomb where the crucified Jesus was buried, and took a number of pictures there. When the pictures were developed, I discovered I had taken a double exposure. In the foreground was an ugly, dirty street in Jerusalem with this pathetic blind beggar in his rags. Super-imposed over it, almost blotting it out, was the open tomb of the risen Christ surrounded by beautiful flowers in full bloom!

This gives us an idea of what the Bible means when it says that the only thing that really matters is whether we are in Christ and Christ is in us. (The New Testament makes this point no less than 172 times.) By this, the Bible means that when we are in Christ and Christ is in us, the divine love of God is superimposed over our old nature. Our old nature is in check, because it is controlled by a higher nature. The portrait of ourselves is no longer a picture of the blind beggar, groping in the dark. Now, it is the picture of "Love Divine all loves excelling" blotting out our old nature and transforming our selfishness into eternal victory!

How does this happen? The Bible says that it happens because God, who is love, comes to our rescue and gives us the kind of love we egocentric human beings do not possess. Because of man's fall we can never love selflessly on our own, but because of God's grace such love is possible for us.

A term sometimes used in psychological parlance is "instrumentation," meaning that a person can be changed by offering himself as an instrument through which good work is accomplished. The same idea is behind the central theme of the message of Jesus, when he says: "You must lose yourself to find yourself."

Jesus is not talking about trying to be more loving or more humble on our own. He's talking about being an instrument for the divine love of God, by permitting God to pour his love into our hearts through the Holy Spirit, which he gives us. He's talking about losing our old selves by super-imposing over our old character of selfishness God's divine character of love. That is the only way any person can ever love with more than human love.

I never say to people anymore: "Now, Christian, you ought to be more loving! You ought to do this and you ought to do that! You ought to love!" For there is no way you can legalize love and make human love into divine Love. That's like telling a cow to be a horse, or a dandelion to be a rose. That takes a miracle! That takes an act of God himself! That takes the in-filling of God's Holy Spirit! That takes the amazing grace of God! Instead, I now simply say to all who will listen, the same good news that John Wesley proclaimed for fifty years. It is the heart of the gospel and the only answer the Bible has for selfishness, and it is this: "The best of all is: God is with us!" And he wants to live in us and love through us!

Everything else is commentary.

XXI   *How to Light up Your Life*

Subject: Boredom

Scripture: John 15:1-11

Text: *These things I have spoken to you, that my
            joy may be in you, and that your joy may be
            full* (John 15:11)

            *I came that they may have life, and have it
            abundantly* (John 10:10b).

            I am the light of the world . . . (John 8:12)

In the 10th chapter of John, Jesus chooses the analogy
of the pastoral setting around him—sheep, sheepfold,
pasture, and shepherd—to reveal to us his mission on
earth. He says that he is like the door to the sheepfold,
where the sheep can go in and out and find pasture so they
can be filled. He says he is like the good shepherd, watching
after the sheep both day and night, so their needs are met
at all times. The highpoint of this message comes when
Jesus says in verse 10:

"*I came that they may have life, and have it
abundantly.*"

He came to give us life that is good, full, and complete,
now as well as later. In fact, he says eternal life must begin
now with the abundant life or it begins not at all. We must
learn how to live the eternal life—the God life—now, if we
are to continue living that life eternally.

The next seven chapters of John, chapters 11 through
17, (a third of this twenty-one-chapter book) are devoted to
revealing how we can experience this abundant life, how all
of our needs can be met. In chapter 11, he raises Lazarus
from the dead and tells us how we too can come to life while
we are still upon this earth. In chapter 12 we're told

about his triumphant entry into Jerusalem and the plot of the rulers to kill him. Then Jesus admonishes his followers in these words:

"The light is with you for a little longer. Walk while you have the light, lest the darkness overtake you. . . I have come as light into the world, that whoever believes in me may not remain in darkness" (Jn 12: 35, 46).

Then, Jesus goes with his disciples to the Upper Room and eats the Last Supper with them. John devotes five full chapters to this—chapters 13 through 17. This passage, called The Upper Room Discourse, consists essentially of the words that Jesus himself speaks, telling how we can "light up our lives," how we can begin to live abundantly right now! Yet each day, we encounter many, many Christians who are living in darkness and have anything but this abundant life.

Although these Christians are very busy, they are terribly bored with life. They find no real excitement and fulfillment in what they do except in spurts, in periodic "highs." Many keep on changing jobs hoping to fill this vacuum of boredom. Others keep on changing marital partners, hoping for the same thing. This boredom is no respecter of age. Of course it often strikes older people when they retire, but some of the most bored people I talk with are teenagers and young couples. In fact, it strikes everyone of every age who has not learned the secret of abundant living! The truth is, it strikes so many people that one well-known doctor says, "It is one of our most deadly diseases, because it drives people to seek their excitement and their fulfillment in ways that are life-destroying, such as drugs, alcohol, and every kind of dissipation you can name."

In order to examine the Bible's answer to this problem of boredom, let's go with Jesus into the Upper Room and listen to him as he gives us the secret to abundant living.

He gives us this secret in the 15th chapter of John. It is all wrapped up in one word and that word is *abide*. This is what the 15th chapter of John is all about. It is about how we can abide in Jesus, the living Son of God, and he can abide in us. We are told here that as the branch must abide in the vine to produce fruit, so must we abide in Jesus, the source of life, to produce abundant living. Listen to Jesus, there in the Upper Room:

> *"I am the vine, you are the branches. He who abides in me, and I in him, he it is that bears much fruit, for apart from me you can do nothing. . . If you abide in me, and my words abide in you, ask whatever you will, and it shall be done for you. By this my Father is glorified, that you bear much fruit, and so prove to be my disciples. As the Father has loved me, so have I loved you; abide in my love. . . These things I have spoken to you, that my joy may be in you, and that your joy may be full!"* (Jn 15: 5, 7-9, and 11).

Here Jesus tells us "the secret of abiding" so that we can experience abundant, joyful living instead of boredom. He tells us this so that his "joy may be in us, and our joy may be full." That is abundant living! That is *How to Light Up Your Life!*

What is the "secret of abiding?" The answer is fourfold.

First, we must have an abiding faith.

We all need a solid, strong foundation upon which to build our lives, a foundation we can trust in bad times and in good times, a foundation which will not crumble and fall when the rains of life come and the ill winds blow.

Jesus tells us here in the 15th chapter of John, that the only place we can find such a solid, strong foundation upon which to build is in an abiding faith! It alone can stand the storms of life; everything else will pass away. Only an abiding faith is grounded in eternal security. Only an abiding faith—a faith that abides in Christ and Christ

207

alone—can give us life and give it abundantly. For only a faith that abides in him as God's perfect revelation of himself to us can show us God's will for our lives. Only a faith that abides in him as God's grace coming to us, can receive the blessings God has for us. Only a faith that abides in him as God in the flesh, our Redeemer and Lord, can align our lives with the rest of God's creation.

Why are so many Christians missing the excitement and fulfillment of abundant living? Read the church publications of most denominations; study most church school literature being published, especially that recommended by the National Council of Churches as International lessons; read the minutes of most denominational meetings; read current books of sermons, and it's obvious why: because the faith espoused is everything but an abiding faith! Instead, it is a faith in church bureaucracy, or in social action, or in liberation theology, women's lib, the quota system, on and on ad infinitum and ad nauseatum!

Now, all of these things may be good, or they may not be; that's not the point. The point is, none of them provides us a strong, solid foundation upon which to build our lives. In Methodism, we call this scattered faith by the name of "pluralism," which has come to mean that you can believe anything you want to believe as long as you have a caucus with enough clout to back you up.

It reminds me of the story of the city school teacher who brought a rabbit to school to show her children. The children were delighted and asked all kinds of questions about the rabbit. Finally, someone asked whether it was a girl rabbit or a boy rabbit. The teacher was flustered, but finally confessed that she didn't know. One little girl solved the problem when she said, "Well, teacher, I know. We can vote on it."

When are we going to learn that there are some things you just don't vote on! The Bible says that the object of our faith is one of those things! The Bible says that to be a

Christian and to experience abundant living, we must have an abiding faith; we must have a faith that is centered in Christ and in Christ alone! He alone must be the foundation upon which we build our lives, or there will come a time when the foundation begins to crumble and ultimately falls, and our lives will crumble and fall with it. The first secret of abiding is an abiding faith.

The second secret is an abiding love.

"Abide in my love," says Jesus, "that my joy may be in you, and that your joy may be full." Many of us have no idea what it means to have the joy of Jesus in us so that our "joy may be full." Actually, we don't like ourselves at all. Memories of our past consist of failures, rejection, and guilt, and our imaginations about the future conjure up a repeat of the same picture. It causes a civil war to be waged within us—a war best described by Paul in Romans 7. We know what we should be, but we also know what we are. We look at ourselves honestly and hate ourselves for what we see. We vow to do better, but we can't. So, we begin to wear different masks; we live a lie. Life becomes a living hell, instead of the abundant, fulfilling life Jesus promises us.

The Bible says there is only one thing powerful enough to redeem our memories so we can like ourselves, and that one thing is the forgiving love of Jesus Christ. What does the Bible mean by this? If we are to experience forgiveness so our memories can be cleansed, then we must abide in the love of Jesus and his divine, redeeming love must abide in us. Before our imaginations can be transformed and the pictures of ourselves can be purified, we must be able to forgive those who have wronged us; only the divine, selfless love of Jesus can do that.

If we are to live with and love ourselves, our only hope is in an abiding love—our abiding in him, so his divine, redeeming, selfless love can abide in us. Discarding one husband or wife and taking another one does not bring the happiness and joy we seek, because we take the same low self-esteem and the same self-centered love into the new marriage that we had in the last one. Only an abiding love can change that! That's our second need if we are to live abundantly: An abiding love so we can live with ourselves.

The third secret is to have an abiding hope.

We all need a goal to point toward if we are to live abundantly, and abiding hope can give us that. When we look to the future we must look expectantly toward joy and fulfillment instead of fear, worry, and anxiety.

For some of us, our present life is constantly corrupted by this bondage to our future. For others of us, it is more like a periodic nagging that slips in and spoils our peace and robs us of our joy. Yet Jesus says:

> *"If you abide in me, and my words abide in you, ask whatever you will, and it shall be done for you"* (Jn 15:7).

Notice the future tense. Jesus says we can look expectantly toward joy and fulfillment. He says the secret of keeping fear of the future from spoiling the present is an abiding hope—a hope in him who has already defeated all of our enemies, including death; a hope in his promise of eternal life. We can have such an abiding hope, Jesus says, by accepting his words about the future as his personal promise to us, and by hiding his words in our hearts so they abide there. Jesus gives us such promises about the future as these:

> *"I will not leave you desolate; I will come to you"* (Jn 14:18).

> *"In my Father's house are many rooms; if it were not so, would I have told you that I go to prepare a place for you? And when I go and prepare a place for you, I will come again and will take you to myself, that where I am you may be also"* (Jn 14:2-3).

> *"I am the way, and the truth, and the life"* (Jn 14:6).

"Peace I leave with you; my peace I give to you. . . Let not your hearts be troubled, neither let them be afraid" (Jn 14:27).

"It is to your advantage that I go away . . . if I go I will send him [the Holy Spirit] to you" (Jn 16:7).

Only an abiding hope in the Risen Christ, who sends his Holy Spirit to abide in us, can free us from the bondage to our future, so we can live abundantly in the present. That's the third part of the "secret of abiding" so we can be free to live life in the present and live it abundantly.

Finally, we must have an abiding purpose.

To escape boredom, life—daily life—must have significant meaning. We must have a goal to point toward—a purpose in life. That's why just changing jobs will not give us the abundant living we all seek, for we take the same old aimlessness into the new work as we had in the past. It takes an abiding purpose to give our life meaning. Jesus says:

"Abide in me, and I in you. As the branch cannot bear fruit by itself, unless it abides in the vine, neither can you, unless you abide in me. I am the vine, you are the branches. He who abides in me, and I in him, he it is that bears much fruit, for apart from me you can do nothing" (Jn 15:4-5).

Jesus is saying that our reason for being is to fulfill his purpose, just as the purpose for the branches is to fulfill the life of the vine. This is why we were created. This is why life was breathed into us. This is why Christ came to redeem us. This is why he created his Church and commissioned it to finish his mission on earth. Our purpose is to be a part of the Body of Christ on earth. According to the Bible, there is only one worthwhile purpose for any of us and that is to be a functioning, healthy, producing member of the Body of Christ on earth.

Our true meaning must be found in him, which means our purpose in life can be worthwhile only when that purpose abides in him. But the good news is, when our purpose does abide in him, he gives us the power, the wisdom, the courage, the love we need to fulfill this purpose! And it is this power, this wisdom, this courage and this love, which makes life exciting and fulfilling! This is why Jesus promised to send his Holy Spirit. This is why he fulfilled that promise for the first Christians and why he is still keeps that promise to his people today. The gifts of the Holy Spirit are given so we can be co-workers with him here on earth and fulfill our purpose in life. This is the calling of every Christian and the only way our lives can have significant meaning. We must have an abiding purpose—a purpose which has eternal significance; a purpose that is fulfilled here on earth, yes, but which has its beginning and ending in heaven; a purpose that produces good fruit because it abides in the vine, the living Christ himself, and receives all of its sustenance and life from the source of all life and power.

That's the four-fold "secret of abiding":

Abiding Faith,
Abiding Love,
Abiding Hope, and
Abiding Purpose.

Only through such abiding faith, hope, love, and purpose can we ever find abundant living—the Bible's answer for boredom.

Subject: Loneliness

Scripture: John 14: 18-30

Text: *I will not leave you desolate; I will come to you* (John 14:18).

What is loneliness? Loneliness is pain, but it is an emotional pain as distinguished from physical pain. It is an ache or a hurting within us that comes from the feeling of being cut off from other people. This feeling of being cut off from other people can be caused by such obvious things as a geographical move from loved ones and friends, death, illness, divorce, language and cultural barriers, children growing up and leaving home, loss of eyesight or hearing which isolates us, and so forth.

But loneliness is more often caused by those feelings which well up inside of us when our relationships are not right. We believe we don't really count because we have been rejected, or at least we feel we have been rejected by others. Or we think we have failed to measure up to what others expect of us; or we feel that others don't understand us; or we feel different from the group that we are in; or for whatever reason, we feel we don't belong.

Past hurts which cause us to be afraid of being intimate again is another cause of loneliness. The feeling of guilt can also be the cause of loneliness when we are so afraid that our past will be discovered that we avoid intimacy with others. In fact, the causes for loneliness are legion. At times all of us experience some of these pains of loneliness.

Why are we lonely? The first thing we need to understand about the "why" is this: we are not lonely simply because we are physically alone! In fact, loneliness and aloneness are totally different experiences. Loneliness is not separation from people in a physical sense, although such separation can sometimes cause loneliness. But loneliness is separation from people emotionally. Strange as it may sound, surveys reveal that some of the loneliest people today are those in the congested sections of our huge population centers, like New York City. So, simply being with other people is not the answer for loneliness; nor is simply being alone the cause of loneliness.

Jesus was often alone, but he was never lonely. Why? Because loneliness is caused by barriers between us and others that cut us off from them. And Jesus knew how to break down barriers. In order to find God's answer for our loneliness, let's go to the life of Jesus and see how he broke down the barriers that cause loneliness.

As I look at the life of Jesus, I see him doing primarily three things that make him victorious over loneliness, instead of the victim of it. If we incorporate these three things into our own lives, we can be victorious over our loneliness too!

First, Jesus used his aloneness creatively and constructively.

Loneliness is an enemy which eats away at happiness, dampens our faith, weakens our body, and stunts our creativity; but aloneness can be a dear friend. It can be the birthplace of creativity, the means for increasing our faith, an ally for productivity, and a source for better health. It was for Jesus. Jesus was alone on almost every important occasion in his life, but he used this aloneness creatively and constructively. For example, Jesus was alone in the wilderness for forty days, but he used this aloneness to settle his life's direction once and for all. He used it to put the temptations of life in proper perspective, and to settle once and for all that God alone would rule his life.

214

- First, he was tempted to be ruled by his physical appetites; that is, to make these physical things ultimate in his life. This was the real temptation when the devil tempted him to turn the stones into bread.
- Next, he was tempted to be ruled by his own ego, by what others thought of him, when he was tempted to jump from the pinnacle of the Temple and win the acclaim of the people.
- Finally, he was tempted to willfully rule with an iron fist over others. During this time alone, Jesus looked at himself honestly, who he was and what his mission was; and he used this aloneness to creatively and constructively set the direction of his life to be totally under God's authority.

Such times alone can be valuable, creative, constructive times for us too, if we will use them to look at ourselves honestly and determine what is ruling us, to discover God's call upon our lives, and to settle the direction that our lives are to take! It takes aloneness to make such important decisions and we should not only be thankful for these times alone; we should actively provide for such times in our busy lives.

Again, after his first day of miraculous healing we are told that Jesus went alone into the arid desert to pray (Mark 1:35). Why? So his strength could be replenished for another day of work and ministry; that's why! He used his aloneness creatively to re-create himself for service. All of us need such times alone each day, so we can be replenished for our work too! Again, when it came time for Jesus to make the most momentous decision of his life, we are told that he went alone to the Garden of Gethsemane to pray. And while he was there he again used his aloneness creatively and constructively as he used it to discover the

Father's will about the Cross and to be strengthened for that total aloneness he would experience on Calvary!

Jesus was alone many times, but never lonely, because he used his aloneness creatively and constructively! He used his times alone to look honestly at his own life, to seek the Father's will, and to be strengthened for the tasks ahead!

We need to do exactly the same thing, if we are to be victorious over loneliness. Instead, many of us do everything we can to avoid ever being alone. If we find ourselves alone, we do everything we can to fill the time, trying to avoid an honest look at ourselves to find God's will for our lives. We watch TV, shuffle cards, or do some other aimless thing we call passing time.

Yet, the basic cause of our loneliness is the barriers in our relationship that make us feel like we don't count or that we don't really fit in. It's axiomatic that before we can begin to break down such barriers we must first know who we are and why we do count and fit in! In order to know this we must begin to use our aloneness creatively and constructively to look honestly at ourselves, to seek God's will for our lives so we can become co-workers with him on earth, and to be strengthened for the tasks ahead.

First, Jesus used his aloneness creatively and constructively; and this is the first step in being victorious over our loneliness.

Next, Jesus was an active part of a dynamic, genuine, support group.

The very first thing that Jesus did when he began his ministry was to create his own support group. He called twelve other men, and the thirteen became a dynamic, sharing, caring support group.

Do you know why some of the loneliest people in the world today are found in the most congested areas of our cities? Do you know why some of the loneliest people in Tulsa right now are packed like proverbial sardines into

216

townhouses, condominiums, apartment complexes, high rises, and crowded nursing homes? It's because, even though they are physically close together, they actually have no one with whom they can share their joys and their pains! It's because their relationships, despite the close proximity, are superficial and don't touch what really matters in their lives. Because they can't share, they begin to feel that no one really cares. And because no one really cares, they draw tighter into their own shells and use their physical bodies as fortresses to conceal and protect their inner feelings of loneliness.

But the Bible says that Jesus created his church to be a dynamic, sharing, caring, support group; because each of us—even Jesus himself—needs such a group. Yet, today, Sunday after Sunday, all across our land, many people sit in church services or in Sunday School classes and feel as if they are the only person in the room, alienated from the others. They never get beneath the surface amenities with other people there.

A Christian psychologist named Norman Wright, who holds seminars on marriage and family relationships all across our country, says he begins these seminars by asking the participants to spend two minutes sharing with two other people their response to his statement: "This is what you need to know about my marriage in order to understand me as a person." After the two minutes, the other two can question the person who shared for one minute. Then they change places and the same procedure is followed until all three have shared and been questioned. Then Dr. Wright asks them: "How long does it take you to become acquainted to this degree with people in your church?" He says the response has varied from never less than six months to as long as ten years!

You see, the answer to loneliness is not built upon the number of casual friendships we have, but it must be built upon what the first Christians called koinonia, by which they meant a dynamic, sharing, caring fellowship—a genuine support group!

The longer I live, the more convinced I become that genuine koinonia is the most neglected, yet the most needed experience of church members today. For you see, genuine koinonia is not a man-made fellowship, but rather it is a Christ-appointed support group just as his first support group was! He is the center of it. He is the redemptive power in the group. He is the source of the healing love experienced there, and it's his love we share with each other. It's his truth we bring to bear upon each other's needs.

This is what Christ intended for the church to be every time that Christians gather together, whether it be in a large sanctuary, a Sunday School class, a choir rehearsal, an Administrative Board meeting, a meeting of the Finance Committee, or just two or three Christians meeting in a home. He intends for there to be koinonia—a Christ-appointed support group. That is, a group where Christ and Christ alone is recognized and praised for his love and redemptive power and where we care enough about each other to share our needs and bring the divine, healing love of Christ to bear upon those needs.

Just this past week God has been showing me some new ways to increase this kind of fellowship in our church. He is still dealing with me about this, but one thing he has made clear is that we must begin using our "Glory Hour" on Sunday evening in a more, dynamic, praising, sharing, caring way, so it becomes a genuine koinonia group. I'll be telling you more about it soon.

Finally, Jesus was victorious over loneliness, because he practiced the presence of God.

The Bible says that Jesus Christ emptied himself of all his divine characteristics and qualities to come to this earth as a human being to be our Redeemer. Jesus had to be wholly human like us so he could be our Savior, yet Luke tells us that when Jesus went into the wilderness to be tempted by the devil, "he was full of the Holy Spirit." By this Luke means that Jesus had all of the Spirit of God in him that it is possible for any human being to have. Jesus was not only wholly human, but he was wholly God too! The exact time when Jesus was filled with the Holy Spirit has been a running argument among Christians all down through the ages. I don't purport to know the definitive answer to that; but that he was filled with the Holy Spirit I do know!

I do know that Jesus was never lonely while he was on this earth because the Bible tells me that. I do know that he was never lonely because he was never alone on the inside where it really matters, for the Father was always with him. Jesus tells us that himself:

> *"The hour is coming, indeed it has come, when you will be scattered, every man to his home, and will leave me alone; yet I am not alone, for the Father is with me"* (Jn 16:32).

I know too that Jesus promises us that we shall never be alone either, that is, alone on the inside where it really matters, because he will come to us:

> *"I will not leave you desolate; I will come to you"* (Jn 14:18).

That's his promise to us—to all of us! To be with us on the inside where loneliness abides. He promises us that he will abide there instead. In fact, his final words in the Gospel of Matthew reiterate this promise. He promises us that we need never be alone on the inside where it really matters:

> *"And, lo, I am with you always, to the close of the age"* (Mt 28:20).

No, I don't know when Jesus was filled with the Holy Spirit or how he was filled with the Holy Spirit; because the

Bible doesn't tell us for sure. Anyway the answer's not really important, for it is only a theoretical question. The important and meaningful fact for us is that Jesus was the very Presence of God upon this earth and did whatever he had to do to be that Presence; and that he died for us, rose from the dead, and ascended into heaven so he could send us his Holy Spirit to be in us when it really matters. The important and meaningful thing is that he told us exactly *what* we must do to receive his Holy Spirit, and *when* we can expect to receive his Holy Spirit. The important and meaningful thing is that he also told us exactly how to practice the presence of God, so we shall never be alone on the inside where it really counts. And, dear friend, that's not theoretical; that is realism personified!

Oh, don't misunderstand me; we can't all be little replicas of Jesus, because he was unique—the only Son of God ever to walk upon this earth. He was never a fallen creature like us, even though he came in the likeness of our flesh. But we can be filled with his Holy Spirit to our own capacity—the capacity of a redeemed sinner. We can practice the presence of God in our own lives and never be alone on the inside where it really matters.

Jesus promises that he will not leave us desolate, that he will come to us. He promises that the Father will send the Holy Spirit to anyone who asks him (Luke 11:13).

All we have to do is to ask in faith, and to receive in faith. That is, to open our lives to him as the divine Son of God, and to accept his Spirit as the divine Spirit of God—as God with us!

John Wesley's final words before he died were, "The best of all is, God is with us!" Certainly this is the best news I can leave with you: God is with us and because of that you need never be alone again!

XXIII   *The Two Shall Become One Flesh*

Subject: Sex

Scripture: Matthew 19:1-9

Text: *Therefore a man leaves his father and his mother and cleaves to his wife, and they become one flesh. And the man and his wife were both naked, and were not ashamed* (Genesis 2:24-25).

Have you not read that he who made them from the beginning made them male and female, and said, 'For this reason a man shall leave his father and mother and be joined to his wife, and the two shall become one'? So they are no longer two but one. What therefore God has joined together, let no man put asunder (Matthew 19:4-6).

The number one problem in marriage breakup is the problem of sex, according to Dr. Philip Rice, the author of several college textbooks on marriage, sex, and child development:

"Over twenty-five years of experience in marriage counseling and teaching have convinced me that sexual difficulties do more to wreck marriages than any other single cause."[*]

Recognized authorities in the scientific study of sex, Masters and Johnson—the directors of the *Reproductive Biology Research Foundation* in St. Louis—conclude that over one-half of all married couples have some serious problems relating to sex.

---

[*] F. Philip Rice, *Sexual Problems in Marriage,* preface, p.9)

Freudian psychiatry says that sex is the strongest drive in all of us, and traces almost all of our problems back to the sexual drive. Certainly, all of us know that sex is one of the strongest drives with which we human beings are endowed. When couples marry, they fully expect that their sexual needs will be met. If they are not met, tension, frustration, anger or hurt is the result. So, as we examine how the Bible can help us with our daily problems, we would be dodging the issue if we didn't look at what so many experts say is our number one problem: sex. Can the Bible help us with our sexual problems?

We might think not from the way both the pulpit and the pew have dodged the subject of sex in the past. But on second thought, we'll see that this dodge is part of the problem. Of course the Bible can help us with the problem of sex. The Bible is God's manual for living, and sex is certainly one of the most important aspects of life.

To find this help, let's go to what Jesus says about it in the 19th chapter of Matthew, the first nine verses. (The same words are also recorded in the 10th chapter of Mark.) The Pharisees ask Jesus, "Is it lawful to divorce one's wife for any reason?" And Jesus answers,

> "Have you not read that he who made them from the beginning made them male and female, and said, 'For this reason a man shall leave his father and mother and be joined to his wife, and the two shall become one?' So they are no longer two but one. What therefore God has joined together, let no man put asunder.

> "They said to him, 'Why then did Moses command one to give a certificate of divorce, and to put her away?' He said to them, 'For your hardness of heart Moses allowed you to divorce your wives, but from the beginning it was not so. And I say to you: whoever divorces his wife, except for unchastity, and marries another, commits adultery'" (Mt 19:4-9).

222

Here, Jesus is telling us three things about sex we need to heed and to mark indelibly upon our minds and hearts.

First, Jesus is telling us that sex is of God.

Sex is part of God's plan, and is good and precious and beautiful and holy. He is telling us that sex is meant to be our #1 source of genuine pleasure and joy in life, not our #1 problem!

In his answer to the Pharisees, Jesus is quoting from the first pages of the Bible, and if you go back and read the whole passage in Genesis, you find this:

"Then the Lord God said, 'It is not good that the man should be alone; I will make him a helper fit for him.'. . . So the Lord God . . . made . . . woman and brought her to the man. Then the man said, 'This at last is bone of my bones and flesh of my flesh; she shall be called Woman, because she was taken out of Man.' Therefore a man leaves his father and his mother and cleaves to his wife, and they become one flesh. And the man and his wife are both naked, and were not ashamed" (Gen 2:18, 21-25).

What the Bible is talking about here is sex in its full dimension—the divine creation of it, the beauty of it, the purpose of it, the joy of it, the fulfillment of it, the sanctity of it. In the beginning, the Bible says, that's what sex was when it was under the lordship of God; but with the fall of man sex came under the dominion of sin and the flesh, which is the non-spiritual part of man. Consequently sex became our #1 problem.

What is the nature of our problem with sex? Sex problems fall into two categories: the physical and the psychological, and the experts tell us that by far the greatest and most prevalent problems with sex are psychological.

Now, the pulpit is no place for dealing specifically and in detail with the physical problems in sex. In the first place it's too complicated, and in the second place it is too delicate; but the pulpit is a place for recognizing such problems and for supplying you with the resources that deal with those problems from a Christian perspective. I want to suggest to you three such resources.

Several years ago, probably six or seven years ago now, on the plane from here to Los Angeles to attend a Christian conference, I sat by a medical doctor named Ed Wheat from Springdale, Arkansas. In talking with him I discovered his medical practice really finances his Christian service. In his office building he operates a free lending service of Christian tapes. When we started our own tape ministry about six years ago, our people made a trip to Springdale to study Dr. Wheat's lending library as our model. On the plane, Dr. Wheat gave me a tape which turned out to be the most explicit, yet delicately stated, discussion of the physical aspects and problems of sex, from the Christian and medical perspective I have ever heard. The tape is by Dr. Ed Wheat himself and is entitled *Sex Problems and Sex Techniques in Marriage.** You may borrow or purchase a copy of this cassette tape by writing his tape loan library. Here is the address: *Bible Believers Cassettes, Inc.,* 130 N. Spring Street, Springdale, Arkansas, 72864.

The second resource is the special book in the Bible which God has given us for the specific purpose of informing us about the beauty, pleasure, and sanctity of sex—the book we call *The Song of Solomon.* Unfortunately, because of the puritanical way the church has looked upon sex in the past, this great book has been twisted into everything but what it really is: God's instructions on how a husband and wife should respond to each other in love. First, the prudish Jewish rabbis began to say that this book was an allegory about Jehovah's love for Israel. Then, the early church fathers, following the same absurd, narrow-

---

* Dr. Wheat and his wife Gaye incorporated this material in a book, *Intended for Pleasure,* Fleming H. Revell, 1977.

minded belief that sex was intended by God only for procreation, concluded that this "Manual on Sex" for God's people spoke instead of Christ's love for his church. It is no such thing! It is simply a picture of idealized married love as God intended it. This picture of married love is written in an idiom and in symbols not familiar today, so you must have a good commentary to understand it. The best one I've found—one which treats it honestly and frankly—was published in 1977 by Thomas Nelson, Inc. The author is Joseph C. Dillow, who was here at our church five or six years ago, and talked to us about it from the manuscript which he was working on at that time. The book is entitled *Solomon on Sex*, and is subtitled *A Biblical Guide to Married Love*.

The third resource, and the best general book on all aspects of sex from the Christian perspective, is a book published in 1978 by Westminster Press. Every husband and wife should own it and read it and continue to refer to it. It's to the point; it's frank; it's clear; it's Christian. It's written by a F. Philip Rice, the Christian marriage counselor I quoted earlier, and is entitled *Sexual Problems in Marriage.*

Because the church and most Christians in the past have treated sex as something dirty to be avoided, a not-to-be-discussed taboo, many adults today grew up feeling that "nice boys and girls don't think or talk about sex," and therefore have found it extremely difficult adjusting to the intimacies of married life. Likewise, they have found it almost impossible to find the freedom which is absolutely essential to satisfactory and fulfilling sexual relations. The consequences have been psychological hang-ups and phobias for many married people, such as fear of being seen nude, insisting upon darkness for love-making, reluctance to discuss sex with their mate, unwillingness to even find out what truly pleases him or her sexually.

Well, the Bible has no such hang-ups. Read the *Song of Solomon* as Dr. Dillow interprets and deals with these subjects frankly, but delicately. The wise author of the

225

Song of Solomon knew that sex is of God. Sex is a part of God's plan. Sex is good, precious, beautiful, and holy. God intends for sex to be our #1 source of genuine joy and pleasure in life, not our #1 problem. Only when we grasp this truth and internalize it into our own way of life can we rise above our psychological hang-ups and phobias about sex. That's the first truth Jesus tells us. The second truth is this:

God created sex for marriage, not to play around with!

Hear what Jesus says again:

"'For this reason a man shall leave his father and mother and be joined to his wife, and the two shall become one.' So they are no longer two but one. What God has joined together, let no man put asunder" (Mt 19:5, 6).

Hear that phrase again: "What God has joined together." Dear friend, that means holy matrimony. God created us man and woman, and the Bible says he provided a way for us to be joined together through a covenant with him, a covenant where both husband and wife are committed to God. Because of this commitment to God, each is then committed to the other. This mutual commitment God blesses with the miracle of "making them become as one flesh." That's holy matrimony!

We noted earlier how our prudish attitude toward sex has caused untold sexual problems, but here we see that the opposite is also true. In an effort to answer this ridiculous prudish attitude toward sex, some shallow-thinking and biblically illiterate intellectuals have gone to the other extreme and said: "Anything goes sexually. Do whatever you feel like doing, with whomever you feel like doing it!" This means, of course, a free license for premarital sex and adultery. As a result, psychiatrists, ministers, and marriage counselors are reaping the catastrophic results of such nonsense as we are being deluged by the battle casualties of such sexual promiscuity.

God created sex as part of his great gift of holy matrimony, and to treat it as simply a plaything without commitment, love, and responsibility, is to invite disaster. To go against God's plan and commit adultery or engage in premarital sex is to invite deep emotional and psychological problems which can keep a person from ever experiencing the joyful pleasure and heavenly bliss God intends for us to have sexually with our God-joined mates.

One reliable, scientific study compared wives who were virgins when they married with those who were sexually experienced. Although those who were virgins were slower in sexual adjustment at first, within two months they had caught up with and then rapidly outstripped the others. (Rice, *Sexual Problems in Marriage* p. 20) Why? The virgins were free of the emotional and psychological hang-ups and could freely mature in their new sexual relationship. While the others were bound to their past by their guilt and fears.

A 1977 survey of one hundred marriage counselors across the country, show that one half of their cases involved adultery. No matter how hard couples try, the marriage is never the same after that. Sex becomes more and more difficult; during sex the mind begins to fantasize what was happening when one's mate had sex with someone else. Only a genuine rebirth experience which gives both husband and wife "the mind of Christ" can clear the past through forgiveness and give sex that stamp of holiness it is meant to have within the marital bonds.

The best insurance you can have against sexual problems after you are married is to resist sex before you are married, and to recognize that God created sex for holy matrimony and not to play around with! If this is true, then why are there still so many sexual problems among good Christian couples, who reserve their sexual relations for their mates and who did not play around with premarital sex?

Jesus answers this question as he concludes his dialogue with the Pharisees about marriage and divorce, and that's the third truth he is teaching us:

Christian couples struggle with sexual problems because of their hardness of heart.

The question the Pharisees asked Jesus was concerning divorce, but remember the #1 cause of divorce is sexual problems. Jesus says:

"For your hardness of heart Moses allowed you to divorce . . . but from the beginning it was not so" (Mt 19:8).

From the beginning God intended for husband and wife to "become one flesh." That is, God intended them to experience a closeness and a oneness which cannot be torn asunder.

When several thousand married women were asked what types of physical expression by their husbands gave them the greatest pleasure and satisfaction, do you know what was #1 by a landslide? They said that the closeness and the warmth or the feeling of oneness with their partner was by far the most important. Men, too, need this same closeness and warmth, this feeling of oneness or something is lacking in their lives.

Yet, so often sex is used for everything else but this. Often we human beings can act more like animals of the field than creatures created in the image of God. When animals get angry and fight, they always go for the genitals because they know this is the most vulnerable spot. Husbands and wives often do the same thing when their hearts begin to grow hard! A woman's most precious possession is her femininity and a man's is his masculinity. A hard-hearted woman will try to undermine her husband's masculinity by ridicule and shame and a hard-hearted husband will try to destroy his wives femininity by his cutting words and acts.

228

Often when a person's heart grows hard, he or she will begin to use sex as a weapon, instead of the tender gift of God it is meant to be. This is sexual sabotage. There are hundreds of ways to do it: picking quarrels, making demands, feigning headaches or other ailments, "It's too late,""I'm too tired," bringing up anxiety-provoking topics like money, watching late TV, being uncooperative, and on and on.

Dr. Rice, the Christian counselor who wrote the book I mentioned earlier, tells about one woman who had been using such sexual sabotage; then she was called for jury duty. The case was the murder trial of a husband who had brutally mutilated his wife with a butcher knife in a moment of rage because of similar tactics. After the trial this woman came to Dr. Rice for counseling and her first words were: "I never realized how important it is, and what a fool I've been. Tell me how I can be a better lover!"

The Bible says there's only one way to be a good lover and that is to be completely aware of your mate's needs and to do whatever you must do to meet those needs without squelching your own deep desires and your own need for fulfillment. This is exactly why God created sex for marriage alone; only the love of God is capable of doing this. Only the love of God is holy and capable of knowing our real needs and completely meeting those needs. Only when a couple has made a holy covenant with God and offered themselves as instruments for his selfless love to each other can this genuine closeness, warmth, and oneness which meets the others' real need become a reality day-after-day. Only when a husband and wife have made such a covenant with God and have actually become instruments for his love can sex become the genuine joy—the pure, exciting pleasure that God wants it to be. But when they do make such a covenant and offer themselves as such instruments for God's love, they begin to experience the closest thing to heaven that is possible here on earth: the miracle of the two becoming one flesh! You see, heaven is being where God is;

and God's eternal love in each of them joins them together in a precious union which God designed for this very purpose! I pray that you will not settle for any cheap substitute for the real thing!

Subject: Homosexuality

Scripture: Romans 1:16-32

Text: *Do not be deceived; neither the immoral... nor*
            homosexuals will inherit the kingdom of God
            (I Corinthians 6:9-10).

            For I am not ashamed of the gospel: it is the
            power of God for salvation to everyone who
            has faith . . . (Romans 1:16).

            Therefore, if anyone is in Christ, he is a new
            creation; the old has passed away, behold,
            the new has come (II Corinthians 5:17).

One of the most explosive questions the church has had to face in our country is one which has come to the forefront in the last decade or so, and is still very prevalent and real today. By explosive I mean something which actually threatens to split the mainline denominations right down the middle. Certainly, no other question has been this explosive since the question of slavery during the Civil War. The question I'm talking about is this: Should the church ordain self-avowed, practicing homosexuals? This question has caused great unrest and turmoil in our own United Methodist Church as it has in the United Presbyterian Church. Almost every main-line denomination as well as the Roman Catholic Church has created study groups to consider the question, and heated campaigns are now being waged by gay caucuses throughout the church-at-large to recognize homosexuality as an "alternative life-style" for Christians.

I can't remember an American entertainer being more harassed and maligned than Anita Bryant was when she took the lead in Dade County, Florida to keep self-avowed, practicing homosexuals from having the legal right to teach her children in school. Because she dared to stand up for her belief in biblical principles, she has suffered much more damage to her career through boycotts and ostracism by certain businesses and networks than did those who openly supported the communists during the Vietnam War.

Only a week or so ago, we read in the paper about a television station denying time to a Texas evangelist simply because he stated in a sermon that the Bible calls homosexuality a sin.

Since 1968, an entirely new denomination of active homosexuals who profess to be Evangelical and Pentecostal in their theology, the Metropolitan Community Church, has gathered congregations in every major American city, including our own. In 1969 a Catholic priest founded a similar church for gay Catholics, called Dignity, and Jews also have their own religious organizations for Jewish homosexuals. In 1973 an ecumenical National Task Force on Gay People in the Church was officially recognized by the governing board of The National Council of Churches.

I say all this to make this point: This is not simply a theoretical or an isolated problem, even if you are not homosexual yourself—and only somewhere between 5% and 10% of our population is actually homosexual in their orientation. This is a real, live problem facing every Christian and every church and it is imperative that we be aware of it, acquaint ourselves with the facts, and know what is the Christian approach to homosexuality and to ordaining homosexuals and the Christian attitude toward the homosexual. That's what I want to deal with now. And I want to do it by asking four questions and going to the Bible for our answers to these four questions.

1. What is homosexuality and what does the Bible say about it?
2. What is the Bible's answer for homosexuality?

3. Should self-avowed, practicing homosexuals be ordained in the church of Jesus Christ? Why or why not?
4. What should be the Christian's attitude toward homosexuality and toward the homosexual?

First, what is homosexuality and what does the Bible say about it?

It's very important that we get our terms straight and know what we're talking about. Homosexuality is an act—it is a sexual act between members of the same sex. The word "homo" means "alike" or "equal to." So, a homosexual is a man or woman who engages in sexual acts with a member of the same sex. I have stated this definition very carefully, so the emphasis is put where it belongs—on behavior, rather than persons, on acts, rather than tendencies or attractions. This keeps us from categorizing and labeling people simply because we don't like their movements, or speech, or dress, or something else about them. Unless you make this distinction between acts and the people who commit them, you can never understand what the Bible says about this subject.

In the Bible, seven scriptures deal directly with homosexuality.

Two Old Testament stories:
Genesis 19:4-11
Judges 19:22-26

Five specific texts:
Leviticus 18:22; 20:13
Romans 1: 26-27
I Corinthians 6:9-11
I Timothy 1:8-11.

There are many other scriptures which deal indirectly with homosexuality, such as the creation story, which shows that the divine order calls for sex only between man and wife. In none of these seven scriptures is homosexuality approved, but rather the Bible specifically speaks of it as sin, as unnatural, and an abomination before God. In Leviticus the penalty for homosexual behavior is death. The passage in Romans is found in what is commonly referred to as "the sin section" of that book, where Paul illustrates what sin has done to man. The I Corinthians passage specifically says that "homosexuals cannot inherit the kingdom of God." The I Timothy passage speaks of homosexuals as "ungodly and sinners." Any person who reads the Bible honestly must conclude that the Bible says homosexuality is a sinful act!

Why does anyone commit a sinful act of any kind? The Bible is clear in answering this question: A person commits a sinful act because he is first a sinner. That is, it's not the sinful act which makes the person a sinner, but it's the fact he is a sinner which makes him commit the sinful act. It is giving that part of his nature which rebels against God control of his thoughts and actions that causes him to sin. It is refusing to give that part of his nature which is God's image within him control over his thoughts and actions that is at the root of his sinning. The sinful act can take many forms, and Paul lists many of them for us in these passages of scripture: idolatry, drunkenness, fornication, adultery, homosexuality, murder, lying, etc. But the basic cause for all of them is the same: our sinful nature.

What causes one person to commit one kind of sinful act such as homosexuality, and another person to commit another kind such as fornication or drunkenness, is basically a study in psychology. Psychology has helped us understand that certain kinds of home environments and experiences will give rise to tendencies for specific sins. And, of course, the devil is going to deal with us at our weakest points. If we have a tendency toward homosexuality, this is where he is going to attack us. If our tendency is toward lying or drunkenness or fornication or adultery, then this is where he will attack us. But, let's not be deceived; the basic, underlying cause for all these sinful acts is the same: our sinful nature. We are sinners! We are controlled by our own "flesh" instead of by the spirit of God!

What is the Bible's answer for homosexuality?

According to the Bible, the way to deal with sinful acts, no matter what they are, is to deal first with the basic problem: our sinful nature. According to the Bible we do this in five specific steps:

- Recognize that we are sinners and the acts we are committing are sinful and contrary to God's will for us. Honestly face up to what we're doing!
- Repent of our condition and our acts.
- Confess to God and acknowledge our weakness.
- Accept forgiveness by accepting Jesus Christ through faith as our own righteousness.
- Begin leading a new life as a spiritual being in the power of the Holy Spirit.

Jesus summed up all five of these in just two steps in his opening words as he began his ministry:

"The time is fulfilled, and the kingdom of God is at hand; repent, and believe in the gospel" (Mk 1:15).

- *Repent*, which includes both recognizing and confessing, and
- *Believe* in the good news, which includes both accepting forgiveness and beginning a new life in the power of Christ.

"Repent and believe" is our Lord's formula for victory over sin—any sin! Repent—turn away from the old life, and Believe—turn to a new life with Christ.

This is all that is needed, because the victory which Christ won over sin on the Cross was a complete victory! There is no aspect of sin that was not defeated there. There is no aspect of sin in our lives he cannot handle and get rid of, if we repent and believe. The only sin in our life he cannot handle is the sin we refuse to recognize and confess

235

as sin. The "unforgivable sin" is the one for which we refuse to repent and seek his help.

Should self-avowed, practicing homosexuals be ordained as ministers in the church of Jesus Christ? Why or why not?

The Bible's answer is an emphatic "No!" Because the self-affirmed, practicing homosexual refuses to recognize that he is a sinner; he refuses to confess his sin and repent of it; he refuses to seek forgiveness for it; and he refuses Christ's Spirit for leading a new life. And this must be the starting place for all who would follow Christ and be his spokesmen on earth!

Dear friend, you can't give to others something you don't have! A minister is ordained to be a leader in the church and to pass on to others what he has freely received, which is the forgiving and regenerating grace of Jesus Christ! A minister is called to preach and teach God's word as truth, and if he refuses to accept it as truth for his own life, how can he proclaim and explain it as truth for others? A minister is called to be an instrument of God's healing love to others, and if he turns his back on this healing love himself, how can he be an instrument for others?

The quickest way to decimate the Church of Jesus Christ on earth is to select leaders who do not accept the Bible as the word of God and as our truth for living, and who turn their back on the grace of Jesus Christ for release from sin and the power to lead a new life. This is exactly the position of the unrepentant, self-affirmed, practicing homosexual person. Now, it's a totally different story for the repentant, non-practicing homosexual.

What should be the Christian's attitude toward homosexuality and toward the homosexual?

At the outset I was very careful in defining homosexuality, to make a distinction between the act and the person committing the act. I said that unless you make this distinction, you cannot understand what the Bible is telling us about this subject. This is because the Bible says that our attitude toward homosexuality and our attitude toward the homosexual himself should be exactly the opposite. We must hate and condemn the act as a sinful act—a part of the work of Satan on earth which must be destroyed. On the other hand, we must love and affirm the person as a person for whom Christ died and who rightfully belongs to Christ.

It is absolutely essential that we get our thinking straight about this distinction if we are to be Christian witnesses for our Lord, and if, as a church, we are to be the Body of Christ on earth. It is essential for our great denominations and other mainline denominations to get their thinking straight about this very explosive question, or it's going to cause catastrophic and tragic splits in the church that will take decades to heal and correct.

So, I want to conclude by simply stating what I understand to be the biblical and Christian position, for both individuals and the church, to this explosive question on homosexuality and the homosexual. It can be summarized in seven brief statements.

Homosexual practice is always sin and we must never compromise this biblical truth by tolerating and encouraging it as an alternative lifestyle. The act of homosexuality must always be hated and condemned by the Christian and the church because it is sin and by sin I mean contrary to God's will.

It therefore follows that **self-avowed, unrepentant, practicing homosexuals must never be put into positions of leadership in the church**, and most especially the ordained ministry, for they would lead the people of God into false teachings and apostasy.

At the same time we must recognize that **in the eyes of God homosexuality is no worse sin than the**

237

other sins listed by Paul in the same breath, such as lying, gossiping, fornication, drunkenness, adultery, idolatry and the like. Christ died on the Cross that we might be saved from all these sins, so we can be God's people and do God's will.

The church must always be a hospital for all sinners, including practicing homosexuals. That is, homosexuals must be welcomed here and affirmed here as persons for whom Christ died, and they should be counseled to search their consciences in order to move toward repentance and a new lifestyle through the power of the living Christ. The homosexual must always be accepted, loved, and affirmed by Christians and by the church as a person for whom Christ died.

When practicing homosexuals do repent and do turn to a new lifestyle in Christ, they should be welcomed into all aspects of leadership in the Church, including the ordained ministry. There can be no better witness for Christ than the redeemed who have found power in him for new life! The Psalmist sings, "Let the redeemed of the Lord say so!" and this should also be the song of the church for all who will sing it! I want to share with you a note I received from a member of this congregation not long ago:

I am a homosexual, have been and will be for the rest of my life. I accepted Jesus Christ eight years ago and haven't been the same since. God is still perfecting me and he's got a long way to go. But I haven't had a homosexual encounter or experience for several years now (used to be several times every week—how's that for a miracle). My marriage is singularly blessed. And growing in God's word is exciting.

Homosexuals do change! But before this can happen there must be both a two-way repentance and a two-way change in lifestyle. That is, there must be repentance both on the part of the church and on the part of its gay membership. There must be a new lifestyle by both church members and repentant gays. By this I mean the church must repent of confusing persons with acts, and thus hating and condemning persons instead of sinful acts. The church must also repent for its failure to minister the redeeming love of Jesus Christ to the practicing homosexual and for casting him out for the wolves of the world to devour with their false teachings and perverted appetites.

On the other hand, the gay membership must also repent of turning away from the word of God and the truth of Christ to try to justify themselves in their sinful acts. They must repent of turning their backs on Jesus Christ, the only name in all heaven and earth who can redeem them and justify them before God and man.

But repentance alone is not enough. The church must turn from a lifestyle of fear and avoidance of the homosexual to a lifestyle of assurance and acceptance that reaches out to bring the healing power of Christ to bear upon their lives. The greatest witness the Church could give to the gay community and to the unsaved world is the witness of the genuine power of the Gospel. As far at the gay community is concerned, this means the power to free the church of its fear and hate and the power to free the homosexual of his guilt and bondage. But there's another side to that coin too.

The homosexual who claims to be Christian must believe in and accept this power of the living Christ—the Holy Spirit—to become a new creation in Christ. "Behold the old has passed away and the new has come" must be his lifestyle!

Finally, all of us must accept the biblical truth that **all of this is possible only through living lives of grace!** The truth is, both the Church and the gay community have approached the explosive issue through legalism instead of grace. That's why almost no progress has been made. The gays have legalistically tried to justify themselves in their sin. The Church has legalistically tried to condemn all gays to outer darkness instead of showing them the light of Christ and how they can follow this light through grace to victory!

If we Methodists would just return to the solid foundation upon which John Wesley founded our denomination we could lead out in solving this explosive problem. That foundation is the proper use of the means of grace as the only lifestyle for a Christian! For example, many practicing homosexuals say they have prayed to change their lifestyle, but they cannot do it; so now they have just accepted the gay life as the lifestyle meant for them. Well, dear friend, there is more to the means of grace than just a fleeting prayer. The means of grace include disciplined and regular worship, serious Bible study under competent leadership, partaking of the sacraments regularly and meaningfully, and genuine Christian fellowship and support in small, redemptive groups. That's what it really means to believe and to put your faith in action!

Again, you can't give away something you don't have yourself; and how many of us—the people called Methodist—honestly and sincerely use these means of grace regularly so we can live a life of grace? Let's resolve to get our own house in order first. Then, as in the first century Christians, and in John Wesley and the people called Methodists in the 18th century, the world will begin to see in us the power they need, and others will begin to seek this same redeeming power in their own lives.

You see, living a life of grace is not only God's answer for the explosive homosexual problem; even more important, it is God's answer for making his church into the redemptive fellowship and the genuine Body of Christ on earth it was created to be!

Subject: Anger and Hostility

Scripture: Ephesians 4:17-32

Text: *Be angry but do not sin; do not let the sun go
            down on your anger, and give no opportunity
            to the devil* (Ephesians 4:26-37).

            *Let all bitterness and wrath and anger . . . be
            put away from you, with all malice, and be
            kind to one another, tenderhearted, forgiving
            one another, as God in Christ forgave you*
            (Ephesians 4:31-32).

How can the Bible help us with the problem of anger
and hostility? Fortunately, the Bible has much truth
for us in the 4th chapter of Ephesians, beginning
with the 17th verse to the end of the chapter, verse 32.
Here, after giving us the key to handling all of our emotional
problems by telling us to put off our old nature, which
belongs to our former manner of life, and to be renewed in
the spirit of our minds, and put on the new nature, created
after the likeness of God, Paul deals directly with anger and
hostility. He begins by saying:

*"Be angry but do not sin; do not let the sun go down
on your anger, and give no opportunity to the devil"*
(Eph 4:26-27).

Then, he goes on to tell us exactly how to deal with this
problem.

What is Paul saying to us? He is giving us the four
truths we must understand in order to handle anger and
hostility in our lives. So let's look at these four truths and
see how we can apply them to our own lives. First Paul
says,

"Be angry, but do not sin" (Eph 4:26a).

Here, Paul specifically distinguishes between anger and sin. The first truth he is giving us is this:

Anger itself is not sin, but unless we handle it right it will become sin.

Most Christians are terribly confused here. Most Christians actually look upon anger itself as unchristian and something they should avoid at all costs. Yet, we are repeatedly told in the Gospels about the anger of Jesus. In the third chapter of Mark, when Jesus enters the synagogue on the Sabbath and finds a man with a withered arm, the authorities prohibit his breaking their Sabbath law and healing on the Sabbath. How did Jesus respond?

"He looked around at them with anger, grieved at their hardness of heart . . . " (Mk 3:5).

Then Jesus heals the man. This defiance of their law, in turn, makes the Pharisees angry at Jesus and they begin plotting how they can destroy him.

Seven times in chapter 23 of Matthew, Jesus' anger blazes forth with the words, "Woe to you scribes and Pharisees, hypocrites!" And all of us know how Jesus angrily drove the greedy temple sellers out of the Temple with a whip and overturned their money tables.

The Bible also tells us that, not only Christ, but also God the Father is at home with anger. In fact, the Bible attributes anger to God five times as often as to man! And of all the targets for God's anger the most frequent is Israel, the chosen people of God.

If we're ever going to learn how to handle our anger, we must begin by dropping the idea that anger itself is sin, for it is not! In fact, it's just the opposite! Anger is power! Anger is meant to be one of our greatest allies, not an enemy! Anger is the emotion God has given us to energize us and motivate us to do what we're supposed to do! Anger is as

244

healthy a reaction to being emotionally hurt as feeling pain is to being physically hurt. Something is wrong with us if we never feel anger. We should love ourselves as children of God and love others enough to "see red" when we're confronted with selfishness, violence, and injustice. Anger energizes us to change what should be changed, to cooperate with God in redeeming this sin-sick world, so his kingdom can come on earth as it is in heaven. I am extremely leery of people who are so even-tempered that they never "see red" about anything! I'm leery of them, because either they are so insensitive to the needs of the people around them and the needs of the Church of Jesus Christ that they don't really care, or they have so repressed their anger that they are eaten up with raging hostility.

This brings us to the other aspect of Paul's exhortation to "be angry, but do not sin." When does anger turn into sin? It becomes sin, says Paul, when either one of two things happens:

You lose control of your anger, or
You repress it and it turns into hostility.

I dealt with the Bible's answer for anger-turned-hostility in the sermon entitled, *God's Answer for Emotional Cancer,* where we dealt with the underlying causes of hostility—resentment and bitterness, the most debilitating and deadly of all emotional diseases. Let me remind you that every experience of anger in which you blame someone else for that anger will eventually become hostility and therefore sin, unless you learn to handle it! In that sermon, we followed step by step the Bible's cure for the disease of hostility. So, take your emotional temperature and if you feel you are suffering from an attack of this deadly disease then refer to that sermon.

As you take your temperature, remember we human beings continually try to disguise and hide this illness from ourselves by using dozens of euphemisms for it. You're coming down with a case of hostility if you find any of these symptoms:

You feel irritated at someone else,
You are frustrated by them,
You are judgmental toward them,
You feel let down, disappointed, critical or used by them.

God's Answer for Emotional Cancer prescribes what you must do to be cured.

We also need to practice preventive medicine, and see what we must do in order to avoid ever being stricken with the disease of hostility in the first place, or with that other malady, an uncontrollable temper, which is just as deadly and, incidentally, incapacitates faster! Paul says we must do three things to keep from coming down with either disease. These are the second, third, and fourth truths Paul shows us.

To keep anger from turning into hostility, or to keep it from getting out of control, we must handle it daily.

Here's the way Paul says it:

"Do not let the sun go down on your anger" (Eph 4: 26b).

The Parable of the Prodigal Son is perhaps the best biblical illustration of "letting the sun go down" on both uncontrollable anger and repressed anger and what happens when you do. The Prodigal Son got angry and couldn't control it, so he stamped off into the far country, eventually becoming mired down in filth and degradation, described by the Bible as "living with the pigs." This must always be the end, when a person permits his emotions to control him instead of exercising control himself.

On the other hand, the elder brother repressed his anger and stayed home. As the days passed his anger turned into the dread disease of hostility, breaking out in resentment and bitterness, and stealing all of the joy and excitement out of his life. This, too, must always be the end when we bury our anger and fail to heed the Bible's admonition, "Never let the sun go down on your anger."

How much better if both boys could have sat down with their father at a conference around the dining room table and said, "Dad, I'm mad and I don't know how to handle it. Help me."

Much of the uncontrollable temper and hostility we find in families today could be avoided, if families would stop eating before their televisions sets and begin using the family meal for what it was intended to be, "The Reconciliation Hour!" This is why Jesus chose a meal for the institution of Holy Communion. The goal of every family meal should not be just to feed our physical bodies, but it should also be to feed our deeper needs, which are right relationships in our families! Before this can happen all members of a family need to understand that the object is not "to tell others off" and vent our spleens, but the object is reconciliation built upon forgiveness, genuine "holy communion." The father, or head of the house, should be in charge and the rules should be kept simple and fair. The motto should be "Our family never lets the sun go down on anger," because as Christians our goal is reconciliation built on forgiveness, not alienation through uncontrollable temper and hostility.

This is the only way I know to actually keep "the sun from going down on your anger," that is, to keep it from becoming sin. If someone else, outside of the family, has ruffled you, and made you "see red" that day, then get in the habit of sharing this and praying about it as a family. Learn to be what the family was created to be: a genuine support group, so "the sun will never go down on your anger." That's the Bible's first prescription of preventive medicine to keep us from coming down with uncontrollable temper and hostility! The next truth is this:

247

Learn to use your anger as it is meant to be used, which is to attack problems, not people.

Paul says it like this:

> ". . . give no opportunity to the devil . . . Let no evil talk come out of your mouth . . . Let all bitterness and wrath and anger and clamor and slander be put away from you, with all malice, and be kind to one another, tenderhearted, forgiving one another, as God in Christ forgave you" (Eph 4:27-32).

You see, anger must have a target and that target is all-important! What you choose as the target for your anger actually determines whether it is your ally or your enemy! The Bible is clear on this, and it says that we must never make people the target for our anger, for that is giving the devil the opportunity he wants to entrap us in sin!

This was the big difference between the anger of Jesus and the anger of the Pharisees that Sabbath day in the synagogue. The target for Jesus' anger was the injustice and heresy of legalism which prohibited healing on the Sabbath. But the target for the Pharisees' anger was the man Jesus himself, and they began plotting his death. The anger of Jesus actually energized him and motivated him to attack the problem of legalism, revealing to us the greatest gift we have ever received: the grace of God, enabling us to live by grace and not by law! On the other hand, the Pharisees' anger zeroed in on a person; it was aimed at Jesus. Therefore, not only did their anger eventually destroy the Pharisees completely, it provoked them to commit the most vile sin ever committed: the crucifixion of the Savior of our world.

What is the real target for your anger? That's the important question. Is it a problem or is it a person? Your answer is the key to whether you are in God's will or out of it, whether you are letting this great emotion be your helper or your enemy.

It's at this very point where so-called "group therapy" often is the very opposite of that, and is "group sickness" instead. Many misled therapists have the mistaken idea that just "ventilating anger so you can get it off your chest" is the real way to handle anger. How absurd! It all depends upon the target for your ventilation, and whether you have control of the ventilation or it has control of you!

Let's take a modern day illustration. A great source of anger ever since I entered the ministry—and it even makes me "see red" just to think of it now—is what the church has done to the healing ministry of Jesus Christ, which Jesus himself bequeathed to the church as his body on earth. The church was commissioned by Jesus to carry on his healing ministry. Yet the church has dropped it like a hot potato, and most ministers and church leaders won't touch it. This is the cause of much impotency in the church today. I look around at people hurting everywhere and I see church leaders looking askance and labeling as fanatic those who follow our Lord's instructions—laying on hands, anointing with oil, and praying the prayer of faith for healing, as God's word commands. I think I know how Jesus felt that day in the synagogue. My anger begins to boil up within me and I begin to see red—bright red! Now, I could ventilate that anger until doomsday by being critical of bishops, district superintendents, brother Methodist ministers, and leaders of boards and agencies and everyone else who happens to be in the way—which, by the way, is what the natural man in me wants to do every time I "see red" about this. But that would only show my own stupidity and my lack of self-control. I would have chosen the wrong target for my anger——I'd have chosen people!

On the other hand, if I make the problem itself the target for my anger, it will energize me. It will motivate me to faithfully obey my Lord in teaching you, our congregation, all of the biblical truths about the healing ministry. It will prompt me to help you learn how to pray for the sick, and actually lead you into doing it here in the sanctuary and in your homes and in our hospitals in Tulsa. Then the Lord will honor that obedience with answered prayer, with healing for our people! Even those who prompted my anger may begin to look at what is happening here and begin to whisper, "You know, God's not really dead. Maybe that's not such a bad idea after all!"

Yes, anger can be one of the greatest weapons in this world for God, when its target is a problem! But it can also be a deadly sin and a weapon of the devil when its target is people!

Finally, the only way we can make anger an ally instead of an enemy is to put it under the dominion of God's Holy Spirit in order to give it divine control and direction.

Paul tells us not to grieve the Holy Spirit, but to:

"Put off your old nature which belongs to your former manner of life . . . and be renewed in the spirit of your minds, and put on the new nature, created after the likeness of God . . ." (Eph 4:22-24).

That's the real difference between a person who cannot control his temper or is filled with hostility, and a Christian! There is lack of self-control or hostility because the person is controlled by his "flesh," which the Bible calls "the natural man." He is controlled by the "flesh" instead of by God's Holy Spirit!

God gave us anger as one of the most powerful weapons we can wield in this earthly battle against evil, but like nuclear weapons of our day, if it is not kept under proper control, it will destroy us instead of the enemy! As far as the Bible is concerned there can be no doubt about what that proper control is: it is the Holy Spirit of God! It is Divine Control!

As long as we remain what the Bible calls "a natural man," refusing the divine control Christ offers us, I don't care how hard you try, your anger is going to be under the control of your "flesh." It will be directed at people instead of at problems. The sun will continue to go down on your anger day after day as it gets more explosive or festers into a deadly malignant growth filled with resentment, bitterness, and hostility until it ultimately destroys you.

The only preventive medicine, says the Bible, is a new nature. You must become what the Bible calls "a spiritual man," under divine control. You can do that, says the Bible, only by a specific act of your will! In faith, you actually will the living Spirit of Jesus Christ to enter your being and to take complete dominion over your mind, body, and emotions. Then, for the first time your anger is under the right control—divine control—and begins to be the powerful ally for you that it is meant to be. Then, when you "see red" you will also "see victory!" Then, Christ Jesus will say to you:

> "Well done, my good and faithful servant, you have finally learned my answer for anger. Enter into the joy of the Lord!"

Subject: Stress and Tension

Scripture: Matthew 12:24-30, 36-43

Text: *Let both grow together until the harvest . . .*
             (Matthew 13:30a).

Medical researchers tell us that even the calmest of us use at least 50% of our personal energy just dealing with the stress and tension in our lives. If we can learn how to stop wasting so much of our energy dealing with the problem of stress, and begin using that same energy creatively and constructively, just think of how much more we can accomplish both for ourselves and for God!

What is stress and tension? (I use the two words interchangeably.) They are simply the names for the civil war which goes on in our minds and our nervous systems when we want one thing but get something else. For example, I always want to have my sermon finalized on Friday, and if something happens on Friday to keep this from happening it triggers a battle within me called stress or tension. Most of us really want to get along with our mate and our children; if we don't, then the battle of stress begins. If you want to get to work at 8:00, but the traffic makes you thirty minutes late, the result is stress! You plan to turn out so much work today, but you're already thirty minutes late starting. Then interruptions steal another thirty minutes from you; so tension is gnawing at you all day long. You plan to have dinner on the table at 6:00, but Johnny has been such a little demon all day that you're already past your deadline and not even started, so you're filled with tension and stress. We all want health, but sometimes we get sickness; and that's not all we get for we get stress along with it.

The cause of stress is usually one of two things, or both of them combined: time and relationships—time deadlines and conflict with people! God created time to be our servant for our good, but so often it's just the opposite. It becomes our tyrant and our worst enemy, simply because we don't know how to handle it!

The same is true with relationships. God set us in community—family, church, society, and nation—because we need each other. But again this community can become the source of our most painful hurts and the cause for constant stress and tension unless we learn how to handle our relationships right.

When we want one thing but get something else, the result is stress and tension. So, it should be apparent why we spend half of our energy simply dealing with stress. Is there a way we can cut this energy loss and operate more efficiently? The Bible answers that question with an emphatic "Yes!" The clearest answer is in our Lord's *Parable of the Wheat and the Weeds*. Jesus says that living in God's kingdom may be compared to a man who sows good wheat seed in his field, but while he is sleeping his enemy comes and sows weeds among the wheat. When the seeds sprout, the servants see both wheat and weeds in the field and say to their master: "Sir, do you want us to go and pull up the weeds?" The master answers, "No, for in pulling up the weeds you will also root up the wheat. Let them grow together until harvest time, then I will make the separation. Then the weeds will be burned and the wheat stored safely in my barn." When Jesus interprets this parable for us, he says that the man who sows the good seed is the Son of man, the field is the world, the good seed are his followers, the enemy is Satan, the weeds are Satan's followers, and the harvest is Judgment Day.

Now, what does all of this mean for you and me in our lives today?

First, Jesus wants us to see that there is no way we can avoid stress and tension in this life!

To live in this world is to live with stress and tension, because there is a real battle going on between Christ and Satan for our very lives. The enemy doesn't lie down and play dead the moment we accept Christ. In fact, that just makes him fight harder for our souls. The first thing we must recognize before we can find God's answer for stress is the fact that in this world there are always some weeds among the wheat! There are no perfect fields!

Some people think that when they become Christians they're supposed to act as if everything were 100% perfect. Consequently, they usually go around with a silly grin on their faces playing "make believe" with the world, while the raging civil war within them gets more fierce and more deadly every day.

Of course, the man in our parable who sowed the seed wanted a perfect field; but he got something else, so there is no way he can avoid stress. But there is a way he can live with it and handle it instead of it handling him. How? First, by being honest and recognizing it rather than putting a silly grin on his face and walking through the field saying, "Why, those sweet little weeds won't hurt anything. I'm just sooooo happy! I can't even see the weeds!" No! That's not our Lord's way. In this parable the sower represents Jesus and he never pretends there are no weeds among the wheat. He knows that to live in this world is to live in the imperfect field of stress and tension, because this world is a battleground and no one can avoid being in the battle. All of us must come face-to-face with tension points every day, because in this world we must live with time and we must live with people.

Those who research this sort of thing tell us that the most dangerous time for blow-ups in every family is right before the evening meal. Mother has about had it, but still she must meet the deadline of dinner. The kids are about

255

played out, but now they are going stronger than ever on nervous energy: interrupting, getting under mother's feet, hungry, and irritable. Dad is exhausted from the harried day at the job and desperately needs some peace and quiet. Instead he finds bedlam and a plea for help from her whom he thought agreed to be his helpmate.

Mother wants to be left alone, but she is getting exactly the opposite. The kids want to eat, but they can't. Dad wants to relax peacefully, but there's a war going on around him.

Now, that's what I mean by tension points: people wanting one thing but getting something else. Right in the middle of it all are the two culprits: time and relationships! Time deadlines and conflict with people! We get tense because we want to do something in a particular time frame and we can't, or we want one kind of relationship but get another. Now, since living in this world means that we must live in time and we must relate to people, it also means that stress and tension are always part of living! There is no way you can avoid it! No matter where you go or what you do, there always will be some weeds among the wheat! That's the first truth to chalk up in your mind and remember. The second truth is the natural consequence of the first:

All of us are naturally inclined to be "weed pickers."

Notice that everyone except the person representing Jesus wanted to rush in and snatch up the weeds. That's natural. When there are weeds in the field, our natural inclination is to think we must go and pick the weeds and throw them out. That's the way it is with natural man. But the Bible says that's not the way it is with the Son of man, or with those who are recreated in his image! "The second lesson we must learn," Jesus tells us, "is to control that compulsion to be a weed picker; for in picking the weeds we will also root up the wheat and destroy the very thing we

256

want the most!" And to follow Christ means to turn from our natural inclination to the mind of Christ.

In our own day, psychologists and psychiatrists are continually reaffirming this truth which Jesus revealed so plainly two thousand years ago. Oh, they put it in different words, but they continually tell us that the number one key to motivation and thus success in life is self-esteem, that is, the image we have of ourselves. Dr. Maslow puts it at the top of our hierarchy of needs, right below self-actualization, which is realization of our potential. For many people, however, this self-image is destroyed at a very early age by parents or parent substitutes who are "weed-pickers." Consequently, the rest of life for these people becomes an uphill climb trying to rebuild this destroyed self-image. Why do we do it? We do it because it's our natural inclination to do it and even after we are Christians many of us know no other way, because we have not permitted Christ to give us his mind!

When you say to a child such things as: "You never do things right! You never do what I say! You're always like that! You're just a trouble maker! How can you make grades like that? Your mother and I weren't like that!" The real tragedy is that, in trying to jerk out these ugly weeds, you also pull up some of the precious wheat—you destroy self-esteem in that child, which will eventually cause more problems and tension.

Perhaps the most pathetic people I see in marriage counseling are weed-pickers—husbands pointing up the faults of their wives, and wives pointing up the faults of their husbands. Of course, by continually harping on these faults they hope to actually pick these faults out of their mate's life and destroy them The trouble is, inevitably it works just the other way! Such weed-picking not only makes that particular fault more pronounced in the mate, but even worse, it destroys a lot of the "wheat" in him or her too! The Lord knows that each one of us has enough faults for our mate to spend an 8-hour day just weed-picking; but

257

the Lord also knows and tells us that this is absolutely the most destructive thing we can do in marriage. The point that Jesus wants us to get here is that weed-picking is not the answer!

It's not only in marriage that we do it; for we see the same kind of weed-picking in the church. Critical minds sitting in judgment of others who are different. Some people act as if their calling in life is to pick weeds. Some people can't sit in a worship service or attend a church program without finding fault. What a pathetic useless way to waste away the precious time and energy that God has given us!

Perhaps we see more weed-picking in business and on our jobs than anywhere else, because we think it is the right way to improve people, to get more production and make more money, when exactly the opposite is true! Unfortunately, many supervisors and executives mistake weed-picking for genuine leadership. Consequently they never are able to motivate the people under them to be loyal, productive employees. How sad!

Some people literally wear themselves out picking weeds out of everything they are involved in. They really don't enjoy their home and family because they're too busy picking weeds. Some people can't even worship God because they are too busy following this natural inclination. Jesus tells us there is another way!

The key to handling stress and tension is to learn how to relax and conserve energy when stress starts firing at us, and direct this energy toward something constructive.

In this parable, Jesus gives us a picture of perfect relaxation and energy conservation in a situation where stress could be at a peak. The householder has just discovered there are weeds among the wheat. That's when he might be the most tense and upset. But what does he do? He puts the situation in proper perspective by recognizing that both weeds and wheat must grow together

258

until harvest time. Picture the situation in your mind. The servants are ready to rush into the field and start weed-picking, but the owner starts walking toward the house to have a rest—to lie down and sleep. Then he turns and says matter-of-factly, "You relax too, and just let the weeds and the wheat grow together until the harvest time."

Here Christ is showing us a way to live with stress and handle it, so we cannot be destroyed by it, but function at full capacity. First, he says, "Let them grow together until harvest time." We must recognize the importance of letting the wheat and the weeds grow side-by-side!

Now, this doesn't mean that we must shut our eyes to the weeds and refuse to recognize them. Far from it! In our parable, our Lord recognizes the difference between the wheat and weeds, but still he says: "Let them grow together!" In other words, We must accept others exactly like they are—even our enemies! Maybe, especially our enemies, for Jesus says that the weeds in our parable represent the enemy. The point is: Time deadlines and people are with us to stay until harvest time and we had better learn how to live side-by-side with them or they'll choke the life out of us.

The very moment I finish preaching each Sunday, I know that I must start thinking about what I'll preach tonight and then next Sunday morning. The deadlines will begin all over again. Seven o'clock tonight and eleven o'clock next Sunday morning and all the other deadlines in-between are as sure to come as the sun is to shine. The church paper must be written on Monday, the bulletin put together on Tuesday, my sermon finalized on Friday and internalized on Saturday. And sandwiched in-between will be the counseling, funerals, weddings, hospital calling, committee meetings, appointments, speaking engagements, administration, and so forth. Each involves both time and relationships. Your schedules would be different only in details, not in principle. Experience tells me I can also be sure of something else and so can you: telephone calls will

259

come at the wrong time; emergencies will happen just when I can't afford for them to happen; time will be wasted by inconsiderate people; relationships will be strained by pettiness. But knowing that these are certainties in life, then there is only one perspective a person can have about them and survive and that is "let them grow together side-by-side!

We must accept things and people exactly as they are and stop burning up all of our energy trying to change them! We must learn to accept others as they are; then we can begin using all that energy we've been wasting in creative, constructive, fulfilling ways! Love must always begin with acceptance, and acceptance means we let the wheat and weeds grow side-by-side. That must be our basic perspective about all of life if we are to handle the stress in this world!

In order to be able to do this and at the same time be able to relax while we're doing it, requires something else; and that's the final truth Jesus reveals to us in this parable:

We can trust him for the results!

We can trust Christ to deal with the weeds!

> *"Let both grow together until the harvest; and at harvest time I will tell the reapers, 'Gather the weeds first and bind them in bundles to be burned, but gather the wheat into my barn'"* (Mt 13:30).

Ultimately, the secret to handling stress is trust. The less we trust Jesus the more stress we shall have. The more we trust Jesus, the less control that stress will have over us. Jesus came to tell us there is really only one true, unadulterated relaxant in this whole world and that is trust in him! In effect, Jesus is saying: "You are to love by accepting others as they are, and trust me for the results!" Trust is the key to relaxing when confronted by stress. Trust is the key to rising above stress!

Of course, there's going to be a Judgment Day when you and I must answer for all of the weeds in our lives; but the Bible says that only our Lord himself has the grace to make this judgment. We don't! Oh, how grateful I am for that! That is truly great news for me!

Dr. Hans Selye, an M.D. at the University of Montreal, has for twenty years done more scientific research on stress and its effect on us than practically all other researchers combined. Dr. Selye has concluded that stress is the number one killer of human beings! In fact, Dr. Selye is firmly convinced—and has been for years—that stress is the ultimate cause of all natural bodily dysfunction and disease. When asked what we could do to keep stress from destroying us, he said, "Since you can't avoid it, then you must learn to handle it; and there is only one way anyone can handle stress and that is with a spirit of gratitude!" He said this because gratitude—genuine thankfulness—is the exact opposite of stress.

As Christians that should be good news for us, for gratitude should be our daily norm. That should be our way of life. Life for every Christian should be a constant demonstration of a spirit of gratitude; because we have something to be grateful for! We are recipients of the greatest news ever proclaimed in this world. Christians, we should shout with gratitude today for our judgment is in the hands of Christ, who is the grace of God and who is Love himself! Jesus came to fill our hearts with gratitude and when he is in our hearts they are filled with gratitude.

Isn't that great news? Oh, how grateful I am for that! I'm grateful I don't have to be judged by the person who writes me those nasty letters or who criticizes my preaching. Aren't you grateful you don't have to be judged by the one who put the knife in your back and twisted it? Oh, how grateful we should be that the dogmatic preacher with blinders on, who lays down all those legalistic rules, won't judge us, nor will the sad-faced saint who wants to take all of the fun out of life! This news is good enough to

261

keep me going even when my field is filled with weeds! For it tells me that he who died on the cross for my sins will be my final judge, and no other! It tells me that he who saw how the weeds were about to take over the whole field and gave his life to stop it, will be the one who deals with the weeds in my own life. I can trust his wonderful grace to do that, can't you? I can be grateful can't you? Jesus wants you and me to realize that trusting in him is really the key to deal with the tension and stress in our life, for trust in him transforms us from weed pickers to lovers! Trusting in him transforms our relationships from adversary confrontations where we think we must do the judging, to love relationships where we leave the results to him, making tension and stress an opportunity instead of a stumbling block. No wonder the hymn writer could sing:

"'Tis so sweet to trust in Jesus,
Just to take him at his word;
Just to rest upon his promise,
Just to know, 'Thus saith the Lord,'

I'm so glad I learned to trust thee,
Precious Jesus, Savior, friend;
And to know that thou art with me,
Wilt be with me to the end."*

That's the Bible's answer for dealing with stress and tension! Is it yours?

---

* *'Tis So Sweet to Trust in Jesus*, Cokesbury Hymnal #135.